BEST LITTLE WITCH-HOUSE IN ARKHAM

BEST LITTLE WITCH-HOUSE IN ARKHAM

WEIRD TALES OUT OF SPACE & TIME

Mark McLaughlin

WILDSIDE PRESS

Published by Wildside Press LLC.
www.wildsidebooks.com

To Michael Sheehan, Jr. for believing in me 24/7.
It's a tough job, but somebody's gotta do it.

To Pamela Briggs, who has known me longer than anyone—
and still likes me! Hurray!

To Michael and Cindy McCarty, rabbit enthusiasts
in pursuit of hare-raising adventure.

To John Betancourt and Wildside Press:
Thank you for your support!

CONTENTS

INTRODUCTION: WHAT'S YOUR PLEASURE?

Welcome to the Best Little Witch-House in Arkham.
What's your pleasure?

In this midnight den of dread and desire, you will find twenty-five rooms, each with a story of its own to tell. Here you will enjoy a delectable variety of otherworldly horrors and delights…enough to satisfy even your most eldritch desires.

You will find evil pop-stars longing to devour their fans. You will find a sophisticated secret agent in search of supernatural super-villains. You will find a futuristic restaurant for alien connoisseurs, where you'll savor the monstrous specialty of the house.

You will learn the vile secrets of Kugappa, the writhing octopus-god, and Ghattambah, an unholy insect deity whose soul dwells beyond time. You will hear the wicked laughter of the Heckler in the Ha-ha Hut, as well as the salacious cackle of the Pecker in the Passageway. You will taste the creamy Milk of Time, served up in a forbidden hideaway known as Der Fleischbrunnen. You will even smell the unhallowed stench of the Odour out of the Terrible Old Man.

But enough of my blasphemous blubbering…off you go! Be sure to visit every room of the Best Little Witch-House in Arkham. Heck, visit them twice, thrice, as many times as you like.

After all, you've paid the price of admission—a shiny little coin known as your *soul*—so you might as well get your money's worth….

A BEAUTY TREATMENT FOR MRS. HAMOGEORGAKIS

"Don't look now," Kyle said, "but that old scarecrow lady is staring at you."

Melina and Kyle were having a cigarette break outside of The Perfect Profile, the most popular beauty salon in the seaside town of Innsmouth. There were three other salons, but they were just part-time operations out of people's homes. Melina took a long drag off of her Belgian vanilla cigarette. They were expensive, but they were smoother than regular cigarettes and not as stinky as those clove things. "What old lady?" she said. She glanced across the street, where some people where talking in front of a doughnut shop.

"Not that way," Kyle said. "Inside. You can look now. She's talking to Marie."

She squinted through the plate-glass window. Most of the women in the waiting area were overweight, so it was easy to tell which one he meant. A bony woman in a simple black dress and heavy black shoes was talking to the receptionist. The woman had long, thick gray hair, done up in a shaggy ponytail. At one point she turned and nodded at Melina. The old woman's face looked like a parchment-covered skull with an eagle's beak for a nose.

"Very scary," Melina said. "I hope she doesn't want me to work on her."

"Well, I don't want to get stuck with her." Kyle flashed his big, lop-sided smile. "Let's both go home sick. Simultaneous food-poisoning. The twenty-hour Ebola virus."

For the third time that day and probably the thousandth that year, Melina thought, *Too bad he's gay*. She still couldn't figure out why any gay man would want to be a beautician, surrounded by women eight hours a day.

"Hey, maybe she wants to be your friend," he said. "You're always saying that you wish you had more friends."

"Yeah, but I'm not desperate. We'd better get back inside," Melina said, "before Midget has a fit." Midget was in fact Midge, their manager, a five-foot-four red-haired dictator. They also called her Little Miss Stopwatch, because she said things like, "You were in the bathroom eleven minutes and forty-five seconds. Did you fall in or *what?*"

"Mel, honey," Marie said as they entered, "this is Miss Papadakis. She asked for you special." The plump, middle-aged receptionist gave her a small, apologetic smile. "She'd like a makeover."

"Lucky you," Kyle whispered as he passed her to go to his workstation.

"Right this way," Melina said, leading the old woman to her area. "So you asked for me? Which of my millions of happy customers sent you my way?"

Miss Papadakis settled into the hot-pink padded chair. "I saw you and decided you were probably Greek, like me, with those big brown eyes and that lovely olive skin. I thought we might have fun talking. Perhaps we are related. You *are* Greek, yes?"

"One-hundred percent. My name's Melina."

"And your last name?"

"We don't give out last names here. Sorry. It's not like I don't trust you, but…"

The old woman nodded. "I understand. Young women these days, they have to be careful."

"Marie said you needed a makeover."

The woman smiled. She had good teeth, even and white. Maybe they were dentures. "I am no Miss America, but do you think you could make me—pretty?"

Melina turned on her best fake smile. "All us Greek girls are pretty. A little make-up's all you need, and I'd love to do something with that hair."

The woman's smile widened. "Very good. You are skilled with the bullshit. You are being kind to an old lady with a face like death." She looked into the mirror. "What is this 'something' you would do?"

"Add some color. Something soft. Muted. Anything too dark might look a little hard on you."

Miss Papadakis thought about this. "Soft, yes. I do not want to look like a tavern whore. You may begin. But first I am going to give you your tip. As incentive." She handed Melina a hundred-dollar bill.

"That's great," Melina said. She slipped it into a pocket. "I hope you decide to become a regular customer." She leaned toward the old woman. "My last name's Theodorakis."

"A name from Crete, like mine. Marvelous!" Miss Papadakis gave her a wink. "Call me Kiwi, please. All my friends call me Kiwi."

* * * *

During the appointment, Melina found out much of the old woman's life story, including why friends called her Kiwi instead of her real first name, which was Angela.

It turned out that many years ago, an old boyfriend, a policeman, had given her a basket of kiwi fruit, and she'd found them to be absolutely delicious. And so every day, she always ate at least three or four kiwis, since they were so tasty and also, they reminded her of her beloved policeman, who had died in a car accident. That was back when she had lived in New York.

"After my Tony died, I came to Innsmouth with a patient of mine, Mrs. Hamogeorgakis," Kiwi said. "I am a doctor, you see. Back in New York, I would drop by her place every now and then—she had many health problems, the poor dear, and she has always been a friend of the family. So when Mrs. Hamogeorgakis decided to come here—she has relatives in town—she asked if I would like to come with her. I was tired of New York, so I said yes."

"You still call her by her last name after all these years?" Melina said as she rinsed out the bony woman's hair. *Kiwi's old enough to be my grandmother,* she thought. *How old is this gal she's taking care of?*

The old woman laughed. "Mrs. Hamogeorgakis is like a queen. Her very presence commands respect."

Finally, Melina finished her work. And the old woman looked—nice. Her hair was now a medium golden-brown and trimmed to shoulder-length. Her gaunt face, through the subtle use of foundation, shadow, lipstick, lip-liner and more, now looked pleasant but dignified. Almost grandmotherly.

Kiwi gasped at her reflection. "My child, this is a miracle! It is like I am only fifty again." She got out of the chair and looked her closely in the mirror. "Interesting, how you've applied the color on the sides of my nose. It doesn't look so big now. I will have to study this when I get home, to see if could do it myself." She turned around. "Or perhaps you could come by sometime and teach me?"

Melina shook her head. "Sorry, we don't give lessons. Otherwise you wouldn't need the salon."

Kiwi pouted. "But I wouldn't have the time to come here every day. And I'd still need you to do my hair." She moved closer to Melina and whispered, "I would pay very well for these lessons. Give me your home number. I'll call you and we'll talk more."

Kyle walked over to Melina's workstation. "Mel, you didn't tell me you had a sister," he said with his usual lopsided grin.

Kiwi ran a bony hand through the male stylist's blond highlights. "This is an interesting effect. Very dramatic. Maybe you could do this for me sometime, Melina."

Melina wrote her home number on the back of a business card and handed it to the old woman. "Whatever you like, Kiwi."

"Your name's Kiwi?" Kyle said.

"Have Melina tell you the story." The old woman put a fingertip on Kyle's cheek. "Such large eyes you have. Are you a Gilman, by any chance?"

He nodded. "Yes, how did you know?"

"The family resemblance is unmistakable." She turned back to Melina. "I must go now—I still have some shopping to do for Mrs. Hamogeorgakis. I pay the receptionist, yes?"

Melina nodded. One hand was in her pocket, touching that hundred-dollar bill.

Later, during their next cigarette break, Kyle said, "That old lady looks about a hundred times better now. But what was the deal with her knowing my last name?"

Melina looked at his big soulful blue eyes and his wide, full-lipped, sensuous mouth. *Too bad he's gay.* "Like she said, a family resemblance. That's not so weird. Most of you Gilmans have the same look. Though you *are* better looking than most of the others. Your uncle Carl looks like a big toad-man."

Kyle grimaced. "Thanks for telling me. Does that mean I'm going to look like an old toad someday?" He threw down his cigarette, crushed it under his heel and went back into the salon.

Melina just shrugged. "Maybe," she said to no one.

* * * *

That evening, Miss Papadakis called Melina. The beautician was lounging in a beanbag chair in her apartment at the time, drinking a glass of wine and doing a crossword puzzle, when the phone rang.

"Mrs. Hamogeorgakis had much to say about your skill—all good, of course," Kiwi said. "I must confess, I had a special reason for coming to your salon today."

God, I hope it's not kinky, Melina thought. "Is that right?"

"My visit was—what is the word I'm looking for?—let me think…"

"I'm good at crosswords—I'm doing one right now. What's the word mean?"

"The word for when you try somebody out, so they can do a task later."

"An interview?" Melina said. She grabbed the wine bottle and refreshed her glass. "An audition?"

"Yes, both of those," Kiwi said. "You see, Mrs. Hamogeorgakis is in need of your services."

"But what about you?"

"I need them, too. But Mrs. Hamogeorgakis needs them even more." Kiwi paused, and then said, "Much more."

"I see." Actually, Melina didn't want to see how ugly the ancient woman in question had to be.

"Mrs. Hamogeorgakis would not be able to visit your salon. You'll have to come here, to 605 Cherrywood Lane. Do you have pen and paper so you can write that down?"

Melina wrote it in the margin of her crossword puzzle. "You know, I *am* really busy these days, and the salon would be mad if they knew—"

"One-thousand dollars." Kiwi stated. "You will receive one-thousand dollars for your visit. Tomorrow night at eight o'clock."

"Great! I'll be there," Melina said. "I look forward to meeting your friend."

"You will like Mrs. Hamogeorgakis. She is a fascinating person, and she will be very grateful. We will see you tomorrow night."

Melina hung up the phone and had some more wine.

A fascinating person.

The old hag probably looked like a mummy. A fascinating mummy.

* * * *

The sky was overcast the next morning. By noon, the clouds were roiling black and grey. Rain was pouring down, accompanied by gale-force winds.

Midge locked the front door of The Perfect Profile and the employees all went down into the basement. It would have been impossible for any of them to go home at that point. Midge was afraid the wind might blow a branch or a trashcan through the salon's plate-glass window.

Melina and Kyle sat away from the others in a corner, smoking.

"I'm sorry about yesterday," Melina said.

"That's okay," her friend said. "It's not your fault. I guess I'm just afraid I'll end up like my uncle. That's all."

"But you really are a lot better looking than—"

"There's more to it than just looks," Kyle said. "Carl disappeared last week."

"Oh no." Melina lit up a fresh vanilla cigarette. "Didn't you have a grandmother who disappeared?"

Kyle nodded. "And my grandmother's brother. What would that be—a grand-uncle?" He reached over and took one of her expensive cigarettes. Ordinarily she'd have complained, but she decided to let it slide this time.

"I don't know why they've disappeared," he continued. "They just go away and the thing is, nobody talks about it. It's like everybody's in on the secret except me."

"Why's that?"

"I don't know. Probably because I'm not like them."

Melina shook her head. "That doesn't make any sense. Do you really think your family is off somewhere saying, 'Let's not tell Kyle the truth about the disappearances because he's gay'? That doesn't make *any* sense."

Kyle's large eyes glistened with tears. "So what's the truth?"

Melina sighed. "Oh, I don't know. Does it have to be something bad? Maybe it's something really cool. Something wonderful and mysterious."

Kyle sat up. "Like what?"

"Well, maybe you're all royalty. Or aliens. Your guess is as good as mine."

Her friend grinned. "Maybe we all grow fingerwebs and swim off to an underwater palace."

"Whoa! Where did *that* come from?"

"I have dreams like that all the time." An oddly blissful look crept across his face. "I dream that my hands are green and there are webs between the fingers, and I've swimming past all these beautiful fish and eels to this big palace, but it's really more of a coral reef. And there are all these green and yellow people waving to me, and I know they all love me. I had that dream again just last night."

Melina looked at her friend's hands. The fingers were long and slender—and between them, there did seem to be a *little* extra skin. Maybe a fourth of an inch. Not much. Certainly nothing freaky.

But when she looked up into his face, it suddenly dawned on her that yeah, she could see a touch of his uncle Carl in his face. That forlorn, toadlike quality. But in Kyle's case, it was more froglike.

Maybe it was just as well that this frog would never be her prince.

* * * *

The storm was over by two-thirty, but the skies still looked terrible. All the day's clients had called to cancel, so Midge told everyone to go home.

Melina had to tell Kyle about her appointment with the old women that evening. It would be best if somebody knew her whereabouts, in case something weird happened. Kyle said, "We have the rest of the afternoon to kill. Why don't we drive around Cherrywood Lane? Check out the neighborhood before your big gig tonight."

"That's in the rich part of town, isn't it?"

"You bet. So we'd better take my car. It's nicer," he said. "Besides, if we took your car, they might recognize it when you came by later and they'd know you'd been snooping around in their neck of the woods."

"Good idea you've got there." She wrinkled her nose at him. "First time for everything, I guess."

"Clever! I should just let those two old witches eat you."

Twenty minutes, Kyle was steering his car onto Cherrywood Lane, which led up a hill overlooking the town. This part of Innsmouth was old and moneyed, and all the houses had winding driveways and expansive, well-groomed lawns. "You'd better scoot down in your seat," Kyle said, "so they can't see you."

605 was certainly the most impressive house on the street. It was a huge, sprawling structure, three stories high and covered with ivy. "Good God," Kyle said. "Yeah, I guess they can afford thousand-dollar beauty treatments. That's the old Marsh place. I used to have a boyfriend who lived on this street. He showed me who lived where."

"*Marsh?*" The Marsh family was one of the most prestigious in Innsmouth. "Kiwi said Mrs. Hamogeorgakis came here to live with relatives. The Marshes aren't Greek."

"Maybe they're related by marriage somehow."

Melina pointed. "What's behind that big wall?"

Kyle looked in that direction. A short distance behind the house was a high wall made partly of large, pale stones and partly of red bricks. "Well, we're right on the ocean, but we had to drive up this hill a ways… Must be a cliff. Let's turn around."

A minute later, they were heading back toward downtown Innsmouth. At the base of the hill, Kyle took a side road to a small seaside recreational area, with picnic benches and a white-painted metal pavilion.

Kyle got out of the car, so Melina did, too. He nodded toward the sun-bleached cliff to their left. "There's what's on the other side of that wall."

She looked up. "Yeah, you can see a little bit of it from here. And some of their roof." At the base of the cliff were rocks and boulders, strewn with green crap. Probably seaweed or moss. "So, Sherlock. What have we learned?"

"Well, Mrs. Hamogeorgakis and her pal live in the old Marsh estate." Kyle looked up toward the house. "They want you to go there late at night. And, they have a big cliff a little ways outside their back door."

"Do you think I'm in danger? Should I tell them to get lost?"

"What, and lose out on the chance to make a thousand bucks?" Kyle thought for a moment. "Take your cell phone with you tonight. I'll be parked down here with my phone. Call me if you think you're in trouble and I'll come help."

"Thank you, Kyle," Melina said. "I'm so lucky to have you for a friend."

He shrugged and smiled. "Hey, if those two old harpies kill you, I won't have anyone to mooch fancy cigarettes off of."

* * * *

That evening, she parked in the driveway near the front steps of 605 Cherrywood Lane, carried a large, red plastic make-up case up to the door and knocked.

A plump, middle-aged man with a jowly face answered the door. "Come inside. You are expected." He picked up her case. "Let me carry that for you."

"Great. Thanks."

As she followed the man down a hallway, she noticed something odd about him. Though he had a big belly, his legs were very thin, and his shuffling gait was slightly jerky, as though simply walking was a strain for him. "So what's your name?" she said.

The man turned his head to reply. "Tyler."

"Is that your first name or last?"

This time he didn't turn his head at all. "Tyler Marsh," he said gruffly.

Melina decided the man wasn't in the mood to talk, so she simply followed. At least someone named Marsh still lived in the house, though he seemed to be acting more like a servant.

He led her up some stairs and down yet another hallway. Here the walls had numerous portraits hung on them. Most of the people in the pictures were fat and toadlike, like Tyler. Others were large-eyed and gangly, with loose folds of skin around their throats.

They came to a room with a black, heavily lacquered door. Marsh tapped on the shiny surface with a knuckle. "Your visitor is here."

The door opened halfway and Kiwi looked out into the hall. "Thank you, Tyler. Please come in, Melina. Come and meet Mrs. Hamogeorgakis."

The man handed the make-up case to Kiwi and shuffled off down the hall.

Melina entered the room. It was very large, with beautiful old furniture, including several bookcases filled with leather-bound volumes. The wallpaper pattern seemed to be either leafy vines or tendrils of seaweed, or maybe both. The carpet's design depicted a scattering of seashells and rounded, multi-colored stones.

Along the far wall was a four-poster bed with sky-blue silk curtains. Lounging in the middle of the bed on a pile of navy blue pillows was a willowy dark-haired woman in a white dressing gown edged with pink lace.

She seemed normal enough—from a distance. But as Melina walked closer, she gradually realized there was something very wrong with the woman.

Mrs. Hamogeorgakis had fine bone structure and large blue eyes. But the eyes had an intense, vicious look to them, like those of a wild animal.

The woman's pale skin had a slight olive cast—and was coated with a shining layer of tiny, iridescent scales.

Her dark hair was full and lustrous—far too lustrous. It glistened with a slick sheen, as though covered with a layer of oil.

Mrs. Hamogeorgakis smiled, revealing a mouthful of yellow, needle-thin teeth. "So this is the fancy expert," she said in a wet rumble of a voice. "The miracle worker. Do you think you will be able to make a goddess of me?"

Melina turned toward Kiwi, who was standing by the door, pointing a knife at her.

"We shall begin very soon," Kiwi said.

Melina stared again at the woman on the bed. Woman? She looked more like some kind of deep-sea creature.

"Do I frighten you, little girl?" Mrs. Hamogeorgakis said. "So sorry. I didn't always look like this. I used to be very pretty, like you. Men used to fight over me. But there are families…" She paused to clear her throat, spitting a thick fluid into a handkerchief. "Families that come from the sea. Some are here in Innsmouth. Some are in Crete. And in other places, many other places. We are all related. We are the children of Dagon, the Sea Father."

Melina realized that these two old freaks were as scary as Hell, and whatever they were planning, they probably had no intention of letting her leave. She had to get to her cell phone, which was in the make-up case next to Kiwi.

"I'll need a few things," Melina said, moving toward the case. She also kept a pepper sprayer in it, for when she had to walk to her car after dark.

Kiwi and Mrs. Hamogeorgakis both laughed as she picked up the case and took it to the side of the bed.

"Foolish girl," Mrs. Hamogeorgakis said. "Your silly powders and notions would only make a ridiculous clown of me."

"Just wait. I've got some great new products here…" Melina bent to open her case, even as Kiwi walked toward her with the knife.

"Don't be foolish," Mrs. Hamogeorgakis said. "We know what we are doing. We have done this many times before. So many times. So many stupid girls."

Melina lifted the case and scattered its contents on the bed and the floor. She found the cell phone and jammed it in a pants pocket. She then spotted the pepper sprayer, snatched it up and fired a stream toward Kiwi's eyes.

"You bitch!" the old woman screamed, dropping the knife. Melina turned and fired the sprayer at Mrs. Hamogeorgakis—and missed. The creature slid off the bed and reached for the blade.

"No you *don't!*" Melina screamed, kicking Mrs. Hamogeorgakis out of her way. The old woman uttered a gurgling squeal, and then turned her head quickly to rake her teeth across the girl's ankle. Melina grabbed the knife with her free hand and ran out of the room.

Tyler Marsh was running down the hall toward her.

She ran to meet him and plunged the knife into his gut. What else could she do? It was her only choice

"Very good!" Mrs. Hamogeorgakis cried from the doorway. "Such spirit!" Kiwi appeared behind the creature, rubbing furiously at her streaming eyes.

The man clutched at the knife handle and fell to the floor screaming.

Melina ran down the hall, looking frantically for the stairs. Finally she saw them to her left. She look behind her—Kiwi and Mrs. Hamogeorgakis were less than ten feet away. The hideous fish-woman was holding the bloody knife.

The girl raised the pepper sprayer and pumped at the cylinder furiously, creating a cloud of the spray between her and the two women. They stopped immediately.

"So clever," Mrs. Hamogeorgakis said. A hard smile played on her lips. "What a pity you must die."

Melina rushed down the stairs, pulling the phone from her pocket. She frantically punched in Kyle's number.

"Call the police!" she screamed into the phone. "The fire department, anybody! Then come help me!"

"Sure! Okay, but wha—"

She cut off the call—there just wasn't enough time to explain. She was about to call 911 when she saw the two old women rushing down the stairs, frantically fanning the spray fumes away with their hands.

She tried to remember which way to turn to get to the front door… Finally, hoping for the best, she chose left. At one point she bumped into a small table and fell down, overturning the table and smashing the vase on top. She scrambled back to her feet and continued down the hall. But soon she saw some paintings she hadn't seen earlier. She must have turned the wrong way. She decided to keep running until she found either an exit or a place to hide and call the police.

After she had turned down a new hall, she came across large double doors with golden handles. Double doors? She opened one and rushed through into a huge hallway, over twenty feet wide with pine-board walls and a cheap linoleum floor. The lighting fixtures were simply yellow bulbs. Maybe deliveries came through this way—which meant it led out of the building. Yes, she decided, that had to be it. She ran on until she'd turned a corner. She couldn't hear them behind her—now she could call the police. She jammed a hand into one pocket, then another.

The phone was gone.

Had she even put it back in a pocket after she'd called Kyle? She must have dropped it when she ran into that table. She couldn't go back. The only thing to do was to follow the hallway.

The floor seemed to slope slightly downward. She rounded a few more corners, and as time passed, it occurred to her that she had traveled a considerable distance. Too great a distance to still be in the house. Was she in some kind of tunnel?

Eventually she came to the top of a spiral staircase made of huge beams and well-worn board steps. The walls here were brick, coated with layers of mildew and cobwebs. The cracked, eroded bricks were probably red, but the light of the yellow bulbs gave them a pumpkin-orange cast.

She followed the stairs downward. They were slippery, so she had to hang on to the filthy banister. Soon her hands were smeared with black mildew.

She walked down another hall. The damp floor was surfaced with thousands of small, flat stones. She began to hear faint splashing sounds. She figured she had to be underground—how far, she couldn't even guess.

Hey, I'm not scared, she thought. She was impressed with herself. Even though she was in some strange underground passage, she really wasn't frightened. That horrible fish-woman had been terrifying, but she'd managed to escape that. Surely she'd find an exit pretty soon. Surely this nightmare was nearing its end.

Then the hall brought her to a large open area.

A cave.

The people gathered in the cave, lounging on rocks around an algae-choked pool, were totally naked. But that was not the most startling aspect of the sight that confronted her.

All of these pale, flabby people had scales and wild eyes, like Mrs. Hamogeorgakis. Then she noticed they all looked a little *like Kyle*—in fact, one of them was his uncle Carl. But he was covered with scales now, and had webbed fingers, claws, and needlelike teeth. She had to cover her mouth with her hands so not to cry out, or scream, or even laugh hysterically. So this was what had happened to those relatives of his. They had…changed…with age. They had to be one of those *families from the sea* the horrible old woman had mentioned…

The sea-people turned and glared at her. But they didn't try to attack her—they didn't even change their positions. A few simply bared their needle-teeth in smiles—cruel smiles that said, *We know something that you don't.*

Then she saw a statue, half-hidden in a shadowed alcove. It was carved from pale yellow stone, and stood almost eight feet tall. It looked like a bloated man with scaly skin and a wide, fish-lipped, horribly pouting mouth. The eyes were huge black gems. She saw gnawed bones piled around the base of the statue. Dry, rotten loops of intestines were wrapped around the body and legs, as though bored, monstrous children that tried to clothe the thing.

She moved quickly along the wall of the cave, desperately hoping to get to the far end without touching any of the creatures. The other side had to have an opening to the outside world. Maybe it led to an opening behind the rocks—the ones at the base of the cliff that she and Kyle had seen from the seaside pavilion.

When she reached the other side, she found only a low passage hewn out of the dirt and stone, shored up with timber and rocks. The yellow bulbs did not go down this path—probably because it was so wet. The muddy walls dripped and ran with moisture. The tunnel led off into midnight blackness.

Tired but determined, she crawled in.

She closed her eyes, even though she was in total darkness, and crawled and crawled, on and on, through mud and slime. Soon her pants were soaked with cold water and filth, and the air in the tunnel took on the stench of rotting fish.

I wish I had my vanilla cigarettes. They'd make this place smell better, she thought. A half-laugh, half-sob escaped her lips. *God, I'm trying to find my way out of Hell and I'm thinking about cigarettes.*

Suddenly she realized: her lighter was in the breast pocket of her blouse.

She dried off one hand as best she could on her shirt, and then found the lighter. She flipped up the cover and lit it.

The tunnel floor was littered not only with dead fish, but with bits of dead dogs and other animals as well. She wanted to throw up. Then she saw that side tunnels branched out from the path every few feet. She had just been proceeding straight ahead in the dark.

There was no way of telling which of the paths led to the outside.

She snapped the lighter shut and stuck it back in her pocket—and kept moving. All her turns before had been bad choices. This time, she was just going straight ahead. She couldn't keep going much longer—the exertion was too draining. She had to find a way out, and soon.

In a few minutes, she could hear an odd, wet, slithering sound. Or rather, a series of sounds. She tried to imagine what it could possibly be. If several people were to start dragging around big sacks of wet laundry, it might sound like that…Or perhaps it was just the echoes of water running and trickling…It was hard to tell.

Soon the floor of the tunnel changed. Instead of mud and rocks, she found herself on a smooth, flat surface. The stench in the air was even worse than before.

She felt overhead—no boards or dirt. She was out of the tunnel. Suddenly she had a horrible thought. Had all her wandering led her right back into the mansion?

She stood up, dug out the lighter and flicked it on again. The small wavering flame cast writhing shadows.

She was now in a small cave with a floor of slick gray stone. To one side was a pool with long bones and chunks of raw meat floating in it. Odd, flat, wet things were moving through the pool and around its rim. They were what made that slithering sound. At first she couldn't tell what they were. They appeared to be shiny blankets—some beige, some pink, some olive-brown—moving aimlessly like misshapen slugs.

One worked its way toward her and she saw it was coated with fine scales, and parts of it were fringed with hair…some parts seemed to be shaped like stockings, and those ended in flattened, boneless *toes…*

She screamed when she realized that the sluglike creatures were in fact *living skins.*

She heard something moving in the passage behind her.

Then something hit her on the back of the head, and she passed out.

* * * *

When she woke up, she found herself in a warm, comfortable bed.

Kyle was standing by the bed looking down at her, and so was Kiwi.

"Oh, no," she whispered.

"Do not alarm yourself," Kiwi said. "I'm not going to hurt you." She put a hand on Kyle's shoulder. "Your friend's uncle brought you to us."

"Where is that thing—that monster?" Melina said.

Kiwi sighed wearily. "I hope you are not referring to Mrs. Hamogeorgakis. That's not a nice way to talk about your hostess. Now follow us. It's time to eat. You've been asleep for quite a long time. Surely you must be hungry."

Kiwi and Kyle then left the room.

Melina got out of bed. Someone had dressed her in a white silk dressing gown.

"Kyle!" she shouted, running after them. "What the hell is going on? I can't believe you were in on this whole thing."

In the hallway, the two turned to face her. "Please," the thin woman said, "there's no need for raised voices. And we won't be having any more calls to the police." She smiled as she looked toward Kyle. "It took quite a while to convince the police that his call was simply a prank. Later he came back, and well—we dealt with him. You know."

Melina shook her head. "No, I don't know. What are you talking about?"

"And to think she said you were a clever girl! Haven't you figured anything out?" Kiwi laughed. "Dear Mrs. Hamogeorgakis should have gone to the sea many centuries ago. But she is in no hurry to do so. So the women of my family have always helped to replace her skin when the scales start to emerge. She heals with amazing speed—she is a living miracle. But the skins become a part of her, so in time, the scales return. The old skins live on after they are replaced, for they have become undying, like her. We put things in their pool for them to…absorb." Kiwi cocked her head to one side and gazed at Kyle. "Her new look is quite *fanciful*, yes? Pretty in a different sort of way."

"Such a lovely boy," Kyle said in a thick, rumbling, yet distinctly feminine voice. His lips parted in a smile, revealing needle-thin yellow teeth. He turned and walked down the hall.

Melina could see the thick stitches in the back of his neck.

"We wanted to use you," Kiwi said, "but it's just as well we didn't. The scales would have emerged far too soon. Just look what her bite—such a tiny amount of venom!—did to you."

Gently, she raised the girl's arm and pulled back the sleeve of the dressing gown.

Fine scales glistened on her forearm, with a slight touch of rainbow iridescence.

"Do not worry. You will make many new friends," Kiwi said. "In the caves."

WHEN WE WAS FLAB

Four astounding musicians. Over the years, they have been called Geniuses. Snake-Oil Salesmen. Superstars. Lard-Buckets. Cutie-Pies. Cannibals. Messiahs. Human Devils. No other musical group in the history of rock and roll has ever inspired more commentary or controversy. Personally—until very recently—I have always called them *my friends.*

They are…The Vittles.

Here are some basic facts about the band, for those of you who have been living in caves or on distant mountain-tops for the past few decades. According to early press releases, they started out as a fresh-faced bunch of kids with guitars, rehearsing in garages and barns in a small rural town in the Midwest. No written records exist concerning their births, grades in school, or any other elements of their early years. That is because after the boys became billionaires, they bought their tiny hometown of Liverpond, Iowa. They paid its citizens to change their names and relocate, and then tore down the buildings and paved over the ruins. Basically, they turned the town into an empty parking lot out in the middle of the cornfields.

A real Nowheres-ville.

None of the boys have ever gone by their real names, whatever those were. Those facts went down with the town of Liverpond. The leader of the group is Popo, the cheery, playful one, he of the bee-stung lips and big puppy-dog eyes. He came up with the tunes, and was usually the lead singer.

Then there's Jones—the sensitive, poetic one, with his little round glasses and serious demeanor. He wrote most of the lyrics, and even penned a few books of short stories and poetry on the side. Those who have read his work soon come to realize that Jones, like so many poets, has his dark side.

Mongo the drummer is…well, he's the ugly one, and the first to admit it. His face is mostly nose, and he has enormous eyebrows—and yet, the girls adored him way-back-when, in the same way a child might cherish a scrawny puppy or a kitten with a missing eye.

Gregor was the intellectual mystic. He was intrigued by esoteric philosophies and religions. Girls called him the smart one, and many fell in love with his brooding good looks.

The boys were always a little chunky, and as the years passed, they gained more and more weight—good living does that to people. Along the way, media wags dubbed them...the Flab Four.

They made a few movies along the way, but eventually stopped. The boys only looked even bigger up on the big screen. When their last movie came out—one with several love scenes—an especially sharp-tongued critic commented, "Who wants to watch a documentary on the mating habits of whales?"

The boys did try to lose weight by various means—in fact, that's how I met them. Years ago, when I was young and needed the money, I worked at a celebrity spa that offered vitamin-enriched colonic irrigations. The Vittles were regular customers, and I learned about the boys inside and out. Later I went into journalism—a line of work not too different from my days at the spa. The boys kept in touch, and even invited me to some of their legendary Hollywood parties.

Along the way, a mysterious woman from a faraway land entered the lives of the Flab Four. Some say she was the one who encouraged them to study the occult. Certainly their music—and careers—took a turn down a darkened corridor after meeting her.

At one point, an assassin shot at Jones as he was leaving a television studio, and since nobody saw him for some time after that, rumors circulated that he had died. In truth, he had gone into seclusion after the ordeal because he'd required extensive plastic surgery to repair damages to his face. After the surgery, he always wore dark glasses during public appearances.

Then came that fateful concert at Monroe Hexagonal Stadium—a night the world will never forget. Fans were shocked by what transpired at that concert, and afterward, bodyguards quickly spirited The Vittles off-stage. The boys quickly left America for a self-imposed exile upon the Pacific island of Pokaluhu, where I recently visited them at their request. It was to be their first interview in ten years. I was not allowed to bring any cameras or video equipment—only a tape recorder.

It would be the understatement of the millennium to say that things did not go as I had expected.

The following is a transcript of the taped interview.

* * * *

MM: Pokaluhu is a beautiful resort island—a paradise of palm trees and exotic flowers. I spent last night and this morning in a wonderful hotel on the other side of the island. A driver brought me to the mansion of The Vittles this afternoon. An elderly blind woman answered the door—she said she was one of the cooks. She was very friendly and cheerful, and we had a nice chat. I asked her if it was difficult being a blind cook, and she just laughed and said, "Blind people have to cook for themselves. Why would it be any harder to cook for others?" Good point!

I am now seated at a little white table in an enormous garden, with fragrant orchids and blossoming vines in every direction. I am in the shade of a huge, flowering tree, dotted with purple and golden butterflies. In front of me is a white gazebo, surrounded by screens of white fabric.

The Vittles are within that gazebo, having their dinner. I can see only their silhouettes. Fortunately there are some torches behind them, so their shadows on the screen before me are pretty sharp. I can even make out the jutting curve of Mongo's aquiline nose. It would appear they have four women at their table as well, and there's a servant standing off to one side. I think there are some big dogs huddled under the table. Or perhaps that's a trunk? The shape kind of reminds me of a treasure chest.

Boys, why are you hiding behind those screens? I can see your shadows from here—you've lost weight. Good for you!

Popo: Yes, we've slimmed down. We've been fighting the flab for years, and it's finally gone. Thanks for noticing.

MM: I believe there are some women in there with you. Are they your wives? Girlfriends?

Popo: To my right is my wife, Laura. She's not having any of the roast this evening.

Laura: I should say not. I keep saying meat is bad for them, but do they listen? I suppose they think they're going to live forever. I simply can't stand the thought of eating anything with a face.

Another Woman's Voice: My, what a sweet little angel you are. 'Oh, my name is Laura and I am so holy, I only eat tiny apples that have already fallen from the tree.' Spare us the sermon! We've heard it a million times before.

MM: Who was that who just spoke?

Jones: My wife Hekuuna. She is from this island. The people of Pokaluhu have a more nature-based philosophy. They see the food chain as—

Laura: They're cannibals. Just say it. Disgusting cannibals.

Hekuuna: Who are you to judge my people, bitch-dog woman?

Mongo: Mark didn't fly out here just to listen to you two argue, you know.

MM: I do want to get back to that whole cannibalism topic at some point. But you still need to answer my first question. Why are you behind that screen? Did you catch some horrible island skin disease or something?

Hekuuna: 'Island skin disease'? No one is ever sick on Pokaluhu! It is a much healthier place than America, where everyone is a bloated pig!

Gregor: You'll have to forgive Hekuuna—she's very excitable. Ain't that right, Jonesy? Actually, we're hidden from sight because we're gods.

MM: Oh? Congratulations, I guess…

Gregor: What I mean is, the locals say we're divine. They don't look at us directly, and they don't want you looking at us, either.

Hekuuna: Your pitiful gaze would defile us.

MM: No offense, but I used to give these guys enemas. I've pretty much seen it all. Besides, there's somebody in with you right now. That guy standing to the side. How come he gets to look at you?

Laura: His name is Ko. He's blind, the poor thing. All of our servants are blind.

Mongo: But it's not like we go around poking people's eyes out. We asked the local islands to send us their blind people. They were happy to oblige.

MM: Hmmm. Back when you were heavier, the whole world was watching you. Now that you're finally slender, no one gets to see you. Pretty ironic. Laura, if I remember correctly, didn't you used to be Popo's dietary consultant?

Laura: He never listened to me. Yet I fell in love with him anyway. He still doesn't listen. But I still love him.

Popo: Those fancy diets of yours didn't do me any good. I was just *big*, plain and simple. We were all big boys growing up. Well-fed from day one.

MM: We've heard from Laura and Hekuuna—who are the other two women at your table?

Hekuuna: They are my sisters, Yilla and M'namma.

Yilla: Hello. I am Yilla.

M'namma: I am M'namma. Hello.

Gregor: M'namma is my wife.

Mongo: And Yilla's my wife.

MM: I'm guessing Hekuuna's sisters were big fans of The Vittles, so she made the introductions?

Hekuuna: That is wrong. My sisters were not familiar with any form of American entertainment. They were priestesses of Kugappa.

MM: Is that a local deity?

Hekuuna: Local? Stupid man! Kugappa is the great god of all the world.

Laura: But he's only worshipped on this tiny hellhole of an island.

Hekuuna: But someday—

Mongo: Now, girls. A little decorum.

MM: Jones, how did you meet Hekuuna?

Jones: It's a long story, so I'll give you the condensed version. Hekuuna's father, who passed away a few years back, used to be king of this island. Her mother was a tourist, originally from Chicago, who met and fell in love with the king. Hekuuna was the oldest of the three daughters, destined to take over the throne someday. Her mother sent her to college in America to receive a more cosmopolitan education.

Hekuuna: America is filled with pigs!

Jones: Yes, my dear—but lucky for me you have a fondness for pork. I met Hekuuna at a concert in New York City. She snuck backstage, and—well, she's just very beautiful. And wise—the wisdom shines in her eyes. I fell in love with her the moment I saw her.

Laura: *Evil* shines in her eyes. I hate her.

MM: I'm not sure if I should bring this up, but—well, my readers would want to know, so here goes. Some people say that Hekuuna is ultimately responsible for the downfall and self-imposed exile of The Vittles.

Hekuuna: Yes, that is true. I made them what they are today.

Laura: Whore. Filthy pagan whore.

Mongo: I give up.

Laura: They came here because Hekuuna told them to. And it's the only place in the world that doesn't mind cannibalism. It's the only place that would *take* them.

MM: Cannibalism. Yes, I wanted to get back to that topic. So that still goes on here at Pokaluhu?

Hekuuna: Food is food. Is that so hard to understand?

MM: Certainly The Vittles sang a lot about food in their early days, with songs like "Submarine Sandwich" and "Captain Bacon's Hungry Chowhound Band." But later—after Jones met Hekuuna—they started to releasing singles like "Eight Plates Of Meat," "I Wanna Eat Your Gland," and "Luigi In The Pie with Diced Ham." Their music grew steadily darker—the *Filet Of Soul* album was awfully grim, but it was positively perky compared to *Monstrous Misery Tour.*

Hekuuna: Yes, that was my doing. I took them to the next level. That is why I told them to destroy the town where they grew up. They were too fond of their old ways. Their old identities. They had to erase the past, so they could be reborn into a new future of great power. An artist must grow—must *evolve!*

Yilla: I started listening to the music of The Vittles after I married Mongo. I like the song "Helena Handbasket."

M'namma: My favorite one is "Buried In Hay Fields Forever." It is very pretty.

Yilla: You mean 'handsome'—it was sung by men.

Hekuuna: No, 'pretty' is more correct. 'Handsome' applies only to the men, never to the music.

Yilla: I see. Forgive my stupidity.

MM: So was it the band's newfound preoccupation with cannibalism that led to the attack on your fans at Monroe Hexagonal Stadium?

(A moment of silence.)

Popo: That's right, Mark.

Laura: Oh, God.

Hekuuna: They were following the way of Kugappa.

Yilla: The way.

M'namma: The way.

Mongo: Yes, the way.

MM: So Kugappa is a god of cannibalism? Just out of curiosity, are you all eating human flesh right now?

Gregor: Is the Catholic deity the god of drunks, just because wine is a part of the religion?

Hekuuna: Yes, we are eating human flesh.

Mongo: It's not that bad, really. It's saltier than you'd expect. I suppose that's because people have too much salt in their diets. The taste is somewhere between turkey and fish.

MM: Laura, surely cannibalism doesn't set well with you. You're obviously not happy with life on Pokaluhu. Why do you stay here?

Laura: I love my Popo more than life itself. I would do anything for him. I did—what I did—so I could stay by his side. I'm a good wife—not some vicious island whore. I'll stay by my man through—through thick and thin—

Gregor: Hekuuna told us how we might achieve godship through Kugappa, and so we…um…

Jones: We climbed onboard. And lost weight in the process. Pretty much a win-win sort of deal. Hekuuna had me convinced long before the others agreed.

MM: What does Kugappa look like?

Hekuuna: A mighty octopus. A beautiful sea-god of knowledge and power.

MM: Oh, I saw a lot of octopus statues today. Were those Kugappa?

Hekuuna: What a ridiculous question! Those were merely *images* of our god.

Gregor: Kugappa is from the same realm beyond the stars as the being known as Cthulhu, daemon-master of madness and dreams, who sleeps in his silent temple on the sunken island of R'lyeh.

Mongo: That's just a few miles from here.

Hekuuna: According to ancient texts, when Kugappa examined this world, he found it to be most pleasing. So much water! So much *meat!*

Gregor: Now here's the really interesting part. There are actually *two* of Kugappa. One is the great soul that exists beyond time and space, and other is the physical manifestation, the body here on Earth—

Popo: Should you be telling him all that?

Gregor: I don't see the harm in talking about it.

Hekuuna: Yes, the whole world will know soon enough. We have much information to share with this writer-man.

MM: Hey, are you talking 'comeback'? Is that why you granted this interview?

Hekuuna: Ah, you are perceptive—not so stupid after all. Yes, The Vittles have been in rehearsal for the past several months. My sisters and I have written some sacred songs for them. Soon The Vittles will be topping the charts again.

MM: You and your sisters wrote the songs?

Yilla: Pretty songs.

M'namma: Sacred songs.

Hekuuna: Songs to enhance, to *multiply* the power of Kugappa. Soon the sacred music will play in every land. The whole world will tremble and kneel before Kugappa. For Kugappa is the great god, the all-embracing god, and he is ravenous. Soon the world will be his for the taking!

Laura: Not if I can help it!

Hekuuna: Dog-woman! Blonde bitch! Shut your mouth! I should have killed you the moment you set foot on Pokaluhu. But the men, they told me you would change. Why do you not succumb to the power of Kugappa? I command you—surrender your soul!

Laura: Never!

Mongo: Here we go again!

MM: It would appear that Hekuuna has lunged toward Laura, and the two woman are wrestling. And yet…It seems like all the figures behind the screen are somehow being pulled into the fight—even the dogs, or trunk, or whatever that big lump beneath the table is. The blind servant, Ko, is trying to break up the fight—that's a mistake! I should warn him. Yo, Ko! *Oh, no!*

Somebody just punched the poor guy—so now he's trying to get away—now one of the boys, I can't tell which one, just—well, *roared*— then reached out to grab Ko. But whoever it was who reached out…I didn't see any legs. Just a long, long body. How—? Oh, now they're really going at it—the servant is screaming and—are they *pulling stuff out of him?*—he's kicking at the screen—it's falling over and—No!—Oh, my God!—

At that point, I had grabbed the tape recorder and stepped back away from the table. But in doing so, I'd accidentally switched off the machine.

The Vittles and their wives stood before me. Ko was dead—torn apart, with bite-marks all over his body. Loops of his intestines were strewn about within the gazebo. His head was practically severed, attached to his neck by only a few shreds of skin.

The eight living people in the gazebo did not have any legs. Below the arms, each one of them was simply a muscular, sinuous tentacle—and the eight tentacles were rooted in the rounded shape under the table. I now saw that the shape was in fact the body of a huge black octopus, which glared at me with bulbous eyes, alight with reddish-orange fire. In a moment, that fierce glow sprang up in the eyes of seven of its people-limbs.

The eighth one, Laura, fought the horrid power of Kugappa. I watched as she writhed in agony, clutching helplessly at Popo's arm. Her eyes rolled up in their sockets as she screamed—and when they rolled back, the fire was blazing within them. The creature had won at last. And what Laura did *then*…I had to look away, because I knew I would vomit if I watched for even a second more.

Hekuuna stared at me with her flaming, almond-shaped eyes. Jones was right: she was a beautiful woman. She had all the cold-blooded beauty of hooded cobra. "Be our messenger," she whispered. Her snow-white teeth were long and pointed. "Tell the world that the hour of Kugappa is near. Go, writer-man, before I gouge out your filthy mortal eyes!"

"Yes," said Jones. "Leave us now." I took a quick look at his blood-streaked face. He had worn dark glasses at the end of his career, so I figured that perhaps there had been some scars from that shooting. But no, the plastic surgeons had taken care of all that years ago. The flesh around his eyes was fine. So he had worn the glasses for another reason. Perhaps his eyes had taken on that glow before the others.

I turned, but I didn't run, despite Hekuuna's threat to blind me. I've seen cats chase mice—predators just love to pounce upon scurrying prey. I simply walked. One foot in front of the other, slowly, so slowly, I walked out of the shade, out of the garden of the octopus, all the way back to the mansion.

I asked the blind woman to call the hotel and tell them to send their driver. She did so.

She accompanied me to the car when it arrived. As I loaded my bags into the back seat, I said, "Do you want to come with me?"

"To America?" she said with a laugh. "Why would I want to go there? A mother's place is with her children."

So the old woman was Hekuuna's mother—the island's actual ruler. "You don't mind what your daughters are doing?" I asked.

"Oh, I don't judge them. I only want them to be happy." Then she smiled. A radiant, crazy smile. "All they need is love."

Yes, I suppose that *is* all they need: the love of millions of devoted fans worldwide, all clamoring to buy the new CD by The Vittles.

Rest assured, I won't be purchasing a copy.

Sometimes at night, I cry when I think for too long about Laura. Kind-hearted, loving Laura, who detested the thought of eating anything with a face....

She was a strong woman, but in the end, she was no match for the power of Kugappa. I will never forget her expression, right after she fell under the sea-god's spell—that look of *bestial hunger* as she reached out, tore Ko's head free of his neck, and bit into his plump cheek with carnivorous gusto.

THE GROVELER IN THE GROTTO

Assuredly I am not a trembling leaf of a man—not the sort who chirps with terror and befouls his dungarees when some weensy, breeze-tossed speck of pollen tickles the inside of his nose on a golden summer's day. No, I am not the sort who waves crucifixes at kittens or calls out the National Guard just because a cricket is nibbling on the crust of his sandwich. And yet I remember a day back in 197-ought, when I did run as fast as my legs could carry me out of the house of my childhood friend Reginald Blathingsmythe. I wore a mysterious black leisure suit, and I ran and ran until I collapsed, and then I got up, ran some more, stopped at a coffee shop for some cappuccino, and then ran for another five minutes.

By then, I was home.

But the next day, while doing the dishes, I thought about what had happened in that accursed house of mind-shattering doom—and the water from the tap suddenly ran cold.

My name is Wintergreen Fortescue St. Valentine, and at that time, I was renting a house in the peaceful town of Dunwich—the sort of laid-back little village where nothing ever happened and people felt free to leave their back doors unlatched at night.

At that time, I was writing a bestselling series of thrillers with the words 'portfolio' and 'death' in the title. *Dr. Portfolio and Mr. Death. Death of a Portfolio Salesman. Ring Around The Rosie, A Portfolio Full of Death.*

I was working on my latest epic, and I needed a new place where I could really think. I was having difficulty coming up with a new title. The best I could think up was *Portfolio, Portfolio, Portfolio, Death, Death, Death.* Not bad, but I felt that I could do better. I found I could no longer concentrate in my lavish Manhattan penthouse. The little cherrywood table next to the bidet had once given me a nasty splinter. Cherrywood. Feh!

My old pal Reginald Blathingsmythe had always spoken well of Dunwich, so when my publisher tapped his wristwatch in reference to my deadline, I decided it was time to roll up my sleeves and get to work in the peace and quiet of Smalltown, USA.

Lars, my live-in butler, secretary, and disco-dancing instructor, took care of finding a house for me. He arranged for some of my clothes and belongings to be transported there. He made sure the utilities were turned on, all the bills were paid in advance, the lawn was mowed, and he even put a chocolate on my pillow (on a doily, of course, so it didn't leave a mark on the fabric).

"This whole moving business has been a terrible ordeal," I said to Reginald on my first day in Dunwich. We were seated in his living room, eating cucumber sandwiches. "But I think I will find the strength to pull through."

"And how does your Lars, your lover, like the town?" Reginald asked, handing me a steaming cup of oolong tea. Reggie was a plain-looking, chubby fellow with thick black hair and eyes of different colors—one green, one orange.

"Lover?" I chuckled dismissively. "You mean 'butler.' Lars is my hired man."

"But he lives with you. Yes?"

"Of course," I replied. "That is what butlers do."

"And he makes your meals. Yes?"

"He is my disco-dancing instructor as well. He keeps track of every calorie I ingest, since a potbelly would ruin the classic lines of a leisure suit."

"And he goes to bed with you?"

"All part of a very specific exercise regimen. He says it loosens up the hips, and I am inclined to believe him."

Reginald choked on his tea and began to blink furiously, so that for a moment I thought he was conveying a message in Morse code.

Reginald's furnishings, I noted, were solid oak. Oak! Now there was a wood you could trust. I noticed something odd about his bookcase—something that caused a small but sharp bell of warning to ring in my mind. Most of the volumes on its shelves were quite old, and bound in rotting human skin. Finally I noticed the thing that had set off my inner alarm: the bookends were mismatched. One was a human skull and the other was a kitschy little plastic owl. Certainly plastic has no place in the decor of a gentleman's study.

Then I saw something else rather unusual. "So tell me, Reginald. That door in the corner—the one marked with that blood-red symbol of unholy dread. Where does that lead?"

The bland, cheery face of my host then underwent a marked change. His plain, dreary features—too boring to be considered ugly, really—suddenly twisted into the spasm-ridden, demon-haunted visage of a doomed soul being relentlessly pricked by the flaming pitchforks of the demons of Tartarus.

"The doorway to the secret grotto—I mean, spare bedroom?" he whispered hoarsely. "Nothing hideous or diabolical about a *spare bedroom,* I assure you." He laughed nervously. 'This relentless questioning of yours is uncalled-for! It really is *too much!*"

What an interesting response, I thought.

"So the door really leads to a secret grotto, eh?"

"Dash it all!" he cried. "Who told you? The shocking legacy of my accursed family has been kept hidden in shadow for well over three-hundred years! And now it seems that everyone with an unusually intimate butler named Lars knows about it!"

I found Reginald's behavior to be disturbing and inexplicable—not 'cool,' to borrow a term from the young people of the time. "So are you going to tell me what's in this grotto of yours or not?"

"No! Never! It is forbidden!" His cuckoo clock then warbled the hour. "My mood-ring discussion group will be here at any moment," he said. "Do stop by tomorrow—so long as you do not mention the black door of the Blathingsmythe family secret, or dance-cults that worship primordial devil-gods!"

"Now why in the world would I mention—" But I cut myself off in mid-sentence. No sense in throwing poor addled Reginald into another tizzy. But I saw he was looking at me curiously, so I thought of a cunning finish to my sentence. "—puppies?"

He smiled pleasantly. "Puppies are fine. Puppies are cute. You may mention puppies as often as you like. Just not devil-gods or ancient scrolls."

"Very well then. Puppies! See you tomorrow, Reggie."

* * * *

Back at the house, I told Lars about Reginald's behavior. He put down his newspaper to listen to me, and also to help me with my grooming. I did not like the paper's lurid headline—GRAVE-ROBBERS AGAIN ABSCOND WITH THE HIDEOUS ROTTING CARGO OF LOCAL TOMBS. People so often jump to outrageous conclusions. Why, maybe the grave-robbers in question were just *borrowing.*

"This matter of Reginald…very curious," my butler stated. "I shall have to ask the group their opinion of the matter."

Lars, in addition to his many other talents, was also a singer with a musical group called 'The People of the Village.' I was forever telling them to shorten that name—to perhaps take out some of the smaller words. But their response was always that 'The People Village' was a bit awkward, so they would be leaving the name as it was.

There were five members, and they dressed in the garb of various professions. Lars, of course, had his butler suit. Gregor wore a pirate's swashbuckling finery. Theodore sported the billowy hat and smart white outfit of a French chef. Horatio's costume was that of a matador, while Calvin favored the multi-colored togs of a circus clown.

"So you will be going back tomorrow?" Lars asked. He had just finished applying a thick layer of wax to my back. "Perhaps I should go with you. This Reginald fellow may be dangerous."

"I don't think I have anything to worry about. Reginald wouldn't hurt a fly." I screamed just a bit as Lars ripped off the wax, along with hundreds of thousands of back-hairs. "You know," I said after I'd regained my composure, "I'm still not sure what back-hair removal has to do with disco-dancing."

"Nothing. I just like waxing people. How hairy is Reginald?"

I ignored the question. "If for some reason I do not come home tomorrow, feel free to come and rescue me. Bring the group if you like. The more the merrier."

"That's what I always say," Lars said with a smile. He aimed a pair of tweezers at my face. "Now let's see what can be done about those eyebrows."

* * * *

The next day, I had to knock several times before Reginald came to the door. I was appalled to see that my friend had experienced a shocking transformation since our previous meeting. His thick black hair was now streaked with white, and his plump face now sagged hideously and was networked with the deep wrinkles of advanced age.

"Great bowls of clam-dip!" I uttered. "I take it your mood-ring discussion group didn't go well...?"

He lead me into the living room, where the coffee table was set up for the dispersal of any sort of drink one could imagine—except coffee. Bottles of gin, vodka, tequila and ouzo cluttered the lacquered surface. Reginald's booze-soaked breath conveyed to me that he was pretty lacquered as well.

"How can a man," he sobbed, "endure the burden of a century-spanning legacy of unspeakable decadence, the likes of which no decent, God-fearing society could ever tolerate?"

"Don't know..." I looked around the room, and noted that the black door was open about an inch. "But I bet this whole legacy of terror rigmarole concerns what's behind that door."

He followed my gaze and, seeing that the door was open, rushed over to shut and lock it.

"Oh, stop being such a mollycoddle," I said with a laugh, mixing myself a Manhattan from the assorted bottles on the table. "Let us see

"Unhallowed centuries ago, my ancestors engaged in numerous hideous acts of carnality with the dread primordial nature-god Shub-Niggurath, who is known as the Goat with a Thousand Young. This fiend is endowed with both male and female…properties. Months later, my female ancestors—and I blush with mingled horror and embarrassment to tell you this—unnaturally spawned the eggs that eventually hatched into the grotto-dwelling spawn you see before you!"

"So you are related to these loathsome beasts?"

"Don't rub it in. And actually, they are called blogdoths." He unrolled the scroll and held it out for my inspection.

"It looks like…" I studied the charts, the graphs, the pictures of little feet, the curved lines, and all the bizarre mathematical formulas and musical notations. "…like some sort of ancient…*dance lesson….*"

* * * *

Suddenly we heard a great shuffling of feet. "Reginald," I whispered, "are more of those blogdoths heading this way?" Then I realized that the noise was coming from the tunnel to the house.

Imagine my surprise when my faithful butler Lars and his musical group, The People of the Village, emerged in full costume from the tunnel's mouth.

"Hello, boys," I said cheerily. "What brings you to the Grotto of Grotesqueries?"

"Well, in the middle of rehearsal, I realized you'd been gone an awfully long time," Lars said. "Nobody answered the phone when I called Reginald, so we all decided to rush over and see if old Reggie had gone crazy and slaughtered you like a pig. Oh, hello, Reggie. Say, where did all the blogdoths come from?"

"You know about blogdoths?" Reginald exclaimed.

All of The People of the Village nodded. "Sure," Calvin said. "We're all descended from good, hearty Lower Belgravian stock!"

"Astonishing!" Reginald enthused.

Horatio nodded. "Yes, we met at a meeting of the Society for the Advancement of Lower Belgravians over in Arkham a few years ago. We found out we shared a love of singing and dancing, and the rest is history."

"I wish I'd known about that society," Reginald said. "Especially since it's dedicated to people from my home country!"

"But aren't you British?" Lars queried. "Heck, I thought you were in line for the throne."

"Look at all these blogdoths," Gregor said. "I was just telling Theodore the other day, what a pity we don't have access to some blogdoths and the Dance Lesson Scrolls of Shub-Niggurath. Why, we could, according to old Lower Belgravian legends, control an eldritch force of unspeakable power. Isn't that right, Theodore?"

Theodore nodded.

"What a mind-boggling series of coincidences!" Reginald marveled. "For here…here in my hands…I hold those very Dance Lesson Scrolls!"

"Quite a coincidence indeed!" Lars said. Then he turned to me. "Well, Wintergreen, we'd better be heading home. You're long overdue for a pedicure."

"Wait a minute," Theodore said as we all turned to leave the cave. "Reginald, can you dance?"

"In my youth, my friends called me Twinkle-Toes."

"I'll take that as a 'yes.'" Theodore grabbed the scroll. "Why, if the six of us—Reginald and The People of the Village—followed the instructions on this scroll, we could harness the power of the blogdoths, and who knows, maybe even the cosmos! But can someone refresh my memory? What part do the blogdoths play in this ancient ritual?"

Reginald rushed over to the alcove and brought out what appeared to be an ancient oil-lantern with a directional visor on one side. He took some matches from his pocket and fired up the wick inside the lantern. He then handed me the relic. "The blogdoths will huddle together to watch when the dance begins. Shine the Lantern of Th'narr directly into their eyes."

I trembled with anticipation. "Wow. My first ancient ritual."

And so it began.

* * * *

The six men of Lower Belgravian descent consulted the scroll, and then started the complex dance, complete with hand gestures and hip swivels. At several points in the proceedings, they spelled out S-H-U-B-N-I-G-G-U-R-A-T-H one letter at a time by shaping the letters with their hands, arms and occasionally even legs.

As per instructions, I directed the light of the lantern into the shiny fly-eyes of the huddled blogdoths. Thousands of beams of multi-colored light reflected off of those multi-faceted orbs, onto the gyrating dancers. I was a little disappointed I couldn't join the dance, since I wasn't from Lower Belgravia—but hey, somebody had to work the lights.

I think the glow of the lantern hurt the eyes of the creatures, because they soon began to cry out, some high, some low, in a complex series of otherworldly rhythms that created an effect not unlike a rather snappy pop tune.

The whole spectacle was pretty entertaining. But then that toe-tapping good time turned into a horrific, soul-freezing nightmare from the mephitic depths of the Devil's own bowels.

For suddenly, the cave walls began to fade away, transforming into the star-spattered darkness of outer space, while the cave floor turned from damp gray stone into a hard black surface spinning beneath us.

"Great Caesar's enema bag!" I bellowed. "What is going on *now?*"

The spin of the black surface, which was disturbingly etched with grooves, threw me right on my backside. But I still managed to hold onto the lantern. I looked up, and saw—saw—

There are some visions that no human eyes were ever meant to see, just as there are certain odors that the human nose was never meant to sniff. Above me towered one such sight, and it reeked of one such scent.

It was a gigantic, goat-headed, snail-antennaed, titanic deejay with a multitude of furry legs, and it was pumping those hairy, behooved limbs as it rocked to the beat of the song created by the mewling blogdoths, who now were scampering all over the giant *record* which the grotto had become. Reginald and The People of the Village were also stumbling around, vomiting in time to the blogdoth-music as they nauseously danced in circles.

I knew then that the ancient deejay had to in fact be *Shub-Niggurath, the stinking Goat with a Thousand Young*—and so I set the lantern by my side and began to grovel—grovel before the primordial god of *getting one's groove on…*

I guess all my groveling must have paid off, because suddenly I was wearing the Black Leisure Suit of High-Priestliness, and Shug-Niggurath was giving me a big thumb's-up—or rather, hooves-up—and the nature god bid me to dance, to show my true talent so that I might become the ultimate power of the Universe. And just as I began my disco-dance of triumph—

I accidentally kicked over the oil-lantern.

The giant record caught on fire, flaming blogdoths were running around bleating, The People of the Village all caught fire, too, since their costumes were made of flammable man-made fabrics—it was just a mess.

Shub-Niggurath waved goodbye with his hooves as the grotto reverse-faded back into place. I found myself standing on damp gray stone again, surrounded by a variety of charred, dead bodies.

The visor from the broken lantern was resting at my feet.

I picked it up and sadly looked at my reflection in its shiny surface—
And ran.

I ran from the grotto, down the tunnel, into the living room, out of the house—and that pretty much brings me back to the beginning of my narrative.

What did I see reflected in the accursed visor of the Lantern of Th'narr? Surely it was a vision of supreme insidiousness, spawned in the bubbling crap-craters of the abyss. I was the Chosen One of Shub-Niggurath, and I would forever wander the Earth with that foetid god's mark upon my wretched brow.

Let me put it this way—

The TV isn't the only thing in my house with…antennae.

ANECDOTE OVERHEARD AT THE
LAST COCKTAIL PARTY EVER

The moon is watching us, my friends. Watching us with enormous quicksilver eyes.

What can be said for the morning news anchorman who delivered his update on Iraq in Pig Latin, with the help of Jeff, the Malaysian hand puppet? And who can fathom the matter of the Sicilian volcano that spewed five-hundred and sixteen gallons of extra-foamy cappuccino while belching out swamp gas to the tune of "Un Bel Di"?

Strange forces were at work that day. Insidious influences of an extra-dimensional nature.

In a village on the Yucatan peninsula, oversized cicadas ate the elastic out of all the white cotton briefs. A British secretary staying in North Rhine-Westphalia was told by the ghost of an insane seamstress where to dig ("Behind the rabbit hutch!") to find a long-lost jar containing half of a cookie that had been nibbled upon by the Marquis de Sade. And at 10:23 p.m. Central Time, a cornfield in Buttercup, Iowa split open and *It* emerged: that selfsame deity that the Pre-Atlantean, Post-Lemurian Serpent Priests addressed by Seven-Thousand-and-Twelve Sacred Names (Number Eleven translating to "Whatever It Is, We Wish It Would Just Leave Us Alone"); that lugubrious critter known to the ancient Aztecs as He-Who-Drips-Sweat-All-Over-Our-Nice-Clean-Temple, to whom they sacrificed the lymph nodes of their enemies after they'd given the hearts to gods they actually *liked.* This entity had the face of a rhinoceros, the wings of an albino fruit bat and the body of a hotel bellboy (It also wore the little hat). It stood eight-hundred feet tall and shot rays out of Its golden-brown eyes that could turn stainless steel into a truly good tapioca.

This being was in fact the odious and horrific Rhinodactyl, Lord of the Absurd, and on the day that It emerged from the cornfield, It screamed and squealed and screeched and caterwauled for—what else?—women's dress shoes. It then added, in a disturbingly conversational tone (for oh, It was trying to lull civilization into a false sense of security), that if It did not receive enough women's dress shoes, and mind you, they had to be stylish, It would coat the entire world with a thick layer of rabbit excrement, ruining TV reception for all eternity. Reporters and channelers and spokesmodels conveyed the news to international heads of state, and so began the mad global dash for shoes, shoes, lovely and delicious and ever-so-rococo shoes. But as soon as the first dump truck load of Italian leather goodies arrived, the fiendish Rhinodactyl requested creamed spinach casserole by the ton.

And the madness continued thusly.

Lava lamps. Couches upholstered in animal prints. Hygiene films. Those little plastic houses that tell you the barometric pressure by whether the little burgomaster or his milkmaid wife pops out of a door. There was no way to predict what the unsavory behemoth would want next.

This nightmare creature shook the world like an aging movie queen shaking the last few drops of hand-cream out of a crystal decanter just before her long-awaited rendezvous with a $150-an-hour male gigolo named Big Johnny. It played with civilization like a garden spider playing with a leprechaun in its web (the afore-mentioned spider thinking, "Gee, a leprechaun, what luck. Maybe it'll grant me three wishes," so the spider asks for three wishes and the leprechaun says, "Oh, okay," and the spider promptly asks for three more wishes and the leprechaun says, "I think not," and the spider says, "Therefore, you *are* not," and begins to suck all the juice out of the poor little leprechaun who only wanted to be loved).

The perfidious Rhinodactyl teased and taunted civilization; It sprinkled itching powder down civilization's back; It slipped a plastic ice cube with a bug inside in civilization's drink; It then told an utterly shocking fib regarding civilization's little sister and a pimply Food-O-Luxe bag-boy (or should I say, comestible packaging engineer) from Wichita Falls, and that was the last straw. The outlandish and superfluous Rhinodactyl was a pest, a bother, a cosmic ne'er-do-well; so actually, no one was surprised when the nations of the world got together and tossed one nuclear warhead, extra-large, upon It.

At this point, one might expect a sweet and dandy resolution, a tidy denouement, a big rubber stamp that reads CASE CLOSED, BABY. But alas, such is not to be. For you see, the atom bomb did what it was supposed to: it atomized the insouciant Rhinodactyl. And the wind carried the monster's atoms through the air into the lungs of people everywhere…from the lungs, the contamination leached into the sweetmeats, into the damp grey convolutions of the brain.

That's the funny, little-known thing about absurdity: it's really, awfully, terribly, implacably, highly *contagious.*

These curious and virulent atoms insinuated themselves into all living things (the catalpa tree outside of my apartment is hopelessly in love with the wire-haired terrier that piddles on it) and into the very workings of our planet…but ah, the grandeur of fuchsia days, the decadence of neon-orange nights! Eventually, these capricious particles seeped beyond the ionosphere to invade the endlessly swirling web of space. Just last night, eyes blinked open in several of the moon's larger craters. And now the moon is watching us with eyes that shine.

So here we are, drinking furniture-polish margaritas and snacking on fricasseed trilobite esophagi. End of lecture…and everything else, for that matter.

Look to the window, my friends, and behold: the full moon, growing larger (hence, nearer) by the second, staring hungrily and grinning with more teeth than I have grubs crawling in the folds of my neck.

CTHULHU ROYALE

I. HER MAJESTY'S SECRET SHOGGOTH

"Bondcraft," said the tall, lean, dark-haired, lantern-jawed man in the tuxedo. Black, of course: a tuxedo of any other color was madness, a veritable mountain of madness. "H.P. Bondcraft."

"Dash it all!" ejaculated W., the Minister of Arcane Defense, a balding, heavyset man. "I know your name! Why, we've known each other since we roomed together at the London Academy for Young Espionage Gentlemen."

Miss Tuppenceworth, W.'s pretty blonde secretary, looked out the window of her office, which served as antechamber to her superior's sanctum sanctorum. "Why is it that whenever H.P. shows up, the sky is suddenly filled with multi-colored silhouettes of shapely women flying about? One can see outlines of guns among the female forms, and hear music filled with saxophones and trumpets. And there's this sort of swirly gun-barrel shifting to and fro…Decidedly odd."

"Not at all," W. said. "It's that private club down the road—the Society for the Advancement of Musical, Gun-Collecting Lady Gymnasts. Their ostentatious laser lightshows happen to coincide with Bondcraft's visits."

Miss Tuppenceworth fluttered her lashes at the spy. "So you went to school with W.? What was he like as a young lad?"

H.P. puffed thoughtfully at his cheroot. "Though Z. is the Ministry's resident expert on curious devices, W. also showed signs of great mechanical aptitude back then. I remember one summer, he bought one of those jolly vibrating massage chairs, and added parts from a milking machine and an automatic taffy-puller, and we took turns—"

"Now, now," W. chided, "Miss Tuppenceworth doesn't have time to stroll down memory lane."

H.P. smiled. "Oh, and once, W. played the part of Juliet in our espionage school production of—"

"Come with me, Bondcraft!" W. led the spy into his office and then locked the door behind them. H.P. headed straight to the liquor cabinet, where he made himself a tequila sunrise. Swizzled, not agitated.

"Drinking on the job!" W. scolded. "And tuxedos, always tuxedos. Why? Explain yourself!"

"Why?" Bondcraft smirked. "Why *not*?"

"You're a spy! You're supposed to blend in with the common rabble."

"Or so one would think!" H.P. drained his glass. "But because I'm usually a little drunk and stand out so, no enemy would ever suspect that I am in fact a secret agent. They'd be expecting someone sober and utterly nondescript."

"I say! I never thought of it that way. Ingenious!" W. sat down behind his enormous mahogany desk, which was littered with stacks of papers and several anatomically correct primitive fetish dolls.

"So what's new in the Ministry of Arcane Defense?" the spy asked.

"Some good news from our research base on Antarctica." W. flashed a merry grin. "We've found and captured a shoggoth! All very hush-hush, of course—top secret! We're still trying to figure out what to *do* with the blasted thing…It's so big and squishy. It eats quite a lot…it can change its shape…perhaps the awful thing has some potential as a biological weapon."

"You could always drop it on an enemy camp," Bondcraft said, "and let it eat everybody."

"Not a bad idea, but afterward, recapturing it would be a problem. Right now it's very sluggish, since it's down at that research base. The thing can't move very fast in that frigid climate. If we let it loose in a warmer spot, we might never be able to pen it up again. We're trying to figure out how to control the beast…perhaps even communicate with it. Maybe we'll find some more—the research chaps say Antarctica used to be crawling with them, back when it was less chilly down there. Anyway, let me tell you about your assignment."

Bondcraft smiled. "Is there an international casino involved? And a sexy double-agent?"

"Silly boy," W. said. "There's *always* an international casino involved. Master-criminals cluster around those casinos like flies around a dead street urchin. And yes, naturally here's a sexy double-agent. Vadda Fookenhottie."

Bondcraft smirked. "Such language!"

W. rolled his eyes. "That's her name: Vadda Fookenhottie. We have no pictures of her on file, but it wouldn't matter anyway because she is a master of disguise. Or should I say mistress of disguise…? Anyway, in addition to Miss Fookenhottie, you will be dealing with—not one, not two, not four, but *three* arch-villains."

H.P. allowed himself a small gasp. "Not…the 3D Cult? Dagon's Deadly Disciples?"

W. nodded. "The very same. Three worshippers of a foul and frightful oceanic deity." He tapped a button on a console on his desk, next to his THANK THE QUEEN IT'S FRIDAY mug. An oak panel on a far wall slid to one side, revealing a large monitor. On the screen, an image sprang up of a grey-skinned creature with a bulbous snout and a tiny, coal-black right eye. The left one was covered by a leather patch. The creature had arms and legs, but a dorsal fin, too, and was pictured stroking a little mutant with the head of a catfish and a human body.

"You'll remember this fellow, Bondcraft, since you're the one who put his eye out. Very clever of you, making him run with scissors. Villain Number One: Blowhole. A half-man, half-dolphin, power-crazed madmerman. His tiny new fish-headed assistant, who I believe you haven't met yet, is the evil Baitbreath. He can fling a fish-hook with deadly accuracy."

The next picture showed a scaly humanoid with flat, fingerless hands and a bumpy reddish-yellow shell on his back. "Villain Number Two: Goldflipper. This ruthless, wealthy turtle-man plots to control the world's finances from his underwater base near the Galapagos Islands." W. shook his head sadly. "Alas, we live in a world where even turtles can go bad."

The final image depicted a slender sea-man in a pin-striped suit. His skin was covered with slimy, iridescent scales. "This is Tunamunga, the Man with the Silver Spear Gun. He is the world's deadliest, most expensive and worst-smelling assassin. We aren't sure which is more lethal: his lightning-quick spears or his garbage-can odor."

"Three bad little fishies," Bondcraft said with a frown. "I see I have my work cut out for me. So where do we start?"

W. hit another button on the console and a panel opened up in the middle of the ceiling. A large plastic model of the Earth lowered on the end of a copper chain. He walked over to the globe and tapped a small land-mass in the South Pacific. The island responded by glowing neon-green.

"That," he said, "is the island of R'lyeh. It rose from the ocean depths a few years back and developers quickly converted all of its ancient architecture into a resort for jaded billionaires. It's the sort of place where the filthy-rich can frolic like satyrs hopped up on Viagra and PCP. It has twenty-seven gambling casinos, nineteen brothels, twelve roller coasters, eight ice-cream shoppes and three amusement parks where you can have sex on a roller coaster while you are gambling and eating ice cream."

"Yum," Bondcraft murmured.

"But the most famous—or should I say infamous?—establishment on the island is a luxury hotel called Cthulhu Royale. Anything goes at Cthulhu Royale—and when I say 'anything goes,' I mean 'warped inhuman perversions.' Why, if you wanted a sixty-three-year-old albino transsexual named Lulu to tickle your nether-regions with a peacock feather while he/she sings *I'm A Little Tea-Cup*, you could easily procure such a diversion at Cthulhu Royale."

"Good Lord!" H.P. uttered. "Do you know this for a fact?"

"Yes." A smile played around the corners of W.'s lips. "Anyway, Cthulhu Royale was recently purchased by the 3D Cult and is now being operated by its unspeakable minions."

"Really," Bondcraft laughed, "what could be so 'unspeakable' about these 'minions'?"

"Three words, H.P.: daily bouillabaisse enemas. Your mission is to fly out to R'lyeh, check into Cthulhu Royale, and find out what the 3D Cult and Vadda Fookenhottie are planning. I have a suspicion they're up to something devilish. Of course, you'll need a new batch of secret weapons. Let's head down to Z.'s laboratory."

II. FOR YOG-SOTHOTH'S EYES ONLY

W. and Bondcraft took the secret elevator in W.'s walk-in cigar humidor down to Z.'s lab.

Z., a bone-thin man with a shock of white hair, greeted them at the elevator doors. "Ah, agent Double-Nought Pi! Good to see you again."

Bondcraft smiled. "You are mistaken. I'm only Double-Nought Three."

"I believe Z. has, as the Americans would say, let the cat out of the bag," W. said. "You are being upgraded to Pi later this month, since you killed so many enemy agents last year. Bravo, old chap!"

The laboratory was filled with shelves of beakers, petri dishes, and electronic components. Bondcraft pointed to a large black door marked with a peculiar symbol in blood-red chalk. "I say, someone has scribbled a bit of graffiti over there," he said.

"That door," Z. remarked, "is the gateway to the dimension of Yog-Sothoth. We're carrying out some tests in that heretofore forbidden realm. That symbol, traced in sacred Tibetan chalk, is the only thing holding back the vile apocalyptic forces of mindless evil and utter darkness."

"Do tell the janitor never to clean that door," Bondcraft said.

"Ah! Good thinking…" Z. pulled out a notepad and scribbled a reminder.

They approached a stainless steel table in the center of the work area. Bondcraft picked up what appeared to be a common cigarette lighter.

"This," he said, "appears to be a common cigarette lighter. What does it really do?"

Z. smiled. "It makes waffles."

"Cyanide waffles, in case I catch an enemy agent at a breakfast buffet?"

Z. chuckled. "Cyanide? Ridiculous! How completely far-fetched. No, that small canister contains, in addition to pressurized waffle batter, time-released mutant scorpion eggs. Simply spray a layer of batter onto a plate. The formulated goo will instantly solidify into a delicious waffle for your target's enjoyment. Later, when he or she is asleep at enemy headquarters, the eggs, warmed by your target's innards, will hatch. Your victim will swell and split open, filling their camp with poisonous little monstrosities. That lighter has enough pressurized batter in it for five-hundred waffles—enough to kill a small, breakfast-loving army."

Bondcraft's next selection was a wristwatch, with two of the legs of cartoon character Oozy Octopussycat as the hands. The other legs were part of the painted background. "How jolly," he said. "Do the little legs spin so fast that the watch becomes a miniature helicopter, capable of carrying me to safety?"

Z. shook his head. "What a crazed notion. Have you been smoking those marijuana cigarettes of which American hipsters seem so fond? No, that watch doubles as a high-power flame-thrower and a bidet. An agent's personal hygiene is always a top priority. My assistant Belasco will give you a comprehensive demonstration later."

"I look forward to it." H.P. next held up a pair of gold cufflinks. One had the letter 'H' on it—the other, 'P'. "Explosives, right? Little nuclear bombs?"

Z. laughed. "Great heavens above! I now believe you have been huffing oven-cleaner, or perhaps smoking crack instead of those smelly cheroots. The 'H' cufflink contains recombinant equine DNA. Make any creature chew and swallow the cufflink and it will turn into a lovely white stallion upon which you can gallop to safety. The 'P' cufflink is a miniaturized nuclear bomb."

"But that's what I said!"

"Not quite. You said *both* were nuclear bombs. How redundant!" Z. took the 'P' cufflink from Bondcraft and popped up its lid. "See this little red dot? Simply tap it once with something tiny, like the point of a toothpick, and then throw the cufflink. You will have three minutes to leave the blast area."

"But it's a nuclear bomb," the agent said. "Would it even be possible to reach safety within three minutes?"

Z. looked with a lowered brow to W.

W. shrugged. "Preliminary testing, H.P., has proved inconclusive. I'm sure you will cross that bridge when you come to it. So! Let's go see Belasco, so he can give you that demonstration. Tomorrow morning, bright and early, he will drive you to the airport and you'll be on your way. I trust you will use all your persuasive powers to assure this mission's success."

H.P. nodded. "Let me at 'em."

III. FROM R'LYEH WITH LOVE

ENTRIES FROM THE PERSONAL JOURNAL OF H.P. BONDCRAFT:

Friday, 9 a.m.: On the plane to R'lyeh, thought the pretty French socialite in the seat next to me looked like a spy. Figured she might be Vadda Fookenhottie. Had sex with her in the loo, to see if that might make her fall in love with me and tell me all her spy secrets. But, it turns out she could only speak French, which is all blah blah blah to me.

2:30 p.m.: Arrived at R'lyeh. Took the shuttle to Cthulhu Royale. Saw the sights along the way. Pretty island. Palm trees and whatnot. The non-Euclidean geometry of the buildings is really quite jolly. Arrived at the hotel and checked in.

Noticed lots of foreigners in the lobby. Multi-colored outfits everywhere. Why in the world can't everyone wear basic black?

Had a few drinks in the bar. Forgot to leave a gratuity. My waitress Helga asked in broken English for her tip, so I took her up to the room and gave her the tip, and seven inches more to boot. But she didn't know thing one about the 3D Cult, so I guess she wasn't Vadda. Blast it all! This case is proving tougher to crack than a granite walnut.

4 p.m.: Saw a display outside the hotel restaurant which read, CTHULHU ROYALE WELCOMES U.N. DELEGATES. That explains all those foreigners. Say, I wonder if there's an American delegate wandering about? Those American girls are dead sexy—I just adore their loud voices and high, nasal accents! How exotic! British women, on the other hand, are dead common by comparison, with their low, purring voices—how dreary.

7 p.m. Had sex with three maids here and there in the hotel, and with a homeless woman, too, out by the dumpsters. None of them proved to be Vadda.

Later, had a lovely chat with a Belgian delegate after we had sex. She hasn't seen the American delegate—oh, poo! And she didn't know anything about the 3D Cult, though she once saw a 3D movie. She said the hotel gave all the delegates a great package deal for a big weekend get-together. The American *must* be here—those Yanks will hop on a plane at a moment's notice, glamorous jetsetters that they are.

11 p.m. Walked around the island for a bit, looking for clues. Maybe tomorrow I'll sneak into Cthulhu Royale's huge central tower. It shoots up way past the rest of the sprawling structure. I'd be able to see the whole island from up there. I wish I had a helicopter—what a pity the watch doesn't turn into one, instead of a stupid flame-thrower/bidet. What if I accidentally got the two functions mixed up? I'd burn my bottom off while giving my enemies a refreshing spritz. Perhaps it's time for Z. to retire.

1 a.m. Showered, brushed teeth, put on pajamas. I've kept the watch on, and have put the cufflinks on my pajama sleeves and the lighter in my pocket, just in case I'm attacked by someone who climbs into my bed to have sex with me.

Just as my head touched the pillow, it hit me: all those U.N. delegates are at the mercy of the 3D Cult! That whole get-together is a trap! Curse those wildly sexy Americans—just thinking about one distracted me so much, I wasn't able to see the obvious danger!

Am writing this with one hand as I use the other to call headquarters. Am punching in the numbers now. Must warn the world! Dear me, white vapors shooting out of phone receiver. Sleepy. Soooo sleeeepy…

IV. DAGON IS FOREVER

When Bondcraft awoke, he found himself in a maze of mirrors.

What have we here? he thought. *Why, I'm surrounded by countless images of me. Look how handsome I am. Hair all tousled. Still wearing my silk pajamas. Of course, I'd rather have my tuxedo on, if I'm going to be doing any spy business. I wonder if anyone tried to have sex with me while I was unconscious?*

Suddenly a booming male voice erupted overhead. "Good morning, Mr. Bondcraft. By now you have discerned that you are within a maze of mirrors."

Bondcraft recognized the voice of the ruthless villain Blowhole. *The devil!* he thought. *It's as though he can read my mind. But he probably doesn't realize that I know about the U.N. delegates.*

"And surely, you have pieced together our little scheme to kill the U.N. delegates and replace them with clones," Blowhole continued.

"Well, actually, I hadn't latched onto the killing or clone concepts yet," H.P. said, "but I'm sure I would have. I'm as sharp as a tack—and twice as deadly."

"While you were unconscious," the villain bellowed, "we scraped a few cells off the inside of your mouth and made a clone of you. We've accelerated its growth and taught it to slowly kill people in pajamas, and right now, it's roaming around in that maze of mirrors, looking for a victim." He laughed maniacally. "A victim in pajamas, Bondcraft! Ha ha ha!"

"Thanks for the warning," H.P. said. He removed the lighter from his pocket and the cufflinks from his sleeves, and then took off the pajamas and put them in a neat little pile by the wall. He was now wearing only his watch.

"I can see you, you know," Blowhole said irritably. "Hidden cameras and all that. Put those pajamas back on. Why, you'll catch a cold."

"Better than being murdered by a clone." The spy began to walk through the maze, surrounded by a pink fleet of nude reflections.

"What are you carrying?" the villain asked. "What are those little objects you have in your hands?"

Bondcraft noticed that some of the reflections farther ahead were wearing tuxedos. He had an idea. "I'm not carrying clone vitamins, if that's what you're thinking!"

"Clone vitamins?" a voice echoed from among the tuxedoed reflections. "Give me one, you handsome naked fellow over there!"

"It's a trick, you stupid clone!" the voice boomed. "You are not to take anything offered to you by a stranger. Especially a naked one."

"Fortunately, I'm not a stranger," Bondcraft said. "I'm your cellular Daddy—one look in any of these mirrors will confirm the resemblance."

"Daddy!" A tuxedoed figure sprang forth from the preponderance of reflections and ran to Bondcraft, giving him a warm hug. The spy popped the 'H' cufflink into the clone's mouth. "Chew. It will make you as strong as a horse."

The clone did as he was told. Soon he began to twitch. "I say, my clothes are getting awfully tight."

"You're a growing boy. Here, let Daddy help you take off that stuffy old tuxedo." The clone disrobed and H.P. put on the garments.

"Putting on the clone's tuxedo isn't going to fool me!" Blowhole cried. "Where are my storm-troopers? Still on their coffee break, I suppose. How am I supposed to get any killing done around here?"

Suddenly, with a loud, wetly explosive sound halfway between a 'pop' and a 'slurp,' the naked replicant biped blossomed into a large equine quadruped.

"Bad clone!" the voice thundered. "I command you to regain human form at once!"

The horse studied its reflection, confused but intrigued. Then it noticed what it had between its hindlegs. "I think I'm going to like this shape much better. It's so well-equipped!"

"A talking horse. How jolly!" H.P. climbed onto its back. "Do you remember how to get out of here?"

"Yes. Right this way." The horse began to trot out of the maze. "So tell me. Do I have a name, Daddy?"

"Let me think..." Bondcraft patted the creature's neck. "How does 'Thunderball' sound?"

"Rather dashing," the horse replied.

Red and blue lights started to flash, and shrill alarms sounded. "Good, because it's about time we dashed out of here," the spy shouted.

The sturdy horse raced through the maze. Several of the mirrors pivoted to one side as doorways, releasing armed storm-troopers. Some of the soldiers were still holding styrofoam coffee cups. The horse simply sped around and past them all, kicking a few along the way.

"Are we the good guys or the bad guys?" the horse whinnied.

"Definitely good," Bondcraft asserted. "In fact, we're fantastic. By the way, I've been told they've taught you to kill people in pajamas."

"That's right!" Thunderball neighed. "People in pajamas! Bloody, hideous freaks of nature, that's what they are! They deserve to die!"

"Not quite. People in pajamas are thoroughly delightful," the spy said. "It's the fishy-smelling villains who created you who are in fact the hideous freaks. Can you remember all that?"

"Oh, yes." Thunderball nodded. "Makes perfect sense, now that I give it some thought. Say, I know a short-cut. Put your head down by my mane, so you don't get hurt." With that, the horse leapt straight through a mirror and landed in the middle of a laboratory. Startled scientists scrambled out the door.

"That was a two-way mirror," Thunderball said. He shook his nose toward a large animal cage in the corner of the room. "Should we let their prisoner go? They've locked her up with some monkeys. I was chatting with her earlier. She's ever so nice."

"That would be the chivalrous thing to do," Bondcraft said. Through the cage's thick screening he could see a young woman streaked with monkey filth. He climbed off the horse and stepped up to the cage door, which was made of cedar. He used several well-placed blasts from his watch's flame-thrower to burn away the wood around the lock and hinges, so that the door simply fell to the floor. All the monkeys happily scampered out.

He used the watch's bidet function to splash the young woman clean. "There. Now you're not caked with poop," he said. "Quite an improvement."

"I should hope so," the prisoner said. She picked a piece of banana out of her short auburn hair. She had pert, mischievous features and bright green eyes. "So I take it you don't recognize me?"

H.P. shrugged. "I guess not. Are you that lady scientist who lives with the chimps…?"

The woman laughed. "We've known each other for quite some time, Bondcraft. We chatted very recently by my desk, outside W.'s office. And we had sex on the plane. And in your room. And out by the dumpsters. And in a few other spots here and there."

Bondcraft stared wide-eyed at the young lady. "Miss Tuppenceworth? Fifi? Helga? Trashcan Suzie? And all those other women? But they were all different ages…weights…*heights!*"

"Mere details. I am, after all, a mistress of disguises, hired by the 3D Cult to keep an eye on a certain spy." She stepped up to him and stroked his cheek. "But they locked me up when I told them I had fallen in love with you."

"Vadda Fookenhottie!" Bondcraft cried, puckering his lips to kiss the alluring double-agent. He leaned toward her and—

"I hate to break up this romantic moment," Thunderball said, "but those fishy-smelling villains just walked in. You know, the hideous freaks of nature."

Blowhole had a pistol in one hand and a laser-gun in the other. Tunamunga raised his spear gun and Baitbreath held out a poison-dipped fish-hook, ready to attack at a moment's notice.

Goldflipper, who would have had difficulty holding any sort of weapon, pointed a mean look at them instead. "Well, if it isn't H.P. Bondcraft…and the girl…and a talking horse!" wheezed the flabby turtle-man. "The Deadly Disciples of Dagon are not to be trifled with. Prepare to meet your doom!"

V. THAT IS NOT DEAD WHICH CAN ETERNAL LIE / AND WITH STRANGE AEONS, EVEN DEATH MAY LIVE AND LET DIE

An hour later, Bondcraft, Vadda Fookenhottie and Thunderball were all tied with thick ropes to the middle of a missile, which was standing inside Cthulhu Royale's lofty central tower.

"You know, I really should have figured out that this missile was hidden in here," H.P. said. "The tower is so much taller than the rest of the hotel, and it doesn't have any windows."

The villains were standing at the base of the missile. "Very soon," Goldflipper said, "we will fire this missile and it will fly off and blow up the home office of Der Moneygrubben, a prestigious chain of Swiss banks. This will throw the world's finances into a tizzy, and I will step forward to take control."

"Meanwhile, all the major powers will blame each other for the explosion," Blowhole explained, "and I will fan the flames of warfare—and sell arms to all the involved parties. And the U.N. delegates won't be able to stop me—for I've fed them to the sharks! Later today, I will fly their clones back to their native lands to replace them."

"Oh, H.P.," murmured Vadda. "Is there no hope for humanity?"

"Or horses?" Thunderball added.

"Leave it to me," Bondcraft whispered, giving them both a wink.

Tunamunga squealed, "At least let me spear one of them! Just one!"

"Yes, and let me throw just one hook," Baitbreath shrilled.

"Why bother?" H.P. shouted down to them. "Nearsighted little fishies like you couldn't hit the broad side of Moby Dick. I bet a million pounds, neither of you could knock the gold cufflink off my sleeve! Left wrist, see it? Shiny little bit of finery?"

"Pompous flounder!" Tunamunga hissed, raising his spear gun. "Eat silver!"

He fired at the cufflink—but H.P. simply turned his wrist so that the tip of the spear snicked open its tiny lid. The projectile then hit the missile's casing next to the spy's arm and bounced off.

"Nice try—for a stupid idiot moron!" quipped Baitbreath. He then flung one of his poisonous hooks. Bondcraft merely turned his wrist again, and the wee point of the hook pressed the cufflink's red button before falling away.

"Farewell, H.P. Bondcraft...and girl...and talking horse!" cried Goldflipper. He pulled a lever on a control panel next to the missile, and then he and the other villains ran off.

"Ten...nine...eight..." echoed a chilling mechanical voice, the sort villains just love to use for countdowns.

A huge panel opened in the tower roof.

"Seven...six...five..."

"Well, at least they didn't—" Vadda began.

"Four...three...two...."

"—feed us to the creature!" she finished.

"...One!"

With an earsplitting roar, the missile flew up and out of Cthulhu Royale.

Bondcraft wriggled his right hand closer to the cufflink. With a brisk tug, he pulled off the bomb and flung it down into the hotel. He looked at the ropes binding him. "What a pity my stupid flame-throwing watch is out of fuel."

"Hey, at least yours shot flames!" Vadda said. "The 3D Cult gave me a secret-weapon, too, but it won't do us any good now." She poked a shapely forearm through the ropes, revealing a gold wristwatch. "The hands go so fast, it acts as a helicopter."

"I've always wanted one of those," H.P. said. "Quick! Turn it on!"

Vadda clicked her fingers three times. Microchips embedded under her nails send a message to the watch and the helicopter action turned on, pulling her wrist out away from the missile. The missile veered ever so slightly in the direction of the pull.

"Ah! The tug of the watch is steering the missile out of its trajectory," Bondcraft said. "The world's finances are saved! Now you can use the watch's spinning hands as a tiny buzz-saw, to cut through these ropes."

"But Daddy!" whinnied the horse. "If she does that, we'll fall off the missile, straight into the ocean, and we'll drown."

"Don't be too sure." H.P. worked his hand through the ropes until he found the pocket holding the cigarette lighter. He dug out the lighter and said, "Quickly, my dear! Begin sawing through the ropes!"

Vadda bore down upon the ropes with the watch's spinning hands, and shreds of fiber flew through the air. On the horizon, Cthulhu Royale went up in a glorious mushroom-cloud of radioactive fire and smoke.

"Good gracious! What was that?" Thunderball shouted.

Bondcraft smirked as he wriggled both hands free. "A fish-fry." He pressed down on the lighter, moving it in a quick circular motion to create a small waffle, which he caught in his other hand the instant it solidified. He continued spraying and adding onto the waffle, always hanging onto one edge, until he'd created a disk as big as a manhole cover. "Thunderball! Help me with this. Grab your side of the waffle in your teeth to steady it—but whatever you do, don't eat any."

He kept spraying and spraying until the thick, resilient waffle was the size of a large raft. Then the ropes gave way and the spy, the girl and the horse all jumped onto the giant breakfast treat, which soared away from the missile like a magic carpet.

"We're free!" Vadda exclaimed. "Where do you suppose that missile is heading now—?"

"We have a bigger worry," H.P. said. "Eventually the waffle is going to land. Or rather, crash-land."

"Before it does," Vadda said, "I simply must tell you the truth. I'm not really a woman. I…I'm actually a small shoggoth. The Russians found me in Antarctica ten years ago and trained me to talk and retain a human form. That's why I can change my appearance so easily." So saying, she transformed into Miss Tuppenceworth.

H.P. took her hand. "I don't care if you're a shoggoth or a jungle beetle or a dancing toaster oven. All I know is this: I love you!" He leaned forward to kiss her and—

"Again, I hate to break up such a tender moment," Thunderball said, "but we've got company."

A huge, scaly claw snatched the flying waffle and its passengers out of mid-air.

Six terror-widened eyes stared up at an enormous face, dripping with seaweed and squirmy oceanic parasites. The face had shining, malevolent red eyes and a beard of flailing tentacles.

"Who's the gigantic bloke?" H.P. finally asked.

"The creature I'd mentioned," said the lovely shoggoth. "That's Cthulhu, a demonic beast-god who, according to ancient texts, has been trapped within the subterranean catacombs of R'lyeh for aeons. They named the hotel after him. I guess that explosion released him."

"Oops! My bad!" Bondcraft said.

One of Cthulhu's face-tentacles snatched up the huge waffle and flung it into his mouth. The creature swallowed the treat without chewing.

"How jolly!" Bondcraft said. "That giant waffle had hundreds of thousands of mutant scorpion eggs in it. The creature will have a belly-ache tonight that he won't soon forget."

"Maybe so," said Thunderball, "but right now—we're screwed."

Cthulhu raised his claw and dropped Bondcraft, the shoggoth and the horse one by one into his slavering maw, much like a lazy Roman emperor dropping luscious grapes into his mouth.

Meanwhile, back in London, W. heard a loud noise and looked out the window, to see if his noisy neighbors were having yet another laser lightshow.

The last thing he saw was the tip of a missile, heading straight for his smug little world.

THE END OF THE WORLD IS BROUGHT TO YOU BY...

7:00 - 7:30 p.m. Central: **My Mother The Shoggoth**

Yep, my mother died and came back as a protoplasmic monstrosity, and now she oozes around town chasing the butcher, the baker and every other lowlife who ever screwed her and blew her off. She's literally boiling mad: her superheated acidic secretions bubble and percolate with insane glee.

Shoggy-Dearest works her old beaus like a nightmare gourmet, frying their skins into crispy rinds, marinating their muscles into soggy ropes of human pâté, steaming their intestines into savory poop-sausages, pressure-cooking their brains until all their lusty memories of her once-lovely body are shriveled into mental raisins within fluffy grey cerebral soufflés. And she doesn't stop there. She keeps boiling and broiling until she's poached them all down to the bone, right down to their squeaky-clean grinning skulls...because old habits die hard.

Mother still likes to leave 'em with a smile.

* * * *

7:30 - 8 p.m. Central: **Rabid Bitch**

What's that you say, girl? A foamy-mouthed kitty bit your ass and now you've gone mondo batshit? You say you've ripped out little Nicky's throat down by the old mill? You say your brain swims in visions of fresh gushing blood, oceans of delicious heat to help warm the cold nausea of your disease?

You say I should follow you into the woods outside of town, the woods where Shub-Niggurath capers like an outsized millipede lined with misshapen goatlegs? The very same woods where your victims go to become doggymen, nasty bloody doggymen who smell like pee and hump the legs and butts and mouths of anyone and anything? You say that soon, Nicky will be joining Shub-Niggurath and the doggymen in a mad dance of red pleasure? You say a sad lonely creature like me would love to join, too...join the lunatic orgy of the doggymen, a mindless bacchanalia of blood-drinking and greasy-assed rutting fury in the deep, dark woods outside of town?

Lead the way, girl. Lead the way.

* * * *

8:00 - 8:30 p.m. Central: **Bottle Blonde**

You thought you could just toss me and my bottle back in the ocean. I loved you, and would have loved you forever. I blinked up a dozen magicks a day to save your bumbling ass, and that was how you repaid me!

Fortunately, a lifeguard, a bronzed demigod with more muscles in one arm than you have in your entire body, found my bottle and now he is my Master—and I am satisfying him in all the ways you were too finicky to ever let me try. He is asleep now, smiling the broad smile of the well-pleasured, so I thought I would take a moment to settle your bland hash.

You wanted me to be a good little show-wife, a prim little ornament to hang off your astronaut arm. When you found you could not tame me, you waited until I had steamed myself back into my bottle and then— chickenshit bastard!—you popped in the cork. When I think of all those wasted blinks, I could scream! You saw my blonde hair and blue eyes and forgot that I am a creature of boundless power—a djinni, and not just one of those cut-rate Persian knock-offs. I am the best of the original breed: an Egyptian djinni-princess, daemon-daughter of the crawling chaos Nyarlathotep. Like my father, who walks among men as a slim Pharaoh, I too enjoy wearing a pleasing human form. But the venom of scorpions flows through my undying veins, and my desert-jackal brain can conceive of a thousand, a hundred-thousand, a thousand-million soul-shredding torments.

You turned my love into hate—now consider this: I can turn your pubic hair into hungry sandworms. I can turn your kidneys into lice-ridden wharf-rats. I can turn the shit in your bowels into red-hot lumps of coal, and the pee in your bladder into liquid nitrogen. I can transform your teeth into wasps, your ribs into lawnmower blades and your spine into a jumbled mass of rusted, twisty bedsprings. I can do it, you know. I can, I most assuredly can, in the blink of an eye....

And certainly, it is time for me to blink away the tears.

* * * *

8:30 - 9:00 p.m. Central: **Flesh-Eating Castaways**

Six weeks after the boat crashed on this sauna-hot Pacific island limbo, we'd eaten all the crabs, all the coconuts, even all the leaves off the coconut trees.

Maybe it was those leaves that made us go bonkers, because soon, we were chomping on that old millionaire's leg, chomping on it and loving it, loving that rich fatty tender meat. That girl from Hollywood gnawed off his pecker at the root and said it tasted like lobster. That other gal, the one from the Midwest, dug her tough farm-girl hands deep into his belly and pulled out his liver and we all broke off chunks for dessert—so rich and sweet, who needs coconut cream pies?

He lasted us for three days. Next, we ate his wife: a touch old bird, but we softened her up by pounding her with rocks. Then we barbecued the college teacher by wrapping him in the chain from the boat's anchor and dipping him for just a few seconds in the volcano's lava. He squealed like a pig, he did. Guess he wasn't all-the-way dead!

The teacher was a pretty smart guy—I miss talking to him. He once said that about four-hundred years ago, the natives of this island worshipped Cthulhu, the tentacle-bearded dream-god of the deeps, who delights in turning men into ravenous beasts.

A lot of time has passed, and a lot of meals, and now it's just me and the captain. He's been protecting me…up to now. He calls me his little buddy, but that look in his eyes tells me that he's seeing his little cock-tail weenie. Well, come and get me, fatboy! I palmed the millionaire's money clip and I've been sharpening the edge of it on a piece of rock. I'll cut you, porky—cut you like the crazed hog that you are. Cut you and roast you on a spit! Roast you golden-brown, oh, you'll taste so good!

I feel the ancient powers of this island flowing through me, and yet I know there is no need for me to make an offering to Cthulhu. For Cthulhu sees through my eyes, feels with my eager hands, tastes with my dripping mouth. But is it my mouth that drips, or perhaps my luxuriant, glistening new growth of fleshy beard?

* * * *

9:00 - 10:00 p.m. Central: **Dunwich Place**

Meet the neutron-hot men and women of Dunwich Place….

Meet Mitzee Pickman, six-foot-one bulimic supermodel: seventy-five pounds of nervous energy with sinuses scrubbed to the bone from a steady diet of nose candy.

Meet Ricky Zann, insatiable, achingly beautiful chorus boy: his backdoor's as nimble as a Czechoslovakian gymnast.

Meet Arkham prettyboy Chucky Ward…med-school dropout Herby West…and Beulah Mae Whateley, a small-town girl with big-cosmos dreams.

When these five Generation Hex love-machines get together, anything goes, including Beulah Mae's hymen. She opened the dimensional gate to her Mystery Date, and before you can say "Sufferin' Psychopompos," she's as big as a bloated hog—and if you listen really close, you can even hear squealy little belly-sounds.

Herby and Chucky assist in the delivery, and both lose a few fingers in the process. The twins, Cletus and Li'l Unspeakable, gangbang Ricky into a puree on their second birthday. The next year, they chop up Mitzee, put her in a food dehydrator and snort up the bits. Chucky and Herby keep losing parts while babysitting, as Beulah Mae pursues a career in interior decorating and performs lavish makeovers on the Shunned House, the Witch-House, and the Strange High House in the Mist.

One day Beulah Mae returns home to find a note from the kids, spelled out on the floor in mingled Chucky and Herby innards. The note explains that the twins have shambled away from home to find their father, even if it means calling his name from atop Sentinel Hill. Beulah Mae recalls there's a television station at that address, and when she gets there, she discovers that Cletus and Li'l Unspeakable have taken over. They've even had stationery printed up, with a three-lobed burning eye as the logo.

The new programming begins to fray the April-fresh fabric of the space/time continuum: soon, housewives everywhere are finding fungi from Yuggoth sprouting in their bathrooms, and windshields worldwide are caked with the shit of shantaks and night-gaunts. Between programs, the twins keep broadcasting the same commercial: that logo, with the brothers gangsta-rappin' the voice-over, "YOG-SOTHOTH…YOG SO-THOTH…YOG-SOTHOTH…"

Inevitably comes that day when the skies turn dark, and all one can see overhead are miles of tentacles as thick as barrels, writhing around dark masses of purple flesh studded with bulging eyes and gaping moray-toothed mouths. Millions soil their slacks and/or die of heart attacks, but Beulah Mae simply looks up, holds out her arms and purrs, "Hey, Big Daddy. Gimme some sugar."

PICKMAN'S MOTEL

Anton Matterhorn Pickman was an eclectic, eccentric, brilliant and yet disturbed and disturbing man of many interests: movies, travel, history, photography, gourmet cooking, Egyptology, astronomy, and all forms of pornography. He owned a business just outside of Arkham called Pickman's Motel, best known for its highly popular comedy shop, the Ha-Ha Hut.

There was once a time when I considered Anton my very best pal in the world, for certainly he was fascinating company, someone with whom one could talk about anything and everything. But then came that hideous night of repellant blasphemy when I learned more than I cared to know about my friend. I discovered the abysmal depths to which he could sink, and after that, he was my friend no more.

His body—or rather, what was left of it—was found stuffed in a dumpster behind the Fancy Lad Male Grooming Emporium. Of his attackers, not a trance was found. I have no idea where they are, and do not wish to ever know.

Several weeks before his shocking demise, Anton phoned to invite me to his home, to show me his latest acquisition. He lived in one of the apartments of Pickman's Motel, and in his rooms he kept an enormous collection of rare, quasi-mystical, and for the most part, sexually explicit films and videotapes. Items in his collection included such controversial works as *Virgin Werewolf in a Whorehouse, I Married a Sex-Pig from Mars, Hitler's Satanic Prom Night, The Horny Revenge of Franken-Caligula,* and that little-known '70s hardcore science-fiction epic banned by the government of Japan, *The Happy Hooker Meets Godzilla.*

When I arrived at Anton's dwelling, he greeted me at the door with an absinthe cocktail and an enormous smile. He was a handsome man in his own strange way, with his wide, flat nose, ruddy complexion, lustrous green eyes, and thick silver hair with black streaks at the temples. One of his front teeth was missing, courtesy of a long-ago bar-fight, but even though he was certainly a wealthy man, he'd never bothered to have the gap mended. I recall he once mentioned the space made it easier to drink Long Island iced teas through a straw. Whenever we dined together and he ate corn-on-the-cob, it was always disconcerting to note one row of whole kernels still girdling the gnawed-upon cob left behind on his plate.

"So what amazing treasure do you have for me to view this evening?" I asked, gesturing toward a stack of videotapes piled on his coffee table. Some appeared to be new, but I recognized some from his previous tape-hunting expedition. Only three months before, he'd returned from a trip to the Forbidden Plateau of Leng, where he'd purchased, from a disgruntled and bowlegged temple acolyte, a copy of the tape, *Why Temple Acolytes from the Forbidden Plateau of Leng are Disgruntled and Bowlegged.*

Anton sat on the couch next to his table-trove of unhallowed goodies. "I just got back from a quick visit to the Nameless City, hidden in a for-midable, windswept Middle Eastern desert. There I learned fourteen of the one-thousand secret names of the fabled deity Nyarlathotep, and—"

"What are they?" I interjected.

"You really want to know?" Anton shrugged as he pulled a crumpled piece of paper out of the stack of tapes. "I wrote them down. It's really no big deal."

"I've always been fascinated by the mythologies of other lands," I said as I took the paper from him and began reading the list....

1. Dark Lord of the Screaming Abyss
2. Protector of the Night-Gaunts
3. Messenger of the Crypt Gods
4. Vile Master of the Blood-Soaked Torments
5. Father of the Black Scorpions
6. Uncle of the Flesh-Eating Hawks
7. Second-Cousin of the Accursed Pharaoh with Pubic Dandruff
8. Niles Lathotep
9. The Killjoy of Kadath
10. Discount Abdul, the Persian Carpet King—Half-Off This Week Only
11. Keeper of the Sacred Camel-Toes
12. He Who Doth Swing Both Ways in Darkness
13. Minty Belasco
14. Big Jake

When at last I looked up from the list, I saw that Anton was loading a videotape into his combination TV/VCR.

"Behold!" he cried. "You are about to witness what may be the great-est find in my obscure-movie-finding career! I have been reading about this little gem in secret-society fanzines for years. I have made hundreds of phone calls and sent countless letters and e-mails, trying to track down a single copy. And now, finally, it is mine! Hurray! Watch, my friend... watch and learn! But first, could you hand me the remote? It's right next to you, on that little table with the blue lamp. Oh, and put a coaster under your glass, please. Thanks!"

On the screen, blood-red letters sprang up on a lime-green background:

NAMELESS CITY FILMS
In Association with
HEADLESS JACKAL PRODUCTIONS
Presents
A Film by
Dzaal Dzoukadzouki, Jr.

DARK SUMMONING
OF THE
INSATIABLE TOMB-LEGIONS

"Great title," I commented.

"Shush!" Anton whispered, turning one admonishing eye toward me as he kept the other eye riveted to the screen. Not many people can do that. "I haven't watched this yet. I've been waiting to see it with you!"

"Really? That was nice of you," I said.

The opening credits rolled on:

Written by
Dzaal Dzoukadzouki, Jr.

Directed by
Dzaal Dzoukadzouki, Jr.

Produced by
Dzaal Dzoukadzouki, Sr.

"Figures!" I muttered to myself, noting the producer's elder status. "Looks like daddy wrote the check for all this. Hope he got his money's worth."

Starring
Dzaal Dzoukadzouki, Jr.
Dzandra Dzoukadzouki
Dzamuel Dzoukadzouki
Dzeke Dzoukadzouki
Kitten DuBois
Raynebeau Catorce
Diamanda Hamogeorgakis
Ming Placebo III
Glork
Hellgar
Krogg
Slobdoth

Yerk

Ghlupp

And Featuring
Attila the Wonder-Goat

The movie began in a torch-lit, subterranean chamber where a tall, hawk-nosed character, presumably Dzaal Dzoukadzouki, Jr., was using a chalice filled with blood and a long-handled paintbrush to paint a peculiar, circular symbol on the filthy stone floor. Around him, robed figures chanted and hummed in low, unearthly tones. I guess daddy's money wasn't enough to buy Dzaal Dzoukadzouki, Jr. a decent musical score for his movie.

"By the Sign of the Messenger of the Crypt Gods," Dzaal intoned, "I call forth the sacrifice! Bring to me the blood-beast!"

At this point, one of the robed figures led Attila the Wonder-Goat into view, and after catching a glimpse of what dangled between his lanky thighs, I could see why he was considered so wondrous.

Dzaal pulled a long, rusty dagger from out of the folds of his robe, and within a few minutes, Attila the Wonder-Goat was reduced to Attila the Generous Serving of Desert Sushi.

As the robed assembly feasted, Dzaal again picked up his paintbrush and used various fluids from the dead creature's carcass to add a few final flourishes to the design on the floor.

"From the dead, velvet blackness of the night sky," he moaned, "the full moon shines its necromantic energy down upon the Nameless City, signaling that this evening, the tomb-legions are ready to surge forth from out of the stinking bowels of the Earth! Arise! Arise, oh insatiable ones! By the power of the desert moon, I bid you to arise!"

At that summons, a fearsome yet oddly muffled howling sounded. Then came a distinct, frantic cacophony of digging and scratching, mingled with more howling and assorted shrieks, grunts, and eager whimpers. Before long, jagged cracks appeared in the stone floor, radiating out from the center of the bloody pattern.

A sinewy, long-taloned claw—a grotesque, bestial parody of the human hand—burst through the stone surface, followed quickly by another. These writhing claws raked and tore at the floor until they had created a hole large enough for the creature to pass through...

Great God in Heaven and all His tiny cherubs! I shall never forget the sight of the monstrous head that poked up out of that rough-hewn hole.

The thing looked like an especially unsavory cross between a mangy hound-dog, a Tasmanian devil, and a scruffy, drug-addled, middle-aged

British rock star. Its thick, drool-flecked lips quivered with rage as it glared, red-eyed and ferocious, at the screaming followers. I noticed that Dzaal was nowhere to be seen. Apparently he'd known what was coming and had left his relatives and extras to their ignominious fate.

The frenzied intruder leaped out of the hole, landing squarely on its misshapen, clawed feet. Its body was an unspeakable, shaggy mass of ferocious muscle and bullish bones. The gigantic phallus that slapped against its powerful thighs made Attila's male organ resemble, by comparison, a quaint Vienna sausage.

"A ghoul!" gasped Anton. "An actual undead entity! I've seen pictures of them in the *Necronomicon*, which I've studied at length at the Arkham Public Library. It has to be a real ghoul—this cheap-ass movie certainly didn't have the budget to create a fake one!"

More shaggy monstrosities, all as well-hung as their leader, squirmed forth from out of the depths until they outnumbered the robed worshippers. The ravenous creatures then threw themselves on the hapless humans and began to rape them, male and female alike, with animalistic gusto.

But the licentious savages weren't satisfied by mere sexual pleasure alone. No indeed. They took huge, flesh-ripping, bone-breaking bites out of the arms, shoulders, necks and heads of their victims as they impaled the poor souls on their engorged, regally empurpled members, thrusting and biting, biting and thrusting, until there was nothing left of the ravaged worshippers from the nipples up.

"The camera-man must be well-hidden," I observed. "They don't seem to be bothering him."

As it turned out, I'd spoken too soon. Apparently one of the creatures must have seen through whatever facade had been used to hide the technician, because at that moment, the savage lunged straight toward the camera—and then the screen went black.

"Oh!" I cried. "Is that all?"

"Yes," Anton said. "It's considered an unfinished masterpiece."

"Well, not sure about the 'masterpiece' part," I said, "but it's certainly unfinished."

Anton scowled at me. "You don't seem all that impressed. Those were real ghouls, I tell you! Real!"

"Oh, I'm sure they were," I said. "But the question is: What exactly is a ghoul? If a ghoul is some sort of huge, malformed human—a monstrosity, but still a part of Nature's grand and yet sometimes ostensibly ridiculous plan—then yes, certainly those were ghouls. But if a ghoul is an undead, supernatural entity...Well, those creatures never actually did anything supernatural, did they? All we saw were freaks on film, albeit oversized freaks with an undeniable taste for cannibalism and necro-philia. Though is it still considered necrophilia if both participants were alive when they started but one was killed in mid-fuck…?

"Perhaps those 'ghouls' we saw were merely escapees from some mental asylum or facility for the incredibly violent and deformed. Per-haps they'd been imprisoned in a room directly below that chamber we'd seen. Maybe listening to that ritual directly overhead had whipped them into a murderously erotic frenzy. We didn't see them do anything that a really strong, crazy, malformed human couldn't do."

Anton pouted. "Oh, poo! Here I thought I'd found something super-incredible! Now you've spoiled my fun. I guess I blew all that time and money on nothing!"

"I wouldn't say that," I replied. "I mean, it's still safe to say, that's probably the world's most exotic snuff film, right?"

Anton's pout turned into a grin. "Hey, you're right! That still makes it highly collectible and well worth the investment. Speaking of snuff films, let's take a look at this other movie I found…"

And so our conversation and evening of movie viewing turned down a different track. Several hours later, I bid my host goodnight and re-turned home.

As time passed, I found my thoughts returning again and again to the videotape Anton had shown me. Could those outlandish flesh-eaters really have been just hungry, overgrown rapists, or had Anton been right all along?

After all, would that many gigantic sex-freaks all look so much alike, and all be so well-hung? Maybe they actually were part of some malignant subspecies, diabolical in its origins. Unsettling thoughts be-gan to fester in my mind. Those creatures did have remarkably brutish, beastly features. But then, I reminded myself, so did my high-school gym teacher…

I happened to run into Anton at the Arkham Public Library just a few days later. I was walking down a shadowy hallway when he came bustling out of the Forbidden, Unspeakably Dangerous, Never-To-Be-Checked-Out-By-Anyone Section with a notepad in his hand and a huge smile fixed on his ruddy face.

"Ah, just the fellow I wanted to see!" he said. "In fact, I was hurrying to find a phone so I could call you. I've just finished taking another look at the *Necronomicon,* and also *The Big Book of Ghouls,* the *Cultus Can-nibalicus,* and *Lord Smudgington's Field Guide to Nasty Things that Eat People.* Based on descriptions from those authoritative tomes from long ago, I can now state without a single reservation that those slobbering bipeds in that videotape meet every single criteria one might expect of a ghoul."

"That might be so," I said, "but I think you're missing my point. Again I must ask the question: What exactly is a ghoul? Consider this! Maybe the deformed, insane, anthropophagous, but definitely earthly sex-fiends of yesteryear were deemed ghouls by the scholars of that time because they didn't know any better. Being less scientific than today's academic types, they would have been perfectly happy to ascribe super-natural traits to said psychopaths."

I must confess, I was taking a perverse enjoyment in countering Pickman's feverish assertions. I did not tell him that in fact, I'd been questioning the validity of my earlier thoughts and theories concerning ghouls.

Again Anton pouted, so I gave him a pat on the shoulder. "Now, now, don't be crestfallen," I said. "Remember: as we discussed, it's still one of the world's most provocative snuff films. Plus, you should be happy that undead ghouls really don't exist—you wouldn't want a batch of them popping up at your place and nibbling on you!"

"Oh, I'm sure they wouldn't care for my meat," he said. "I eat a lot of garlic and onions and seafood. They'd probably find my flavor very peculiar!"

"Now, let's not give ghouls and cannibalism and all that mumbo-jumbo another thought," I said. "Let's head back to the motel and have some gin-and-tonics at the Ha-Ha Hut."

"An excellent idea," Pickman said with a tepid half-smile. It was clear he was still chagrined by my input regarding his rare videotape, and probably would be for some time, in spite of his efforts to try to be positive about it all.

I decided to drop the matter entirely. If he ever brought it to my attention again, I would change my stance and, in the spirit of camaraderie, agree with his point of view. After all, I didn't want to lose his friendship over such a trivial matter—or so I thought at the time.

But then...

Then came that terrible night of ultimate horror—a night of the full moon, I might add—when I came home from a restaurant dinner with a group of friends and found the most mind-boggling message conceivable on my answering machine.

The message chilled my blood through and through, and caused even the shortest of my short-hairs to stand on-end. Needless to say, I never actually saw what was going on at the other end of the line—I only heard it. But what I heard was enough to make me fill my stylish slacks not only with the steaming No. 1 of fear, but also the stinking No. 2 of terror.

"Damn you!" shrieked the voice of Anton Matterhorn Pickman. In the background, I overheard the most awful screaming…and howling… and yes, assorted shrieks, grunts, and eager whimpers. "Damn you for drumming those damned doubts of yours into my damned head! Because of you, I simply had to know the truth—I had to try the ritual with a full, necromantic moon looming high in the sky. In the basement of my own business, Pickman's Motel, I gathered a motley assortment of lowly vagrants and ne'er-do-wells to help me with the summoning. I even had to buy a goat!

"But now—! The goat is dead and the worshippers are being eaten and fucked to death even as I speak!"

Causing the death of vagrants is one thing—but dealing death to a poor, innocent goat is quite another. That was a sin I could never forgive, and at that moment, Anton stopped being my closest friend. But considering that I'd found out about his sin from a message, and that his life was obviously in mortal danger during the time he was making the call (the guy pretty much had one foot in the grave and the other on a greased Slinky), there was an excellent chance he was already dead by the time I'd listened to his words, so it's not like I would've had to worry about running into him at parties.

The message continued. "I'm calling you from the basement phone—it's all happening right behind me! Why the Hell am I even jeopardizing my life by taking the time to call you, when I should be running to safety? It's like I'm some sort of witless character in some sort of melodramatic horror story!

"My God—those things, those ghastly things! If you were here, trembling in their horrendously demonic presence, you wouldn't doubt their supernatural origins for two seconds! And by the way, when they dug up through my basement floor, they didn't emerge from some underground prison that just happened to be down there. You've got to admit, that was a pretty stupid theory you had about where the movie's ghouls came from. What are the odds that there'd be a room right below the ritual filled with super-strong, sex-crazed cannibals? Come on, give me a break already!

"But what's this? One of the ghouls is shambling this way! Get away from me, you red-eyed, sharp-toothed devil! Get your damned paws off me! Get away! Get—"

Oh, if only those words had been the very worst of that madness-inducing message! For after a series of shocking screams, followed by a great deal of bone-crunching and what sounded suspiciously like intestine-slurping, I heard a different voice on my answering machine.

This new speaker's sepulchral tones rumbled with the repugnant vehemence of a plateful of rancid crab-salad working its way through the coiling intestines of a flabby casino waitress who always hits the buffet after her shift, no matter how long the food has been sitting out. The voice was gloatingly wicked—wickedly gloating—and altogether bloatsome, loathsome, insidious, lugubrious, and a lot of other snazzy adjectives, and this is what it said:

"Blecch! Your buddy sure tastes like crap!"

SQUIDD, INC.

Henderson snapped one day in the department head meeting and began speaking in tongues: "Ulala pizani! Y'kha Shub-Niggurath ghakala! Azagga pupago ma'azu!"

Henderson's seat is right under the huge chrome Squidd, Inc. logo mounted on the wall, and his outburst was more than a little blasphemous—an affront to our disciplined business world. Or so I thought. We all looked to bulbous-eyed Old Man Squidd, our flabby corporate pooh-bah, to watch the fireworks.

The Old Man sat up in his chair (a formidable task for one so huge) and said, "By God, Henderson, I like a man with Spunk."

* * * *

Spunk. Spunk. Spunk with a capital S became our watchword, our password, our office shibboleth.

At that time, Squidd, Inc. specialized in the production and distribution of pharmaceuticals, with interests in medical equipment and bio-chemical research. I was Director of Sales, and I longed for Spunk like the cartoon coyote longs for roadrunner meat.

I'd been with the company for twenty years; my hair had turned grey and my skin had grown spotty in the service of Squidd. My chair at the meeting table was choice: only three seats down from the Old Man. But did the younger Directors have any respect for my years of experience? Sorry, no. Whenever they deigned to speak with me, their smug expressions told the story too well. They saw me as nothing more than a corporate leftover—a dried-up old piece of sushi.

I wasn't about to let the matter of Spunk, and my lack thereof, cripple my standing with the company. I prayed at my desk: Gods of Commerce, I need more than just daily bread. Lead me deep into temptation and give me a magnum of champagne, a midnight-blue BMW, a penthouse office, a stock portfolio to die for, and most of all, a generous helping of high-energy, high-octane, high-and-mighty Spunk.

Amen.

* * * *

McCallum, Director of Public Relations and the youngest of our lot, tried his hand at Spunk the next week. He entered the department head meeting wearing a studded black leather collar and an orange Mohawk.

Old Man Hawthorne gave him the big thumbs-up. "Spunky," he said, winking one of his staring sea-green eyes. "Damn Spunky."

Each executive at Squidd, Inc. took their own personal walk on the Spunky side (except myself—my time had not yet come, my glorious dawn of Spunk). Abernathy patched his pinstripe suit in gingham and replaced the handle of his briefcase with a corncob, like the mayor of Dogpatch. Van Doring donned the robes of a Tibetan monk and delivered his marketing report in a complex but undeniably Spunky combination of Morse code, sign language, and hula dance. Johannson filed his teeth to points, then decided to get in touch with his feminine side by personally designing a red velvet, off-the-shoulder business suit, perfect for the office or a night on the town. Ms. Devlin, the only woman in the group, thrilled the Old Man with a brilliant display of Spunky initiative. She shaved her head, carved notches in her ears, and had a blue-green dragon tattooed across her face. She chain-smoked clove cigarettes and insisted that we call her 'Lobo.'

* * * *

I was sitting at my desk, thinking about Spunk, when I began to make paper airplanes. As I folded in the wings of my seventeenth memo pad stealth bomber, I stopped to consider the printing at the top of the sheet. The stylized cephalopod depicted in the logo stared back at me. Its gracefully curving tentacles seemed to be reaching out…but not to crush me. To embrace me.

I put in a request for an extended leave. And not for just a week. This particular leave would eat up all of my vacation time. Sick time. Holiday time. Personal time. I had to pull some strings and cash in some favors, but I finally managed to swing it. I then arranged for my work to be covered by several efficient but lackluster lackeys (Rule No. 1 in the white-collar jungle: never hire anyone with more Spunk than yourself). I divided my duties among these underlings in a complex, piecemeal fashion, to prevent any one of them from attempting a coup in my absence.

Having battened down my administrative hatches, I began my sabbatical. I had a lot of accrued freedom coming, and would need every second of it for what I had to do.

* * * *

When I returned to work, a delivery boy standing in the front lobby screamed and fainted. The copying machine repairman flew under a desk and began to whimper.

My entire life savings had gone into my transformation. Skin grafts. Hormone injections, both natural and synthetic. The removal of certain bones. Tendon and cartilage augmentation. Gland transplants. Extensive redistribution of muscle tissue. And more. *Much* more.

I was supreme, imperious, an industrial juggernaut: the Squidd, Inc. logo incarnate.

I slithered into the department head meeting and stopped in my slime-streaked tracks. Abernathy, he of the gingham-patched suit, was sitting *in my chair*. With a squeal of outrage, I lashed out a tentacle, knocking out his teeth from across the table.

He rushed out of the room, his mouth gushing blood. I then looked to the head of the table, anticipating a big thumb's-up.

It was then that I saw the unthinkable.

Next to Old Man Hawthorne sat McCallum. The Spunky young Director of Public Relations had given up his orange Mohawk and dog collar. Now, he too sported a slick, cone-shaped head and a writhing cluster of sinuous appendages —

Six inches longer than my own.

McCallum wriggled up to me. "Nice try, my friend," he said with a gurgling chuckle, "but I'm afraid that mine is just a bit...nicer."

A red mist of fury seethed across my vision.

"I have news for you, McCallum," I stated, whipping my two largest tentacles into the air. "It's not the length that matters..." I lashed my mighty musculature around his thick throat. "It's what you do with it."

And then I squeezed...and *squeezed*...and SQUEEZED...

First, his cone turned dark purple.

Then his eyes bugged out of his skull.

I decided to let go when his brains started to squirt through his thin vestigal nostrils.

Old Man Squidd bared his dark teeth in a crazed grin. Later, he took me aside for a man-to-monster chat.

He said he admired my drive and ingenuity. He told me about a special clinic in his hometown of Innsmouth that could fit me with gills, making my transformation truly complete. He then lifted his flabby jowls, revealing shallow, green-edged fissures just under his jaw line. He explained that this sort of thing happened to the men of his town when they reached a certain age. And someday, after his gills finished growing in, he would take me down, down, down to the ocean floor, to visit the sunken Home Office. There we would pay honor to our Chief Executive Officer: mighty Cthulhu, power monger of the deeps.

But in the meantime, there was work to be done.

* * * *

I have become the prototype for an exciting new product line. The Old Man's empire is expanding, taking the world of plastic surgery by storm. Around the globe, Squidd BioMorph Clinics are currently under construction.

Are you tired of the same old body, day in and day out? In the market for a new look? Our skilled specialists know how to bring out the real you. Ladies: fuller lips and bouncier breasts can be yours for the asking. Men: there's certainly no need to suffer the shame of, shall we say, *tentacle envy*...

But don't stop there, my friends. Try fangs. Pincers. Ghoul claws. Night-gaunt wings. Let your imagination run wild. You will love what we can craft out of you.

We'll have you looking smart and sassy —

And as Spunky as hell.

SHOGGOTH CACCIATORE

Serving unit Romeo14 watched the dented blue-green shuttle descend into Parking Sector H. At one point it jerked awkwardly, hitting a lighting pole. He wondered what sad ambulatory bits of space-trash were navigating this sorry craft. Probably Ong-Ponthians. They were the worst. Tacky, ignorant mutants that couldn't decide if they should select from the carbon- or silicon-based entrees.

When at last the craft had settled, the door slowly creaked open and—

Romeo14 emitted a soft electronic whistle—his version of a gasp. Earthlings? Yes indeed. A man and a woman: a couple.

The slender silver bot had been modeled after a handsome male humanoid—from the waist up. Waist down, he was simply a pillar with three silver wheels at the base. He turned and glided into the Golden Nebula restaurant, almost bumping into a busbot with dish-filled prehensile arms. He veered past it, moving with graceful speed along the back wall of the dining area, in the shadows so as not to disturb the patrons. He sailed through the kitchen doors and headed directly to the preparation area.

"Caesar72, you will not believe who has just landed," Romeo14 uttered in his chirping tones.

The squat golden cooking unit beeped irritably. "Who indeed? The Prime Modulator, perhaps, descended from Great Matrix of Time?" Both Romeo14 and Caesar72 had been programmed with male personalities, by a scientist who'd been fond of the works of an ancient Earth playwright. But structurally, both bots were as genderless as any of the pots, spoons and strainers floating above them in a handy theta-energy hover-field.

"Do not be facetious!" Romeo14 said. "I'll have you know a real Earthling couple is heading this way at this moment."

Caesar72's ocular lenses began to pulse with blue light. "Earthlings? How exciting!" An extender claw shot out of his body and grabbed a Tyvarrian deboning knife out of the hover-field. He used it to subdue an unwieldy entree-to-be that he was still in the process of killing.

"Why, that pretentious old beverage-preparation unit down at the Solar Flare will turn rusty with envy tomorrow when I tell him we had humans here this evening. Oh, you should have heard him crow when those fungus creatures from Yuggoth had a few drinks at his place. Ha!

Let's see if he can top an *actual human couple*." Romeo14 released a low hum of satisfaction. "I must rush back to greet them. In the meantime, think of something spectacular to serve them. Remember, no ammonia or arsenic or plasma waves—"

"Please, I know the dietary requirements and limitations of thirteen-thousand life-forms. As if I would serve plasma waves to a carbon-based being!"

"I am sorry. I did not mean to insult your fine memory matrix. I just want everything to be perfect for the humans." So saying, Romeo14 hurried out of the preparation sector and back to the restaurant entrance, just as the couple had reached the base of the building's steps.

It was difficult for Romeo14 to contain his excitement. He wanted to buzz, to chirp, to spin. Earthlings. There was no mistaking the placement of the ears, or the subtle curve of the cheekbones. "Good evening, sir and madam," he purred. "Welcome to the Golden Nebula."

The heavyset Earth male shot him an irritated glance. "A good evening? Maybe for you."

The Earth female, whose damp eyes were rimmed with smeared makeup, shot the male an angry look. "You have to give everyone a hard time. Leave the nice whatever-it-is alone. He's just doing his job."

They are displeased! Romeo14 realized. *This must be corrected.* "You have had a long voyage, yes? Let me show you to a table, where you can have relaxing beverages as our skilled massage units apply their talents to your tense muscles."

"Oh, that sounds wonderful," the female said. She gave the male another look. "Tell the nice thing how wonderful that sounds!"

The male shrugged. "Yeah, wonderful. All I want is a gin and tonic—with Earth gin, none of that Zorvonian crap."

"Earth gin! Yes, we always have plenty," Romeo14 said. "Right this way. How marvelous that you have selected the Golden Nebula. My name is Romeo14, and I will be coordinating our services to meet your needs this evening."

The Earthlings followed the serving unit into the dining area. "You sure seem happy to see us," the female said. "Like we're celebrities or something. I'm Mella and this is my husband, Squinn."

"He doesn't really care," the male said.

Romeo14 led them to a table. "Oh, I am indeed very happy to see you," he said. "Earthlings invented restaurants. Your civilization led to my creation. In a way, you are my—" He searched his memory matrix for an appropriate term. "—parents."

"Oh, geez," Squinn said.

Mella patted Romeo14's cheek. "Aren't you precious! I wish you were my son."

"Mella, he's not even alive," the male said. "You want a bucket of bolts for a son?"

"He's nice. Nice is better than nothing," the female said angrily.

"I will summon the massage units," Romeo14 said. He wheeled away from the table to a control console on the wall. He pressed a button to alert the massage bots, then entered the coordinates that would direct them to the right table. He pressed more keys, instructing the beverage-preparation unit to send gin-based drinks to the couple.

He then glided back to the preparation area. "Caesar72! The Earthlings are not pleased. They are experiencing interpersonal difficulties. I trust you have given considerable thought to their dinner selections."

"They are just hungry," the squat bot said. "They will feel better after they have eaten."

"The female seemed upset because they do not have young," the serving unit noted.

Caesar72 mulled over this fact. "This scenario is not unknown to me. Are they older creatures?"

"I believe so."

"Certain carbon-based life-forms cannot have offspring after they have passed a certain point in their reproductive cycle. Perhaps they delayed such matters for too long—and now it is too late."

Romeo14 considered this information. "But medical advancements exist that—"

"They are extremely expensive. Also, there may be other matters involved. Do not question them: they do not need to address those issues tonight." Caesar72 held out two plates piled with greens, lightly drizzled with an amber dressing. "Take them their salads. Make sure they have plenty of alcoholic beverages. They need to forget their life difficulties if they are to enjoy this evening."

"How do you know so much about Earthlings?" Romeo14 said, taking the plates.

"Have you ever heard of 'movies'? An emotion-based audio-visual artform of the Earth culture. I own a small but choice collection. Very informational." Caesar72 pulled several kitchen tools out of the theta-field with extender claws. "Endeavor to direct their entree selection to the shoggoth cacciatore. They will not be disappointed."

A smaller cooking unit rolled into the preparation area. "Is there anything else with which I can assist?"

"Please wash some more dandelion greens, Hamlet5," Caesar72 said.

"Shoggoth cacciatore! Made with those marvelous red tomatoes. And they're from Earth, too, like these lovely greens. One cannot go wrong with the right ingredients." The serving unit buzzed happily as he wheeled away with the salads.

* * * *

"That's just what I needed," Squinn said, taking a long draw from his drink. A small, multi-limbed massage unit had removed the male's shoes and was rubbing his feet.

Mella munched at her salad as her massage unit worked at her shoulders. "I didn't realize how hungry I was," she said.

Romeo14 nodded. "Excellent! Are you ready to make an entree selection? For a truly memorable dining experience, I would suggest the shoggoth cacciatore."

"Shoggoth?" Squinn said. "You're not talking about those monster-amoeba shoggoths, are you?"

"Indeed I am," the serving unit said happily. "Though actually, their bodies are more like sea cucumbers than amoebas. In their natural state, they have a flexible, muscular infrastructure—and it's delicious!"

"The shoggoths we're talking about came out of the Antarctic when it thawed out many centuries ago." Mella said. She bit her lower lip fretfully. "Big acid-blooded blobs. They killed millions of people."

"I am surprised anyone still knows of the shoggoth attacks. That was so long ago," Romeo14 said. "In fact, the only reason I know is because I am required to have a thorough knowledge of all our house specialties. Of course, my knowledge base is nothing compared to our lead cooking unit, Caesar72. "

Mella sat up and pushed away her massage unit. "Well, none of your other fancy diners may know about the shoggoths, but Squinn and I do. I'm a librarian. I have access to tons of old books, back from the days when they were bound sheaves of paper and not brain-implant chips. You want us to eat those horrible, savage monsters?"

"Beings from all over the galaxy praise our shoggoth cacciatore!" the serving unit said. "Do you recall how the shoggoths were defeated?"

Mella shook her head. "The books I have only chronicle the shoggoth uprising. Actually, I would like very much to know how they were destroyed. They seemed to be practically invincible."

Romeo14 had no real reason to clear his spitless electronic throat, but he did so anyway for dramatic effect. "Remember: they only emerged from the Antarctic, their ancient base on Earth, after it thawed. Shoggoths cannot withstand extreme cold. Some rich Earthlings simply hired a service from KromTek, a planet of robots, to freeze them with liquid nitrogen blasts and ship them away. Robots hate to waste anything, so they experimented with the creatures and found that they could be… farmed. Isn't that interesting? They found that after the acidic ichor was bled from a shoggoth, the remaining meat was in fact delectable.

"Shoggoths can take the form of any life-form they touch—they absorb and assimilate DNA quite easily—and this fact is taken into consideration at the shoggoth-farming facilities. They often introduce new DNA, to flavor and soften the tissue to perfection. Rest assured, the meat loses this recombinant quality when it is cooked."

"That's all really fascinating," the female said, "but it still sounds awfully scary."

Squinn laughed bitterly. "'Scary'? Oh, isn't that rich. Everything scares you. We didn't move to Pharnok while land prices were low because it was 'scary.' I didn't take that job at—"

"Don't you start blaming me for your crummy career in sales!" the woman cried. "I'm not even sure I can call it a 'career.' That would imply some kind of direction."

"So, now it all comes out!" The man's round face was red with anger. "Here I'm trying to save our marriage by bringing you to this fancy restaurant and all you can do is make fun of me. You're the one who's been holding me back all these years!" He turned to Romeo14. "For once I'm going to make a decision and not take any lip about it. Yes, we will *both* have the scary shoggoth cacciatore!"

The serving unit noted with unease that other diners had turned to watch the arguing couple. "Trust me, it is a mouth-watering delicacy," he said softly to the female. "And it is cooked *through and through.* As a dining experience, it is unique and completely safe. You have nothing to fear!"

"Well, if you say it's okay…" Mella grasped the serving unit's hand. "My idiot husband seems to think one night at a fancy restaurant is supposed to make up for twenty years of crap." She began to cry. "We don't even have any kids. So many wasted years and nothing to show for it."

"Now I've heard everything!" Squinn said. "Let go of that damned machine. He has to go fetch our food."

Romeo14 patted the female's hand. He searched his memory matrix for something to say that might console this devastated Earthling. Suddenly a possibility came to mind. "You must love each other very much if you've been together so long. You are very lucky. The vast majority of organisms are incapable of experiencing love."

"Really?" She let go of the robot's hand and looked around at the various aliens at the other tables. "Did you hear that, Squinn?" she whispered. "Most organisms can't feel love."

The serving unit spun around and headed off to place their meal order. But his hearing was very sensitive, and he heard the man say, "I bet that old tin can has never been in love. Hell, he's not even alive."

* * * *

"But it is true," Caesar72 said as he chopped at a large piece of bled shoggoth tissue. "You have never been in love. And you are not alive. Why should these facts bother you?"

"Because they seem unfair," Romeo14 said. "I can think and move like a living creature. I am smart enough to discuss love. And yet because I am a machine, I am denied life and love."

Hamlet5, who had been listening, tapped the serving unit's smooth, featureless pillar. "You do not have the gonads of a living being. It would do you no good to feel love. You cannot bring physical pleasure to your-self or anyone else."

Caesar72 pushed the smaller cooking bot away. "I should never have allowed you to watch those movies! You are using the facts they have taught you to make hurtful comments."

The serving unit thought for a moment. "Interesting…We can be hurt. We do have feelings. So perhaps we can feel love." He pointed to the small bot. "You do not know everything. Love is not all about gonads. Look at your mentor, Caesar72. See how he enjoys coating that shoggoth meat with herbs. He loves his craft. I love my work. One does not need gonads for that!"

Caesar72 slid a panful of shoggoth into the oven. Though he had many technological options from which to select, he still favored cook-ing with actual flame. "They should be ready in twenty minutes. That should give them enough time to roast completely."

"Oh!" Hamlet5 rolled up to his mentor. "Is that important?"

"Of course. The shoggoth is an insidious replicant," the golden bot said. "It downloads the DNA of other life-forms to suit its own purposes. We, of course, have nothing to fear, being machines. But if a living creature ingested the raw flesh of a shoggoth…There is no telling what would happen."

"Oh no!" the small bot cried. "I have made a serious error! I ne-glected to consult the data files! Please, do not dismantle me!"

"Hamlet5, what are you talking about?" the serving unit asked.

"I made the Earthling salad from the dandelion greens, and then I looked around in the refrigerated locker and—" A red alarm light flashed on top the small cooking unit's head. "—I added bits of diced raw shog-goth to the salad of the Earthlings. For flavor, only for flavor!"

* * * *

Filled with dread, Romeo14 rolled slowly up to the table of the Earthlings. "Here is the shoggoth cacciatore," he said, trying to make his voice sound cheerful. "The pride of the Golden Nebula."

He noticed that Squinn and Mella were now sitting side by side. Perhaps that was a good sign. He set down his serving tray and gave each of them their plate. "Is there anything else I can do for you? Would you like another beverage?"

"Our water pitcher is empty," Squinn said. "We would like more water."

"Yes," Mella said. "More water."

The Earth couple stared at him with wide eyes. Romeo14 took his tray and the water pitcher and rolled off.

A Graaldoth at a corner table tapped him with its silicon tentacle as he rolled past its table. "I am so glad," whispered the slick creature's top head, "that those loud, uncouth Earthlings have stopped their bickering."

"Indeed," agreed its lower head. "We could barely hear ourselves think. Your skill with uncultured clientele is admirable, Romeo14."

The serving unit nodded. "Thank you. I do hope the rest of the evening proceeds…smoothly."

"Earthlings are so unpredictable," the top head said. "I cannot understand why. They have only one brain. Life should be easy for a carbon-based creature with a single brain."

"One would think so," Romeo14 said.

He filled the pitcher and returned to the Earthling table. Their plates were already empty. Squinn had his arm around Mella's shoulders.

"Here is your water," the serving unit said.

The male stared at him. "We want more food. More shoggoth."

"More shoggoth," the female echoed.

"As you wish."

For the next two hours, Romeo14 wheeled back and forth between the Earthling table and the food preparation area. The couple simply could not eat enough shoggoth. They required pitcher after pitcher of water, too. To his credit, he did manage to also serve his other tables diligently.

"This is the last of the shoggoth," Caesar72 said, loading two steaming plates onto the serving unit's tray. "And we're out of tomatoes, too."

"Are they manifesting any strange symptoms?" Hamlet5 said.

"They are behaving without emotion," the serving unit said. "I find that very disturbing." He looked at the thick, golden-brown slabs on the plates. "Plus, they have ingested a great deal of food and water and yet

I have not seen them go to the bodily waste facilities. I am sure they are well past the normal nourishment capacity for beings of their size."

Suddenly one of the busbots sped into the preparation area. "Romeo14, please attend to the Earthling table! We have an alarming development on our hands."

"Oh no!" cried Hamlet5, his red light flashing.

Romeo14 set down his tray and rushed to the dining area. Caesar72 followed close behind.

Upon reaching the Earthlings, the serving unit emitted his soft whistle of surprise—three times. The clothes of the couple were scattered on the floor. The two of them were locked in a tight embrace on top of their table. Thick, pulsing red and green veins laced in and out of their bodies. A huge, bushy yellow flower was pushing its way out of the wife's mouth.

The Graaldoth oozed up to the table, slapping its tentacles together. "Romeo14, you jolly trickster!" it cried, loud enough for the whole dining area to hear. "At first I'd thought these bipeds were simply noisy Earthlings. But now it is very clear that the antics of these creatures—whatever they are—have been part of a clever dinner-theatre experience!"

Oooh's and aaah's sounded from all the tables.

A Klarbvog diner stood up on its hindlegs. "What an extraordinary performance. Truly memorable! Romeo14, you have outdone yourself! What sort of finale do these stars of yours have in store?"

The Earthlings began to rock back and forth, faster and faster.

"Whatever it is," Romeo14 said, "I believe it should take place in the parking area. Caesar72, please assist me in carrying this table."

"An excellent suggestion." Together, the two bots picked up the table, with its hideous burden, and rushed it out of the building.

"Let us follow!" the Graaldoth cried. "I do not want to miss a single moment of this splendid drama!" All of the diners then left their tables and rushed out into the parking lot.

The serving unit and his golden colleague set down the table at a distance from the building and any of the vehicles. By this time, the couple had transformed into an enormous, misshapen tomato, topped with an enormous dandelion blossom. It continued to pulse and gurgle savagely. Spurts of pinkish foam began to shoot from small cracks in the surface of the obscene fruit.

"Wonderful," breathed the Klarbvog. "My spawning partners will be sorry they missed this!"

With a gush of froth and pent-up gases, the huge tomato burst open, releasing a teeming swarm—thousands of tiny, frantic creatures. The elfin shapes had thin, vine-like limbs and wee, blubbery red bodies, topped with billowy wads of fluff, like those of dandelion seeds. A gust of wind caught the swarm and whirled the tufted mutant shoggothlings throughout the parking area. The ruined tomato-husk that had been Mella and Squinn quickly turned to coarse, greenish-gray dust and a few ragged ribbons of dried plant fiber. A moment later, the wind blew the desiccated refuse away.

The diners clapped and hooted and squealed with applause. Finally they filed back into the building to finish their meals.

The airborne shoggothlings drifted and swirled with every passing breeze.

Romeo14 and Caesar72 looked toward the shuttles in the parking area. Dozens of them. All from different planets. Most of the diners had left some hatches on their vehicles partially open, so that their stuffy travel quarters could air out. Such a shockingly careless thing to do. Of course, neither bot would ever dare mention such a concern to their customers. Why, that would be tantamount to calling them idiots, right to their faces! An unforgivable faux pas.

The bots quietly carried the empty table back into the restaurant.

HOUND-DOG MCGEE AND THE GHOSTPUNCHER GANG MEET THE BLUBBERING BLASPHEMY IN THE BED & BREAKFAST OF MADNESS

"How interesting. How very, very interesting," said Louise, the smart one, as she read the message on her computer monitor. She pushed her heavy glasses back up her freckled nose.

Winston, the handsome one, leaned over her so that his fashionable scarf brushed her neck and shoulder. The thrill of that silken touch, along with his sweet, slightly musky scent of after-shave, made her tremble. "Looking at some e-mail, Louise?" he said. "Who's it from?"

She tapped the screen of the monitor. "A potential client! He thinks the farmhouse he inherited may be haunted. Look's like another job for the Ghostpuncher Gang!"

Monique, the pretty one, looked up from her fashion magazine. "Yeah, but it's too bad we never find any real ghosts. They're always—well, criminals. Old men trying to pull off some kind of real estate scheme. Or diamond smugglers. Or kidnappers. Or pimps in vampire disguises running secret whorehouses out of abandoned mansions. Gosh, I hope it's not another secret whorehouse. Frizzy just can't keep his hands off of those awful whores."

Frizzy had entered the meeting room through the door behind Monique, so he heard the last part of her speech. "Hey, can I help it if I have an eye for the ladies—along with a few other body parts?" He turned toward Winston. "You didn't seem to have any problem keeping your hands off those scantily clad hotties. Why is that?"

Winston ran his fingers nervously through his blond highlights. "I'm a gentleman. Not some over-sexed hippy, like you."

"I am rightfully proud of my hippy upbringing and heritage, thank you very much," Frizzy said, smoothing a wrinkle out of his tie-dyed t-shirt.

Louise turned away from the screen to face the others. "Cut Winston some slack, Frizzy. I mean, sure, he's never groped any of those whores, even though they practically threw themselves at him because of his movie-star good looks. But it's not a crime for a guy to have manners. In the five years we've been working together, solving mysteries, Winston has never laid a finger on either Monique or myself." She looked up at her handsome coworker and smiled. "Of course, if he ever did, I wouldn't be too upset. I mean, we've known each other a really long time, and… well…oh, never mind…" Her voice trailed away as she turned back to the computer.

"So tell us more about this farmhouse," Monique said.

"Ah, yes!" Louise tapped the screen again. "This man is trying to operate a bed & breakfast, but an eerie presence keeps scaring away the customers."

At that moment, Hound-Dog McGee walked in on his hindlegs. "Sounds like another secret whorehouse. Try to keep it in your pants this time, Frizzy."

The enormous hound trotted up to the table, picked a bagel off a tray with his teeth, and began to gnaw on it. "Hey, Louise, how come we only have bagels out? I'm a dog. I like meat. How about a big, juicy bone every now and then? Of course, I'd probably have to fight Winston for it."

Winston gasped and put a hand to his chest. "Now what's that supposed to mean?"

"Am I the only one who finds it odd," Hound-Dog McGee said, "that Winston goes to meetings of an alleged 'stamp-collecting club' every Tuesday at Club Manhole? On the same night that the club has its all-male dance revue?"

"That club is centrally located to all the stamp club members," Winston said. "We're all dedicated philatelists!"

Hound-Dog McGee nodded. "My point exactly."

"This guy asks a question about you, Hound-Dog," Louise said. "He says he was looking over our website, and he wonders why our team includes a huge talking dog that walks around on its hindlegs. He also mentions that he has never seen a dog with eyebrows before."

The dog sighed wearily. "Oh yeah, I get questions like that all the time when I'm out shopping, or when Frizzy and I go out to a restaurant and order a super-long sandwich so we can both take an end and eat our way to the middle. Personally, I don't understand why people are so surprised to see a human-sized dog on his hindlegs who walks and talks and has eyebrows. I mean, it's not like I can fly. Oh, well—just give the guy the facts, Louise."

"Yes," Frizzy said. "Let him know that Hound-Dog is a mutation with unusually humanoid characteristics who is probably the next step in dog evolution. It's as simple as that."

Winston smiled. "Yes. Perfectly natural."

Monique agreed. "Not scary at all."

Louise concurred. "Logical, too."

Hound-Dog strutted up to Frizzy. "May I sniff your rear end? It's been a while since the last time I sniffed it, and I just want to see how it's doing these days. It's a dog thing."

"Sure, buddy," the hippy said. "You don't even have to ask."

* * * *

The next day, the Ghostpuncher Gang loaded all their equipment into their van, which they lovingly called the Spookster Express, and began the long trip to the bed & breakfast in the small New England town of Dunwich. Frizzy and Hound-Dog McGee agreed to take turns driving.

On the way there, Louise went over the specifics of this particular case. "The owner, Jake Whateley, age twenty-seven, inherited the farmhouse, as well as the family fortune, from his reclusive, mysterious grandfather Zebekediah Whateley last year—"

"This Jake…" Winston said. "Is he single? What does he look like? I bet that old farmhouse is filled with some great antiques."

Hound-Dog McGee rolled his big, brown puppy-eyes, but said nothing.

"Jake is in fact single," Louise said. "I saw his picture on the website for his bed & breakfast and he's a real hunk. Almost as handsome as you, Winston, except he has more of a tan and the clearest blue eyes I've ever seen. He must work out all the time, because he has a huge, muscular chest and biceps that look like they were carved out of boulders."

"Winston, are you okay?" Monique said. "You're breathing heavily and your face is all sweaty."

"Am I? Is it?" The handsome man brushed his silk scarf over his forehead. "This van is so stuffy. Can someone open a window?"

"No need," Frizzy said. "The air conditioning is on full-blast."

Monique opened up her purse. "Well, if this Jake is as handsome as all that, I'd better touch up my make-up."

Frizzy smiled. "Already I can tell this is going to be a pretty interesting weekend. Now about that farmhouse…?"

"Well, I've been doing a little research," Louise stated, "and back when Zebekediah was alive, that house was considered a source of great evil by the locals. It was rumored that the Whateley family worshipped devil-gods from beyond. Gods with eldritch names like Yog-Sothoth and Azathoth, and sometimes even just plain old Thoth. Strange, lurid lights flickered in the windows of the farmhouse at odd hours."

"I still think it's a secret whorehouse," Hound-Dog said.

"Zebekediah's daughter Asmodarla eventually became mixed up in all this mumbo-jumbo," Louise said. "She was a shy, bookish girl who was ignored by all the local boys, so everyone was surprised when she became pregnant."

"Sure," Monique said, powdering her cheeks, "who'd want to do it with some dried-up, near-sighted old brainiac? I mean, they'd have to be pretty desperate to—" She then looked at Louise. "Umm, sorry to interrupt. Go on."

Louise stared back. "Well, I bet Asmodarla wasn't some tarted-up bitch who never did her share of the work around the office." She reached into her sweater pocket, pulled out a pack of clove cigarettes, and lit one up. That was her only vice: three cloves a day. She used to be a chain-smoker, and had never totally rid herself of the habit. "Anyway, the records state that she'd given birth to twins, but one had died at birth. She herself died during the delivery, and the surviving child—Jake— was sent to live with relatives in Boston."

"Poor, motherless child." Winston dabbed at his eyes with his scarf. "He must be lonely. So very lonely."

"The rest you know. When Jake inherited the family farmhouse, he opened up the bed & breakfast, which he called the Dunwich Arms. But a disturbing presence has been driving away all the guests."

"Do we have a description of this presence?" Frizzy asked.

Louise nodded. "Yes, we do, and it's very peculiar. Its appearance suggests alien or perhaps even extra-dimensional origins. According to reports, this large, mysterious creature is covered with clusters of thick, prehensile protuberances. These long, smooth, fleshy shafts are covered with bulging veins, and—What's wrong now, Winston? You're starting to sweat again."

* * * *

The farmhouse was a loathsome, rambling structure, nestled amidst overgrown thorn bushes atop a weed-choked hill. The front windows seemed to stare into space like the eyes of a skull. The building had been white-washed, but that only served to strengthen its resemblance to some bony remnant of a long-forgotten cadaver.

"Charming place," Frizzy said, shortly after he had parked the van in front of the house's deceptively cheery sign, which read: THE DUN-WICH ARMS—A GOOD NIGHT'S REST WITH NEW ENGLAND'S BEST. "The owner should just send us home and burn the place down for the insurance money."

"Now Frizzy," Louise said, "that's not a good Ghostpuncher Gang attitude. Has anyone seen Hound-Dog?"

"Here I am," the talking canine said, emerging from some bushes. "I just went off for a moment to urinate on a tree. That's what us dogs do."

Winston studied the sign. "Interesting. I wonder if this Jake really is New England's best?"

"Simmer down," Frizzy said. "I think it's referring to the bed & breakfast."

"Look who's coming this way," Monique said breathlessly. "The master of the manor himself."

A tall, tanned young man was descending the porch steps. He waved to the gang and flashed them a perfect smile.

Monique exhaled into her cupped hand to check her breath. Winston turned away from the house and raised an arm slightly, sniffing to make sure his deodorant was still working.

"So who do you think is going to bed the Dunwich dimwit?" Frizzy whispered into Hound-Dog's ear.

The dog shrugged his narrow shoulders. "Hard telling. I think they're both ready to start leg-humping any second now."

"Hello, everybody," Jake Whateley said. "I'm glad you got here so quickly."

Louise stepped forward. "Hello, I'm the one who responded to your e-mail. Louise Slapowski. I'm the business manager. These are my colleagues, the Ghostpuncher Gang. Monique LaRue can sense the presence of the dead, and also handles some secretarial duties. Winston Prescott is sensitive to psychic vibrations—he takes care of promotions, too. Frizzy Phelps is our electronics and science expert and resident mechanic for the Spookster Express. And Hound-Dog McGee can actually sniff out danger."

Jake grinned as he looked into Louise's eyes. "Oh, don't you have any special powers, like the rest?"

Louise bit her lower lip. "Well, I hate to brag…"

"Go ahead. Tell me."

"When I get really mad, I can concentrate and make people bleed from their nostrils and ears."

"Oh." The grin slowly faded away. "I'm sure that must come in useful from time to time." Jake stepped up to Monique. "Are you sensing any dead people right now?"

"Goodness, no," she said. "If anything, I'm sensing a lot of life. Hot, pulsing life."

Jake turned his attention to Winston. "How's the place doing in the psychic vibrations department?"

Winston shook his hand. "Right now I'm picking up some really good vibes. Oh yeah."

Finally the young New Englander turned his attention to Frizzy and Hound-Dog McGee. "Well, you don't have any equipment set up yet, so I don't suppose you've had time to gather any information. But what about you, Hound-Dog? Smell any danger?"

"No," the dog said, "but would it be okay if I sniffed your rear end, and perhaps your crotch, too? I don't have to do it right now, but I would like to get around to it eventually, since we've just met and that's how us dogs get to know strangers."

Jake gestured toward his hips. "Do it right now if you wish. I should smell pretty good. I've had my morning shower."

Hound-Dog McGee began sniffing, savoring the young man's warm, slightly spicy natural aromas.

"Lucky dog," Winston whispered to himself.

* * * *

That night, Hound-Dog McGee had a dream.

Jake Whateley had given him a bedroom that looked out over the town of Dunwich. It was a brooding, mysterious town, filled with low, dark buildings, cobbled streets, and neon-lit adult bookstores.

Before retiring, he had enjoyed a bowl of scraps mixed with dog food, so that might be what gave him such an awful, vivid nightmare. Minutes after his furry head hit the pillow, bizarre visions filled his animal brain. He dreamed of rats with the faces of old men, and giant worms that walked around with human masks. Winged fungal beings soared between the stars, and tentacle-bearded monstrosities slumbered in giant temples on the ocean floor. Then a deep, booming voice intoned an unspeakable couplet:

That is not dead which can make people sick,
And with strange aeons, dogs may have a lick.

Then he awoke, and found that his legs were twitching like crazy. When at last he went back to sleep, he had a perfectly normal dream about chasing a bunny through a tunnel. At some point, the bunny turned into a tree and he peed on it. Then he remembered that he had to take a test, but he hadn't studied for it. Fortunately, the classroom was filled with big, juicy bones, and he gnawed on them as angels sang about the price of a doggy in a window.

* * * *

Meanwhile, in the room next door, Louise Slapowski was also having a dream. Her usual dream.

In it, Leonardo DiCaprio was wearing a black rubber suit covered with silver zippers, and he was dancing. Dancing to that old disco song about a cake being left out in the rain. And he was saying, "Solve the mystery, Louise. Come on, you can do it. Just search my pockets. You'll find lots of clues along the way. Do it, girl. Do it."

And so she jumped out on the dance floor and unzipped the first zipper—the one that ran along his left shoulder. She then reached into the pocket and pulled out a hot dog.

"Pretty good," Leonardo said. "Keep searching."

She then tried a zipper on his right bicep, and found a big, juicy bratwurst.

"Try lower down," the movie star whispered. "Much lower."

She tried a zipper on his calf and found a firm, exceptionally long zucchini.

"A little too low," Leonardo whispered. "Try again."

By this time, Louise's heart was beating like a conga drum. She reached out for that special zipper, the one that she knew held a wonderful mystery just for her, and—

Here her usual dream changed into something very unusual. All the zippers flew open and writhing tentacles emerged. These sinuous appendages wrapped around her limbs, and Leonardo began to laugh with insane glee.

"You wanted to stay in the Dunwich Arms. Well, how do *these* arms suit you, Louise?"

Louise woke with a start and sat up in bed. She looked up and wondered if she was still asleep and dreaming, because there in the air above her hovered a dim, translucent apparition—a writhing mass of tentacles and eyes and, and…

There was more to see, but before she could make out any details, the spectre began to fade away, until at last it was gone.

She thought for a moment. What was it she had just seen? Was it the ghostly presence that haunted the bed & breakfast, or just a waking carry-over from the nightmare? Certainly her research on the bed & breakfast might have influenced the content of her dream.

Finally she decided not to tell anyone about what she'd seen—at least, not yet. To do so might taint the objectivity of the others.

She then went back to sleep and dreamed that Dorothy and the Scarecrow were flying around Oz on the Witch's sturdy broom.

* * * *

For the next two days, the Ghostpuncher Gang tested and calibrated every imaginable property of the house. They studied blueprints and searched the halls and all the rooms for secret passageways. Jake was disappointed that the usually mega-obtrusive spectral presence that haunted the Dunwich Arms was now being inexplicably bashful.

Jake had told his cook to take some time off while the Gang looked over the place, and so he had to wait on them by himself. One morning, Winston lingered at the breakfast table after the rest of the Gang had left.

The young innkeeper sat down across from Winston. "You guys must think I'm making this whole thing up. I can't understand why the creature hasn't shown up yet."

Winston gave him a coy smile. "Oh, I don't mind. I find this whole New England gig totally charming. And you've been such a marvelous host. I wish there was some way to show you my appreciation…"

"Well, I am paying the Ghostpuncher Gang, but your rates are extremely reasonable—you are certainly worth much more. And I am extremely grateful for all your time and attention. Why, I'm the one who should be showing the appreciation around here! Is there anything I can do for *you?* Just name it. Say what you want and I'll do it. No questions asked. My reply will be an automatic, enthusiastic 'Yes!'"

Winston mopped at his brow with his scarf. "My goodness…"

"Just say the word!" Jake said. "Anything at all!"

"Well, hold on a second. Let me think…"

"No need to be shy! Come now, you must have *something* in mind!"

"Now that you mention it—"

Suddenly Louise came running into the room. "Jake! Winston! Frizzy's equipment is registering something. It happened only a few seconds ago. Winston, you're all sweaty again. Maybe you should see a doctor."

She led the two men into the large sitting room, where Frizzy, Monique and Hound-Dog were standing around a large metal console with numerous dials, a control panel and a monitor.

"It's the strangest thing," the hippy science expert said. "No more than a minute or so ago, I was getting strong energy readings. They seemed to be coming from below ground level—the basement, perhaps, or even lower. Is there anything below the basement that you're aware of, Jake? A tunnel? A cave?"

"Not to my knowledge," the New Englander said, "but then, maybe it's something I don't know about."

"I'm wondering what triggered those high energy levels," Hound-Dog said.

"Perhaps strong emotion," Monique said. "Anger or fear or even lust can set off paranormal activities."

"Winston, you looked pretty flushed when I entered the dining area," Louise said. "Where you in the grip of some strong emotion?"

"In a way. Jake had some kind words to say to me, and I was feeling—appreciated." He nodded vigorously. "Yes, I was overwhelmed by feelings of appreciation."

"Interesting. How very, very interesting. Now that I've heard that," Louise said, "I think it's time to tell you all about a dream I had on our first night here. I was very excited in the dream, and that may be what caused me to see...what I saw." She then described her dream, but instead of Leonardo DiCaprio dancing, she made the focus of the dream an attack by a sea monster, because—Well, they'd just make fun otherwise.

Hound-Dog thought about sharing his dream with the others, but then decided against it. He still wanted to think more about the special significance of that mystic couplet...

"We should check out the basement again," Louise continued. "We've gone over it once already, but there must be something we missed. And we must all keep our emotions in check while we are down there, so we don't disturb some potentially dangerous force."

"Sounds good to me," Jake said. "Winston, I'll try not to make you feel appreciated while we're down there."

Winston sighed. "Whatever."

* * * *

Jake and the Ghostpuncher Gang searched the basement carefully, sorting through dusty antiques, leather-bound books, and dozens of huge jars. Some jars held herbs and nails and other common items, while others held disturbing biological specimens pickled in brine.

"Look at this," Louise said. "This jar is filled with flaming red, three-lobed eyes—what animal do you suppose they came from?"

"This one has some rotten old vegetables in it," Frizzy said. "They seem to be glowing a color I've never seen before. It's certainly not a color from Earth."

"That's ridiculous," Winston said. "So where did the color come from? Out of space, perhaps?" He looked into the jar. "That's puce. Yes, definitely puce."

Monique circled around the granite altar in the center of the basement. "I have a sneaking suspicion that this has something to do with those energy levels."

"Now that you mention it," Hound-Dog said, "I don't think I've ever seen a basement with an altar in it before. I'd better give it a good sniffing."

He lowered his nose to the surface of the altar and sniffed every square inch. "I think people used to get killed on this thing. There's a faint but definite whiff of murder here—but nothing recent. This dip in the stone here is probably where they put sacrificial hearts, and maybe some other chopped-off bits, too."

"Sniff around the bottom. That's what you're good at!" Frizzy said.

"Oh, look who's starting a career in comedy. Okay, Mr. Funnyman, I'll sniff the base of this thing. I bet it'll smell better than your—" Suddenly Hound-Dog recoiled. "Hey, there's a little stinky air coming out of a crack down here."

Louise lit up a clove cigarette. Then she had an idea, and put the cigarette near the crack indicated by Hound-Dog. The smoke was blown away from the base. "He's right. So there's definitely a lower level. But how are we going to raise this altar?"

"Maybe the altar is part of a secret passageway," Winston said. "There must be some hidden way to open it up. Try pressing stones in the walls."

Frizzy examined the surface of the altar. "Where's that dip in the stone you were talking about, Hound-Dog? I don't see it."

The dog touched a circular depression in the granite. "Here."

The hippy shook his head. "There's nothing there."

"Are you blind?" the dog said, exasperated. "Should I give you a white cane and start leading you around? Look here. Right *here*." So saying, he pounded the indicated spot with a forepaw. The depression sank a half-inch with a loud click. Then the entire altar began to slowly tilt back, revealing an opening in the basement floor.

"Hound-Dog, you did it!" Louise said. "Let's get geared up for an exploration!"

* * * *

Later, flashlights in hand, they descended the stone steps beneath the altar. Winston said to Jake, "You know, I bet this supernatural presence is probably your twin brother. I bet he didn't die at birth. That was probably just a cover-up."

"Hmmm…" Jake thought about this possibility. "That's an interesting thought. But would he still be human, or some kind of ghost or zombie?"

"Your mother and grandfather used to engage in strange worship," Monique said. "Maybe your dad was one of those alien devil-gods. Maybe you're the more human sibling, and your brother looks more like your dad."

"Oh, that kind of stuff could never happen in Dunwich," Jake said. "I mean, sure, everybody around here worships weird demons, and sometimes folks are arrested for cannibalism, but still, what you're talking about is just too…sci-fi."

"It does sound a little farfetched," said the talking dog with eyebrows.

Finally they arrived in an enormous cave filled with huge mounds of bones. The canine eyed these delicacies rapturously.

"Now Hound-Dog, don't get any ideas," Louise said. "These are human bones, and chewing on them would be bad. Besides, they all look pretty old, so the marrow would be dried out anyway."

"So where's the monster?" Frizzy said. He opened a packet he'd taken from the Spookster Express when they'd geared up for their descent. "I have a bunch of tranquilizer darts here, and a dandy blow-gun, too. I sure hope it's a real monster this time. I'm so tired of dealing with old men in rubber masks."

"Now that we're ready for him, how are we going to make the creature appear?" Winston said. "Maybe Jake should show me some more appreciation…"

The bones suddenly reminded Hound-Dog of his dream, and that brought to mind the seemingly inexplicable couplet:

That is not dead which can make people sick,
And with strange aeons, dogs may have a lick.

"You say strong emotions will bring out the critter?" Hound-Dog asked. "Then I know just what to do: something that will elicit definite reactions from all of you…"

"You don't mean—? No! Don't do it!" Monique hissed.

"Lord, not again!" Louise moaned.

"Yes, indeed. I'm going to lick myself!" the dog cried. And with that, he got to work.

"Oh my God!" Jake shouted.

"You're freaking me out!" Frizzy said.

"Lucky dog," Winston whispered, dabbing at his face wildly with his sopping scarf.

"Oh, you poor humans," Hound-Dog said between licks. "What a pity you can't do yourselves this delightful favor! It is fantastic! It is marvelous! It is, quite simply, *bliss!*"

Suddenly the cavern grew much warmer, until it was as hot as a tropical island. Blasts of wind swirled the bones through the air. Jake and the Ghostpuncher Gang dropped to the floor and covered their heads.

Then a sound like hot tar speaking—a bubbling, blubbering torrent of lunatic words—echoed through the cavern. And those words were these: "*At last I am strong enough! I now have the power to fully materialize! I am coming, father! Yog-Sothoth! Yog-Sothoth! YOG-SOTHOTH!*"

A misty, misshapen form began to take shape in mid-air, gaining more and more definition and density until at last it became a solid entity.

Jake and the Gang looked up in terror at the hideous being. It had dozens of long, fleshy, sucker-lined tentacles, covered with bulging veins. Blue eyes weaved back and forth on the ends of fleshy stalks. Numerous mouths puckered their full, red lips. A half-dozen massive breasts swayed and jiggled, slapping lewdly against the tentacles.

Clearly Jake didn't have a brother.

He had a sister.

With a squeal of delight, the she-monster stormed out of the cavern, grabbing a souvenir on the way out.

* * * *

"Because your sister had a lot more alien devil-god in her than you," Louise said, "she had difficulty materializing on this plane. She needed a great deal of emotional energy to fuel her full corporealization."

"So that's why she only appeared as a spectre," Jake said.

"Yes—and then, probably only after a couple of your guests had argued, or made love," she explained.

Jake was walking with the Ghostpuncher Gang through the ruins of Dunwich, under a clear night sky. After his sister had fled the cavern, she'll bopped into town to do a little celebratory rampaging.

"So when Hound-Dog started licking himself," Monique said, "that created strong psychic waves of feelings—mostly disgust. Our combined emotions were enough to give your sister the power she needed."

"I am nothing if not helpful," Hound-Dog said.

"It's a pity Dunwich is destroyed," Jake said.

Frizzy patted him on the back. "You can't make an omelet without breaking a few eggs."

Louise lit a fresh clove cigarette. "I must say, your sister is a real go-getter. She was quick to snatch up Winston on the way out."

"She was pretty gentle with him," Jake said. "Did you notice how she lovingly held him out of harm's way as she destroyed the town?"

Louise looked up at the stars. "And now she's taken him to another dimension…Do you think they'll be happy together?"

Hound-Dog and Frizzy both rolled their eyes. Then the talking canine said, "Oh, I suppose anything's possible."

NO PROMOTION FOR PITT

"You are very late," Cord said, glancing up from his monitor. A puzzled expression crossed his round, bland face. "Oh. You have hurt your forehead. Are you all right, Pitt?"

Pitt put a hand to the bandage on his white forehead. "A rock hit me as I was leaving my lifespace. I am going to see a doctor about it later."

Cord blinked. "You should go now. Why wait?"

"I like the young doctor on the afternoon shift. He tells amusing stories as he performs his examinations."

"Really?" Cord was not sure if that sort of behavior could be considered professional. Perhaps it put the patient at ease..."Did someone throw the rock at you?"

"There was no one in sight," Pitt said, taking his place at his control panel. "The rock was very small. It still hurts, though. I think a small bit of it is caught under the skin."

"I hope the discomfort does not interfere with your work." Cord watched briefly as Pitt pasted sensors onto his temples. He then returned his full attention to his monitor. Earlier he had envisioned an overhead view of the proposed 138kh lifespace plan onto the screen. Very nice— but the placement of the lighting fixtures in relation to the windows was slightly amiss.

After correcting the problem, he saved the file back into d8055, the main data nexus. A large d8055 processing column filled the entire other end of the station Cord and Pitt shared. This column was one of three-hundred and twenty in their work precinct.

Cord moved on to his next project—the 138kh.c. food preparation area. Certainly the angle of the air vents could be improved upon...

Later, as he was imaging new designs for the air-plant employee washrooms, Cord heard Pitt gasp—with pain? His coworker did seem even paler than usual. "Is something wrong, Pitt? Should I alert a medic?"

Pitt looked up from his monitor, his face long with anxiety. "No, I am fine, Cord. But the image I have called up does not..." He began to gnaw on a fingernail. "...does not appear to be work-related."

Cord removed his temple sensors and walked over to the pale man's side. "I hope this will not take long. I am working on an important—" His brow furrowed as he took in the scenario on the screen. "Pitt! This landscape is completely inefficient. I do not recognize the sector."

The monitor showed three tall hills, all laced with twisting footpaths. A large, dark house stood on the middle hill. Suddenly the image changed to a close-up of the house.

"This baffles me," Cord sighed. "The lawn is half-dead and the sidewalk is broken and uneven. And the building…the doorway is too wide. There are far too many windows. What are you trying to picture here?"

Pitt rubbed worriedly at the sensors on his temples. "I do not know, Cord. I was designing a sector 150dh warehouse facility when this suddenly came into view."

"I should inform our supervisor," Cord said as he reached for the interoffice communicator.

"Please do not, Cord. I am being considered for a promotion and I would not want this aberration to weigh against me." Pitt put a hand on Cord's wrist. "I should like to be a class-5c designer like yourself. My family would be so pleased." He shot a fretful glance at his monitor. "Maybe I should simply disconnect my sensors for a moment…"

Cord rubbed his chin thoughtfully. "Not just yet. Since we are overlooking protocol, we might as well explore this aberration in detail." He gave Pitt a small, stiff smile. "This scenario piques my curiosity. Someday I shall become a supervisor, so perhaps I could use similar images to illustrate poor design to trainees."

Pitt nodded, but said nothing.

"Now tell me," Cord said. "Why are the sidewalk tiles all of irregular shapes? And why is the roof so steep?"

"I do not know. I am imaging it, but I cannot control it."

"How eccentric. No wonder you fear for your promotion. Your visions are usually so practical." On the screen, the building's wide door swung open. "Did you do that?"

Pitt frowned. "Not consciously."

"Perhaps if I saw more, I could fathom this abnormality. Can you direct the image through the doorway?"

"I will try. I hasten to remind you that I did receive a blow to the head this morning. That rock—it was purple, and roughly textured. Very unusual."

On the monitor, the image blurred for a split-second, then came back into focus. Beyond the building's entry stretched a long carpeted hallway lined with doors.

"The pattern of the carpet…" Cord tilted his head to one side. "Tentacles? How disturbing. Why not something tranquil, like interlocking circles? I see a large room farther down. Please direct the vision in that direction."

The screen's perspective swept forward. At the end of the hall was a room filled with large wooden boxes, strapped shut with metal bands.

Pitt gently peeled up the bandage on his forehead and began to poke gingerly at his sore. "No doubt about it," he said. "There is a tiny bit of stone caught in there."

Cord pointed to the screen. "There is a rope tied around the largest box. A rope with knots tied in it at regular intervals. And it leads through a hole in the wall..."

The view moved along the rope and through the gaping hole, into—

"Pitt! This is extraordinary!" Cord clapped his hands together. He was gazing down upon a vast marble platform floating in a gray void. Two objects stood on the platform: an enormous coffin, on end, and a tall, curious—Objet d'art? Idol? Cord had no idea what this strange item could be. It was a black, metallic pillar topped with a sphere of rough purple stone. This sphere was covered with a network of wormy, pulsing veins. The knotted rope led down to the platform, where it was tied around the base of the pillar.

"Down the rope to the platform, Pitt," Cord commanded.

"But Cord—that purple globe. Small chunks of it are shooting off into space. Surely that is significant...?"

Cord thought for a moment. "Purple was once considered the color of royalty. Now down the rope." With a small wince, Pitt directed his attention down the rope to the platform.

"What fools we have been, Pitt." Cord reached over his shoulder and touched a button on the control panel, activating the continuous data-save. "We should be saving this aberration of yours to study."

"But my promotion!" the pale man wailed. "The project review officials might come across the file. They will be conducting an audit in a few days."

"Really, Pitt. We can always erase it before then. Now to open that casket!" Cord grinned with anticipation.

"There is a little window on the lid, Cord. Let us peek inside first."

In a moment the dark, octagonal window filled Pitt's screen. The two imagers leaned closer, trying to catch a glimpse of the box's contents. Suddenly something loomed forward within the coffin: a misshapen lump of blue flesh dotted with yellow eyes. A puckered opening in the lump twitched once, twice, and then dilated, revealing a ring of dark, rotted teeth.

"Pitt! Remove your sensors, Pitt!" Cord cried.

"I cannot," Pitt moaned. "They will not come loose."

Cord looked down at his coworker and screamed. The sensor wires had become ropy veins leading into—or out of—Pitt's forehead.

Cord reached out to turn off the continuous-save function, but too late; a froth of blue liquid was oozing up from around the control panel buttons. As he watched, the froth solidified into thick blue tissue. From where he was standing, he could see a similar blue mass growing over his own control panel.

"No, no…" Pitt whimpered, his eyes wide with fear. Cord followed his gaze.

The lid of the coffin, hinged at the bottom, had fallen open—or more probably, had been pushed from within. The occupant of the coffin was an absurd creature—very inefficiently put together, Cord thought grimly. Too many eyes, too many antennae, far too many limbs. A horrible calm came over Cord. He was not even surprised when the cables leading from their work station to the d8055 processing column turned into huge, pulsing veins.

"Now, do not worry, Pitt," Cord whispered. Where was that strange sucking noise coming from? Best to ignore it for now. "What have we done, really? Transferred a bit of jelly from a small box to…a larger one." The d8055 column began to rumble and throb. "Correct?"

The shriveled, papery husk once known as Pitt rustled in lieu of a reply.

THE EMBRACE OF KUGAPPA

Jasper Dunlap gazed up at the enormous statue of metal, glass, plastic, dead insects and more. It stood about thirty feet high and was situated in the Pavoni Gallery's atrium. Huge ferns stood behind the statue, with a faux creek burbling through a pebble-lined plastic canal encircling its base. The work depicted an enormous octopus-like creature, coiling around a crude brass skeleton. The complex curves of the monster's tentacles seemed to suggest the spiraling double-helix of DNA.

The tentacles were studded or otherwise adorned with all sorts of curious items—gems, rings, baby toys, bottles, condoms, books, shoes, even moths and beetles stuck on pins.

Jasper began to write in his notepad, looking back and forth from the art to his notes, back and forth, until suddenly he realized with a start that someone was standing next to him, watching him.

"Hello. How's every little thing?" the woman said. Her voice was low and raspy—a chain-smoker's voice. But she didn't smell like smoke. Actually, she smelled like…He couldn't place it, but it was sweet and somehow familiar. She was pale, thin and angular, and she wore black horned-rim glasses and a navy-blue business suit. Her thick black hair was gathered up in a loose bun, with two yellow pencils stuck through it. She tapped his notepad with a shiny blue fingernail. "Taking lots of notes, I see."

"This piece…" Jasper said. "It's ridiculous. Trite. Eccentricity for eccentricity's sake. Do you see its name anywhere?"

The woman pointed to an engraved rectangle of dark gray plastic mounted on a small stand next to the statue's base.

Jasper squinted at the tiny white letters: *The Embrace Of Kugappa. Vyvyka Megamega. 2001.*

"The artist's name is just as stupid as the—" He stopped and turned toward the woman. "Oh, great. I bet you're this…Mega-mega."

She managed a small smile. "It's pronounced Muh-GOM-muh-guh. You're Jasper Dunlap, aren't you?"

He closed his notepad. "have we met?"

"No," she said. "But I've read your arts column, and you bring out that phrase all the time—'eccentricity for eccentricity's sake.' You use it in about every other column."

"Oh, so now you're attacking me?" Jasper said. "Criticizing the critic?"

The artist shrugged. "Just stating a fact. That's all."

Jasper waggled his pen at the statue. "Well, since you're here, perhaps you can tell me, if you can, what this…object…means?"

The woman laughed—a loud, rasping bray. "'Means'? It is a representation of Kugappa. What more could or should it mean?"

"And what exactly is Kugappa?" He opened his notebook to a blank page. "Tell me. I'll try to work it into my column."

"Yes, I'm sure you will." The woman laughed again. "I'm afraid I don't have the time or patience required to give you an explanation. But—" She stepped up to the statue, looked it up and down for a moment, and then plucked a small blue bottle out of a slot in one of the tentacles.

"The stars are right," she said. "Take this."

Jasper shook his head. "No way. I'm not going to drink it."

"Did I tell you to do that?"

"Well, no—but that comment about the stars. This must be one of those designer drugs that movie stars take." He gave her what he hoped was a hard look. "Movie stars—and artists?"

"The stars I'm talking about have no use for drugs." She slipped the bottle into the breast pocket of his shirt. "You claim to be a critic. If an artist offers you some valuable insight into a work, you must evaluate that insight before you write about said work, yes?"

He fished the little bottle out of his pocket. It looked to be half-full of some sort of foam. "A bottle of insight? It looks like rabid dog spit."

The artist pointed to the empty slot. "If you think that little bottle will hurt you—if you are afraid of it—just put it back in its place."

He glanced at the slot, and then noticed that all of the arms of this creature, this Kugappa, had several slots on them, filled with similar bottles of different colors.

"Of course I'm not afraid," he said. "I'll take your little bottle. But can you at least tell me what I should do with it?"

Vyvyka Megamega gave him a wide smile, revealing a mouthful of small, square, very white teeth. "I can think of many things you can do with it."

Before he could say a word, she turned and walked briskly away.

* * * *

That night, in his office—the spare room next to the bathroom—Jasper had to admit: that girl knew how to push his buttons.

He held the bottle up to the bulb of his desk lamp. It was half-full of froth—he'd noticed that before—and now he saw it also held dark little bits of something. Black thread? Tiny buggies? Could this stuff be some sort of bio-hazard? Surely the gallery wouldn't allow that. Surely they would check out the bottles first. Wouldn't they?

He wanted to call the gallery, but then he realized that if he did, they would only call Vyvyka to find out what was in the bottles, and then she would know that he had called them…

Called them out of fear.

And she'd have the last laugh.

Finally, he decided to call his mother.

After listening to Mary's usual ten-minute stream of boring neighborhood anecdotes, he explained the bottle situation to her.

"She sounds like a nice girl," his mother said. "Ask her out."

"That's not going to happen, Mary." His brothers used to make fun of him for calling their mother by her first name, but he just couldn't bring himself to call her 'Mom.' That would've been such a sitcom thing to do.

"She likes you," Mary said. "That thing she said about the stars. That spells romance. She was obviously flirting with you."

"Oh, I really doubt that," he said.

"Why? Are you that ugly?"

He looked at his reflection in the window to his left—no light outside, so the image was a midnight version of himself in shades of blue and gray. Though that made the picture more dramatic, it still wasn't more enticing. He was simply a stocky, plain man with a pudgy face. "A girl like her wouldn't want a guy like me," he said.

"Jasper, you call tell your mother. Are you gay?"

"No!" he cried, exasperated.

"Well then, why do you find it so hard to believe this girl likes you? You're a man. She's a woman. For Christ's sake, Jasper. When are you going to make me some grandkids? All your brothers have kids."

Jasper sighed as he stared at the bottle. That stupid, trouble-making bottle. "This conversation is going nowhere, Mary."

"What a way to talk to your mother! Just open the bottle and smell what's inside. Maybe it's perfume. If it is, that means she likes you. Then you can write a good review of her statue thingy and ask her out. She sounds like a nice girl."

"Good Lord, Mary," he said. "I would never, ever write a review just to impress a girl. I have my integrity. The community depends on me for cultural guidance."

"Now I've heard everything," she said. "You're just a computer fix-it guy with a little column on the side. People are going to like or hate stuff no matter what you say. You know that. Don't get all fancy-schmancy on me."

"But—" Jasper shook his head. "Whatever."

"Now while you've got me on the phone, open the bottle," Mary said. "If it's poisonous and you faint, I'll call 911. See? I'm looking after you. You need your old mother after all. Now open the bottle. That police show starts in about two minutes and I don't want to miss it. The one with the police driving around. Do you watch that?"

"No, Mary. I don't watch that. I hate police shows. Hold on, I'll open the bottle so we can just get this over with." He had to admit, if only to himself, that he liked the idea of smelling what was in the bottle while he had Mary on the line. He grabbed the bottle, pulled out its little cork, and held it cautiously under his nose. "It smells...like..." He sniffed a few times. "...Like nothing. No, wait, maybe...just a little like...strawberries?"

"See? She likes you." Mary was triumphant. "Finally, a girl who likes you. Ask her out, for Christ's sake. I gotta go, my police show is starting."

She hung up.

Jasper noticed an empty plate on the corner of his desk. It had a few crumbs on it, from some sandwich past, but he brushed those away and poured out the bottle's contents. He swirled the plate a little to make the little puddle of froth spread out.

But actually, it wasn't a froth—he saw now that it was a watery, light-blue gel filled with tiny translucent globes. Fish eggs? He couldn't tell what the black bits were.

He picked up the plate and held it under his nose, trying to figure out that smell. It really wasn't strawberries, though it was certainly that sweet...

He brought the plate closer, and finally recognized, with a sting of dismay, the fruity aroma.

Decay. Rot. A bad meat smell.

A cold wetness touched his chin. To his horror, he realized he'd brought the plate too close to his face. But that close? He wondered, in a mad rush of absurd panic, if the substance had somehow jumped onto his face.

He wiped his chin on a sock he found on the floor. He threw the sock in the trash can. Then he took the plate into the kitchen and rinsed it off in the sink with hot water. He wondered what to do with the plate. At last he tossed it in the garbage. When in doubt, throw it out.

He went back into his office and grabbed the Arkham phonebook. He could not find Megamega in the listings—but then, it had to be a pseudonym. No one could actually be born with a name like Vyvyka

Megamega. And really, what could he possibly have to say to the woman? He wanted to scream something at her—but he wasn't sure what.

It then dawned on him that he hadn't washed his chin off. He should have done that first! He went into the bathroom and washed his whole face with bar soap and the hottest water he could stand. Then he rubbed his skin with an astringent—he always kept some on hand because he had oily skin, though he hated the vanity behind worrying about such things. He looked at his chin in the mirror.

His chin had a tiny cut on it, from shaving that morning. Oh God. Did any of that goo get onto the cut? He looked up into the reflection of his eyes. They were completely dilated. His heart was beating like a jungle drum. He was right in the middle of a full-blown anxiety attack, and he usually passed out when that happened.

And that's exactly what he did.

* * * *

Jasper always knew when he was dreaming, and yet the realization never woke him up, like it did most people.

He dreamed that he was on the beach of an island with bone-white sand, and before him stretched a horizon of dark green sea.

Sinuous—vines?—stretched up out of the water, huge vines overgrown with many smaller vines, and all those vines held an abundance of small, squirming things.

One of the vines swirled up out of the water close to shore, and he saw that it wasn't a vine after all—how silly, how stupid, vines didn't grow in oceans. It was a huge tentacle, overgrown with smaller tentacles, and those had even smaller tentacles on them, and so on in a sort of biofractal progression.

He knew he should be afraid, but he wasn't. Not really. Because.

Because they.

They wanted.

Wanted him to be happy. Yes, the Great Old Ones wanted him to be happy, and Kugappa was one of the Great Old Ones, and the best way to be happy was to be like them.

Be.

Like.

Them.

Who'd told him that? Who'd told him about the Great Old Ones? He giggled—the initials of that spelled 'goo.' Why, that was who had told him. The goo had told him.

Before he knew it he was swimming in the dark green sea, even though he didn't know how to swim, and tentacles and tentacles-upon-tentacles were handling him, exploring him, sliding into every part of him, even into his pores, infiltrating his cells, embracing his soul—

* * * *

In the morning, he woke up curled on the bathroom floor, cuddling some used towels he'd thrown in a corner.

It took him a moment to figure out why he wasn't in his bed. Then he remembered the whole bottle incident.

He stood up and looked in the bathroom mirror. He vaguely recalled that he'd had some sort of dream about octopi and tentacles, and he found himself worrying that something might be growing off of his chin. A beard of tentacles, maybe? What a stupid idea. What sort of ridiculous creature would have a beard of tentacles?

Nothing was growing off of his chin.

There was, however, a small, gaping hole there.

A hole wide enough to accommodate the head of a pin. It went into his chin like a tunnel.

He looked at his eyes in the mirror, but they weren't dilated. He wasn't having a panic attack.

In fact, he was okay with the hole.

He took a shower, had breakfast, then called Mary just to hear her voice. It was Saturday, so he didn't have to be at work. His column was only a little job on the side. His real job was—

He thought for a moment. What did he do for a living? It was pretty important—it provided most of his money. Something about computers, yes, that was it. Funny he couldn't remember any more. Computers, they had to do with the internet—maybe he did internet stuff, too. Probably. The internet was like a monster octopus, big wires like tentacles reaching out, branching into smaller tentacles, smaller and smaller still, until each was wrapped around some poor fool with a computer.

Lots of things were like octopi that way, he thought. Business. Money. The food chain. Reaching out. Grabbing. That's what life was all about.

He was walking down the street. Streets were like that, too. Big streets branching off into little streets, onto sidewalks, into doorways, down halls, right up to some little idiot staring at the TV. TVs, phones, faxes, all sorts of systems, connecting the world in a multi-tentacled embrace.

And now he was walking down a sidewalk into a building. Statues and paintings all over the place.

He found himself standing in front of a huge, glorious statue of a mighty octopus, which was lavishing its affection, its loving caress, upon a skeleton that surely represented all of humanity. Humanity wasn't dead, but it really wasn't altogether alive, now was it? People simply went through the motions, like sleepwalkers—no, more like puppets, wooden-headed little morons who didn't realize that the universe was a grand system of interconnected patterns and forces, swirling and moving together. And the little icons on the statue, the tokens, the treasures on the sinuous limbs, they represented those patterns, those systems, those majestic eternal forces, so powerful, so wondrous—

Someone was standing next to him, watching him.

A beautiful woman.

"Hello. How's every little thing?" she said. Hers was the voice of a goddess. Or maybe a priestess. She tapped his chin with a shiny nail. "Ah, I see some little thing has gotten into you."

He felt his chin. The hole was now big enough to hold the tip of his pinky.

"Is something in there?" he said, messaging his chin, his jaw, feeling around. He knew the answer, but it was still a thought or two away, like an unspoken truth on the tip of his tongue.

"There's nothing in there." Vyvyka Megamega took his hand. "And the nothing is growing. Come with me."

They walked out of the gallery. A teenage girl happened to notice Jasper's face, and she gasped and hurried away.

"Ignore her," the artist said. "The stars are right, and that's all that matters. Soon Kugappa shall be able to plunge from world to world, spreading joy and knowledge. And you—oh, harshest of critics!—you shall help. Won't that be fun? I've figured out why you're such an ass-hole—you've never really had any fun. You've never been given permission to *have* fun, even by yourself. But we'll soon take care of that."

* * * *

Vyvyka led Jasper to her house, which was only a few blocks from the Pavoni Gallery. The walls needed painting, the grass needed cutting. and a crack in the front door's windowpane had been covered with duct tape.

In the living room stood a statue made from gardening tools and pieces of bicycles and tricycles. It resembled some sort of gigantic centipede. The artist's home was more of a workshop than a dwelling. All of the rooms held statues in progress, as well as materials, welding equipment, tools. In the corner of one room Jasper saw a hotplate, a make-up kit, a refrigerator and a futon mattress with a few quilts piled on it—Vyvyka's combination kitchen/bedroom. She led him to the mattress pushed him down onto his back.

She helped him out of his clothes, then removed her own. Soon she began to pleasure him. He tried to kiss her, but she simply shook her head. He wanted to say something—to whisper some gentle words—but found it impossible to speak. But, maybe that was just as well. He didn't want to scare her off by saying the wrong thing. So Mary had been right: the girl liked him after all. A few seconds later, he wondered, who was Mary? And this girl, what was her name again?

Now the girl was upon him, riding him, her eyes closed, lost in her own world of bliss. Jasper squirmed with pleasure—but not too much, he didn't want to throw the girl off. He saw something twinkle out of the corner of his eye. He looked to the left. The girl's make-up kit. A navy-blue plastic box overflowing with tubes and little brushes. A mirror was leaning against the side of the box, and his reflection stared right back at him.

Hair, brow, eyes—those were all the same. But the nose, cheeks, mouth, chin—all gone, swallowed up in a slowly swirling vortex of blackness, dotted with shimmering stars.

Suddenly the mirror shattered—the girl had thrown a shoe at it. She climbed off of him, and no wonder: the sight of his own ruined face had dwindled his erection to a puny mushroom-cap.

"So much for fun," she said with a sigh, "but at least Kugappa will get to have his way with you. Or rather, through you. Shouldn't be long now." She crossed to a toolbox by the wall and began looking inside. "I managed to give up smoking about two weeks ago, but you know..." She found a silver cigarette case and clicked it open. "...I think the occasion calls for a little lung candy. What the Hell. I'd offer you one, but, well..." She laughed as she lit up.

He didn't know what to do, but since he was having difficulty thinking, he decided to just do nothing. Nothing at all. He stared at the naked woman as she sucked on her cigarette, blue smoke swirling around her face and shoulders. She really looked quite lovely. Her expression was one of...What? Amusement? Anticipation? Were they waiting for someone?

He felt a light touch on his shoulder. Now what was this little thing called? A fly! Yes, he remembered that. What a pretty thing it was, black and shiny, so small and yet so complex, so—

Suddenly his vision was filled with sinuous, swirling flesh, flowing out of him at lightning speed from just below his eyes. The tentacles and tentacles-upon-tentacles flexed and flailed, ripping apart the living gateway of Jasper-flesh, making way for the bloated body and ravenous mind of Kugappa.

The critic didn't even have time to form an opinion.

THE HECKLER IN THE HA-HA HUT

I. WHAT LURKS WITHIN PICKMAN'S MOTEL

I arrived in the mystery-shrouded, fear-spattered community of Arkham hoping to make a name for myself in stand-up comedy, my career of choice. But though I had chosen that line of work, it had not yet decided to embrace me to its bountiful bosom.

Previously I had dwelled in the seaside city of Innsmouth, where I had plied my trade in a damp, ramshackle nightclub called Dagon's Den—but alas, my material was not to the liking of its fish-eyed patrons, and they simply regarded me with blank stares as thin lines of watery drool spooled down from their flabby lips.

Arkham, I hoped, would treat me a bit better, since it featured not two, not four, but three comedy clubs. There was Wilbur's Hideaway on the corner of Squamous and Rugose; Shoggy's Bar & Grill next to the Plateau of Leng Travel Agency; and the Ha-Ha Hut, inside Pickman's Motel. All three were considered prestigious venues—especially the Ha-Ha Hut. Certainly Arkham was the place for me. If I made it there, I could make it anywhere.

I found a quaint, furnished apartment two floors above a bar called The Blasted Heath. I would need some humble income to float me while I perfected my act, so I found a low-stress office job at the Arkham Public Library. The library closed at 6:30 p.m., so that would give me plenty of time to zip off to any late-night comedy gigs I might have scheduled.

On my first day at the library, I met a young coworker named Dilbert East, who seemed immensely interested when I told him of my humor-spawned aspirations.

"A comedian?" he exclaimed in a nasal, aristocratic tone. "How immensely interesting. I admire anyone who would try to pursue such a calling. I could never engage in such a fear-fraught endeavor. I am terrified by the very prospect of public speaking, of rising to address an assembly of potential critics who might ridicule the nervous gibberish shambling forth from my palsied lips." The fine-boned man shivered visibly and blinked his sky-blue eyes repeatedly. "I only hope you are never tempted to…to…But no, I dare not tell you!"

"Oh, give me a break," I replied. "You can't just say, 'I only hope you are never tempted to...' and then not finish the sentence. Not only is that rude, but the sight of your impossibly neat desk over there by the window, with seventeen piles of paperclips arranged by size and color in a navy-blue plastic tray, tells me that you must be so insanely obsessive-compulsive, the very thought of not finishing a task you have started—even the completion of a sentence!—would surely drive you to madness. And it would be a short drive indeed. So come on, spill your guts, shaky-boy."

Dilbert let loose with a shrill gasp, much like the sort an effete monkey might release upon discovering he has eaten the last banana in the Congo. "Curse you, ummm—whatever you said your name was. I have such a poor memory for names."

"Winthrop Goiter," I reminded him.

"Oh yes. that's right. So...Curse you, Winthrop Goiter! You have discovered my most lamentable weakness—my puritanical need for closure!" He shook his head sadly. "Very well. You win. Here is the end of that sentence. I only hope you are never tempted to venture into the library's Forbidden, Unspeakably Dangerous, Never-To-Be-Checked-Out-By-Anyone Section to peruse our secret copy of that most shocking and insanity-inducing of ancient tomes, typeset at a point-size convenient to those with impaired vision—the *Large-Print Necronomicon!*"

He paused to wipe a trickle of sweat from his pale brow before continuing with his babbling. "The book of which I speak features the most frightening joke in the known cosmos—a joke so fiendishly effective, the very telling of it would flail to bits the fragile fabric of the space/time continuum. Beware! Promise me you will avoid that joke, which can be found on page 637, a couple inches down from a woodcut depicting Cthulhu's half-sister Catherinulhu."

"Never fear, Dilbert," I said. "My latest material is so strong, I shall never need to destroy the cosmos just to get a laugh. But tell me this: why is this copy of the *Necronomicon* set in large print?"

"Most scholars of ancient lore do not know this," Dilbert said, lowering his voice, "but the author of the *Necronomicon*, Abdul Alhazred, wrote the book not for humanity, but for a pantheon of intergalactic demon-gods known as the Old Ones, who shared their mind-snapping extra-telluric knowledge with him. He was their scribe, and he created the book for them in case they should ever forget the details of their own eon-spanning history."

"That's all well and good," I said, "but again I must raise the question: why was this accursed volume, created for the Old Ones, set in large print?"

"Quite simply, the Old Ones…are *old,*" Dilbert said. "Thusly, they cannot see very well." He leaned closer. "Alhazred himself wrote on page 248 of his macabre masterwork: 'He who asketh a stupid question, verily shall receive a stupid answer.'"

II. OPEN-MIKE WALPURGIS NIGHT

A week later, I performed at Wilbur's Hideaway on an Open-Mike Evening, which happened to fall on Walpurgis Night. I was in top form, opening my act with the jaunty tale of a golf outing attended by the Pope, a bishop, a rabbi, and the King in Yellow. I won first prize, which was a seventy-five dollar gift certificate for fiddle lessons at the Erich Zann Conservatory of Music.

Two nights after that, I hit another open-mike event at Shoggy's Bar & Grill. I treated their patrons to a saucy anecdote concerning a necromancer from Nantucket with a penchant for speaking in rhyme. Again I won first prize—this time, a coupon good for a rubdown and colonic irrigation at a nearby health spa called the Towel & Bowel.

Four days after that, still riding high with confidence from my recent performances, I entered an open-mike contest at the Ha-Ha Hut. The emcee was a cadaverously thin old chain-smoker named H.P. Lungflapps, who started off the comedy night with a joke of his own.

"One morning," he wheezed, "an old witch had this to say to her husband, the warlock. 'Honey, I had a very strange dream last night. I was at an auction where penises were being sold. The longest ones went for about fifty dollars each, and the thick, meaty ones went for one-hundred dollars apiece.'

"The warlock raised an eyebrow. 'What kind of a price were they asking for cocks like mine?'

"The witch waved a hand dismissively. 'Oh, they were just giving those out as free samples.'

"'I also had a dream,' her husband said. 'But in my dream, they were auctioning off vaginas. Normal-sized ones sold from about three-hundred dollars each, and the tight, muscular ones had bidders spending up to a thousand dollars.'

"This time it was the wife's turn to raise an eyebrow. 'And what about vaginas like mine?'

"'Where do you think they held the auction?' the warlock replied."

The audience roared with gusto, relishing the ribald jest. And as soon as the laughter began to die down, the emcee announced the first performer of the evening—

Me.

"Winthrop Goiter," he wheezed, "let's start with you. Get your ass up here and make us laugh! Remember, first prize is a haircut, shave—face or legs, your choice—and cappuccino at the Arkham Unisex Grooming Boutique & Coffee Shoppe, where the elite gather to blather and be coated with lather."

I climbed the steps up onto the stage and looked out over the murky gloom of the club. As I regarded the misshapen lumps that passed for audience members, a tremor of dread scampered up and down my body like a tarantula on crack.

I decided to follow the emcee's example and lead with an anecdote of an adult nature. "So! A lady of the evening and a winged night-gaunt walk into a bar—"

"Impossible!" thundered a hoarse, impossibly low voice from the shadows at the back of the club. "A night-gaunt cannot pass through a typical door. Its huge membranous wings do not fold in against the body all the way. It would be able to pass through a garage door, but no bar would have an entrance that wide. Huh! It is clear you did not do your research!"

I found this bizarre and overly long outburst so disconcerting, I was only able to choke out a few more feeble witticisms before I finally returned to my seat, saddened and humiliated.

I stared into the shadows which housed my tormentor. The darkness was too complete for me to discern his form, but I could sense he was still there. Veritable waves of contemptuous psychic energy seemed to wash over me from out of that lightless limbo.

Later that evening, huddled under threadbare blankets in my drafty bedroom, I could still hear the malignant "Huh!" of my unseen abuser, echoing in my gooseflesh-flecked ears.

III. HORRORS OF THE HECKLER

In the library's employee lounge the next morning, I told Dilbert of my ordeal.

"Truly, it sucks to be you," he intoned. "It is a pity your performance has invoked the contempt of the Heckler in the Ha-Ha Hut!"

"And exactly who," I asked, "is this alliteratively titled individual? Does this insidious interrupter have an actual name?"

"Vince, the bartender there and a close personal friend of mine, has informed me that the Heckler is a creature of great antiquity," Dilbert whispered. "The index of the *Large-Print Necronomicon* lists thirty-seven references to the Heckler within its panic-plagued pages. He is the one whom the serpent-priests of Lemuria dubbed 'the Killjoy of

Kadath'—but other, less reptilian but more lemurlike primordial scholars knew him as Nyarlathotep, Dark Lord of the Screaming Abyss!"

"This nightmarish scenario gnaws at my soul like a hungry trucker chewing on a spicy-hot buffalo-wing!" I cried. "I wish to appear at the Ha-Ha Hut again, but how can I, knowing that this vile nemesis with such a preposterously polysyllabic name is waiting to lay waste to my next performance there?"

Dilbert's frantic eyes rolled up and down, back and forth as he pondered my predicament. Finally he said, "You simply must strive to be funnier, my friend…so funny, you can actually bring laughter to the vicious lips of a creature that has not even chuckled since its shocking and sacrilegious genesis, millennia ago."

"Wow," I said. "Talk about a tough audience."

The next week, I showed up again at the Ha-Ha Hut, my mind buzzing with a teeming swarm of new jokes. And again, H.P. Lungflapps started the evening with a tale of libidinous humor.

"One afternoon at the nudist colony," he said, "a necromancer and his beautiful young wife were walking along, having a nice chat, when a huge honeybee flew straight into the wife's pussy. The frightened couple put on some clothes and headed off to their doctor's office. The sick people in the waiting room were terrified by the furious buzzing echoing forth from the depths of the wife's uterus.

"After a thorough examination and a few x-rays, their doctor shared his professional opinion. The insect, he noted, had crawled a good distance into the woman's reproductive tract. He then said, perhaps the necromancer could put some honey on his tallywhacker, slide it all the way into his wife, and then pull it out. The hungry bee might then be tempted to follow the honeyed boner.

"Unfortunately, the thought of a south-of-the-border bee-sting took the romance right out of the necromancer's erection: it refused to become as stiff as the desiccated old corpses used by the magic-man in his rituals. Finally the physician, a braver fellow, said he would be willing to give it a try. With no other options, the couple agreed.

"The doctor opened his pants, dribbled some honey on his rigid tool, and slid deep into the woman's buzzing snatch. Soon he began thrusting vigorously, and the necromancer shouted, 'Hey, what's going on?'

"'I changed my mind,' the doctor announced. 'I've decided to drown the little fucker!'"

Again, the audience hooted and hollered with unbridled mirth. And again, after the laughter had faded away, I was the first performer called up onto the stage.

I gave the audience the biggest, brightest smile I could muster. I clutched the microphone and cried out, "So! How about this unseasonably chilly weather? It reminds me of my early days as a traveling brush salesman, and of the time I stopped at a shunned and shuttered farmhouse in Dunwich, where—"

"Enough!" cried a hatefully hoarse voice from the far shadows. "Proceed no further! Boy, I thought I was an entity of incredible antiquity—but in comparison with the age of that cobweb-strewn knee-slapper, I am but a mere embryo! I have heard it a million times, and it has never made any sense to me. A brush salesman would not be able to make a decent living selling his wares to a backwoods clientele. Plus, the farmer's daughter is altogether too compliant. Away with you, you tedious teller of tepid tales!"

I could feel hot tears streaming down my cheeks as I rushed off that accursed stage, across the club, out the door and into the night. What was I to do? In truth, my version of that particular joke, admittedly a rather timeworn jest, was going to take a more modern and naughty turn a few sentences into its telling, but—woe unto me!—the Heckler had not allowed me to proceed that far.

As I stumbled through the night, I suddenly saw before me, glowing yellowish-white in the moonlight, the venerable pillars of the Arkham Public Library, my place of daytime employment.

I thought back to what Dilbert East had told me of the *Large-Print Necronomicon*. He had mentioned that it contained within its wickedness-warped pages the most effective joke in the entire cosmos, the telling of which would rip asunder the fragile fabric of the time/space continuum...

I stood and stared, stared and stood before the library, pondering my options. I was an employee and the key to the side entrance was in my right-front pants pocket. I knew exactly which basement room held the Forbidden, Unspeakably Dangerous, Never-To-Be-Checked-Out-By-Anyone Section. I didn't have the key to that, but I knew where it could be found: hanging from a nail on the wall behind the coffee machine in the employee lounge.

That night, a solitary figure (namely, me) entered the library and emerged, a few minutes later, clutching a certain large-print book to his chest...

Later, that same desperate character (still me) opened the book to page 637 and found a certain doom-fraught rib-tickler—a joke so effective it could reduce the known universe to a steaming pile of baboon flop...

At this point, the afore-mentioned protagonist (yep, still me) decided to switch back to telling his—I mean, my—story in the form of a first-person narrative. I carefully crafted a new version of that cosmically injurious jest. My subtle adaptation, I believed, would considerably reduce the joke's destructive power. At the very worst, it would probably give a few audience members heart attacks and maybe knock over a few tables. Nothing too serious.

As for the Heckler in the Ha-Ha Hut…Surely he would be impressed by my newfound comic acumen. Who knows, perhaps he'd even buy me a congratulatory cocktail. Maybe one with a festive little umbrella!

I arrived at work a half-hour early so I could return the *Large-Print Necronomicon* to its shelf before the other employees arrived. Around noon, I bumped into Dilbert in the employee lounge.

"You know what I just noticed?' he said. "The key to the Forbidden, Unspeakably Dangerous, Never-To-Be-Checked-Out-By-Anyone Section's room doesn't have any cobwebs on it today. And yet yesterday morning it was positively festooned with spider-exuded gossamer. What do you suppose is the reason behind this disturbing new development?"

"I'm sure I do not know!" I replied. "Maybe one of the other librarians did a little light dusting. Maybe somebody opened a window and an unseasonably chilly breeze blew away those pesky cobwebs. Who knows? My storehouse of knowledge in the matter of the now inexplicably clean key holds no inventory! Okay?"

Dilbert, apparently, had stopped listening to me at some point during my discourse, because he then turned to me and said, "Hey, we're out of creamer."

IV. AT THE MICROPHONE OF MADNESS

At last came the fated evening of ultimate destiny: the next open-mike contest at the Ha-Ha Hut. The withered old emcee opened the evening with yet another salacious story. It was clear there was no end to the old coot's inventory of smutty utterances.

"A blind mystic showed up at a furniture factory," he said, "sat down in the owner's office, and asked to be interviewed for the position of quality control manager. The owner asked, 'But how can you do your job? You won't be able to see the wood.'

"The blind fellow assured him that he could do the job by smell. His ultra-sensitive nose, he stated, could not be fooled.

"'Is that a fact?' the owner said. He took a piece of wood from a table near his desk and held it under the man's nose. 'What kind of wood is this I am holding in front of you?'

"The mystic took a few sniffs and said, 'Ah, that is clearly a fresh piece of Norwegian pine!'

"'Very good!' the factory owner said. He grabbed a small piece of wood out of his wastebasket and held it out for the mystic's nasal consideration. 'How about this one?'

"The sightless gentleman announced, after just one sniff, 'That, I am sad to say, is an inferior grade of mahogany.'

"'Absolutely correct!' the owner cried, quite impressed.

"At that point, the owner's wife entered the room. The owner put a finger to his lips to let the woman know she shouldn't speak. He then gestured for his wife to stand in front of the mystic and lift the front of her skirt, and being a saucy lady, she did so. 'Now what can you smell?' the owner said.

"The blind man sniffed once. Twice. Three times. 'Hmmm, this is rather unusual. Can I smell the other side?'

"The wife turned around and lifted the back of her skirt. 'Okay,' said the owner, 'try another sniff.'

"The mystic took a good, deep sniff, gave the matter some thought, and then smiled. 'Ah, I have it figured out—though it took me a moment. That rotten plank came from the shit-house door of an old tuna boat!'

"Audience members howled with merriment, and some even fell out of their chairs. But I was far too nervous to share in their amusement. Sweat seeped forth on my forehead and in my armpits; from those fleshy locales, it flowed down my body and pooled coldly in my trembling belly-button, under which, butterflies of nervousness fluttered in my acid-addled stomach.

I let out a wee burp of mingled apprehension and indigestion when H.P. Lungflapps called me up onto the stage. My hands shivered like twin albino bats in an Antarctic ice-cave, assuming such caves served as lodging for such bats. I'm not really sure. They'd have to be pretty hardy bats. What would they eat? Maybe baby penguins.

My hands shook so ferociously, I practically knocked the microphone to the floor when I went to grab it. I managed to take a firm hold of the auditory appliance, and with a deep intake of breath to steady my jangled nerves, I delivered my scaled-down version of that unspeakable joke from the pages of the *Large-Print Necronomicon*.

I dare not share the punch line with you, but I can tell you this: the set-up involved a creature belonging to a non-extinct species of Atlantean poultry, trying to cross an avenue of traffic on a moonless winter's night.

I was able to tell my joke from start to finish: the Heckler did not interrupt me once. When I had finished my comedic tale, I looked out over the room to witness the results of my performance on the audience and of course, the time/space continuum.

Apparently, it was the sort of joke where the complexities of its elaborate plot had to really sink in before any sort of response could be expected. A full minute of complete silence passed. Suddenly, I heard a shrill squawk of what I thought sounded like laughter—then another and yet another. Soon the entire room was filled with wild, unbridled cackles of raucous mirth.

As the piercing cries of my audience continued to peal forth, it gradually dawned on me that those loud squawks weren't really laughter at all. They were just...

Squawks.

The folks in the audience were actually squawking like common hens. When they began to shrink and grow feathers, beaks, and scaly, clawed feet, I realized that perhaps my revision of the joke had concentrated just a little too heavily on the poultry-related aspects of the plotline.

I gazed into the inky blackness at the far end of the club. What, I wondered, had become of the Heckler?

Leaving the stage, I grabbed a cigarette lighter off one of the tables, flicked up a flame, and kicked hens and roosters out of my way as I walked to the back of the room.

A thousand mixed emotions swirled through my brain when I saw the thing seated at the lone table I found there.

I approached the table and did something rather curious...altogether unusual...

Then, I left the building and strolled the streets of Arkham, trying to gauge the extent of my joke's influence.

It turned out my joke only had a three-block range. Some folks living on the fourth block had sprouted a few feathers, but those dropped out almost immediately.

But as for me...

On the chair next to that lone table in the shadows of the Ha-Ha Hut, I'd found a single egg, large as a melon and as black as a raven's wing. The otherworldly Heckler had undergone an exceptionally complete metamorphosis.

Ordinarily, I'm not a vengeful man, but you must understand: the Heckler had vexed me beyond the limits of human endurance.

Taking a butter knife from the table, I'd tapped a hole into that oversized ovoid and greedily sucked out its contents, so that I might experience the ultimate victory over my tormentor.

But as it turns out, the yolk was on me.

It's a good thing I'm getting close to the end of my narrative, because it's getting pretty hard for me to type as my fingers slowly turn into ebony talons. Good God, my emerging feathers, darker than the night sky, are really starting to itch! I know I shall have to leave my current dwelling, since the business across the street is a chain restaurant specializing in fried chicken. The very thought of what goes on in there makes my vermilion comb stand on end.

Where shall I go? The answer is ridiculously clear. I don't know how to get there, but I shall. I shall.

I must go to the dimension from which Nyarlathotep came—that dreaded domain of grotesque dreams and arabesque nightmares known as...

The Other Side.

FINESSE

"I need something special for my show tonight." Zannika tap-tapped her nail-thin heels down the aisle, past monkey-fur miniskirts and sequined bustiers. The artist bit at the tip of a black-lacquered fingernail. "Something delicious. Nasty. To die for."

Her manager adjusted the lavender rose in the lapel of his lemon-yellow blazer. "Ernst told me they've got some new fishnets in every neon imaginable."

"Earth to Yoyo: neon is out, out, out." Zannika sighed hugely. "This place is full of whore clothes. Let's try somewhere else."

"In a minute. Ernst went to get us some Dust Bunnies." Yoyo glanced over a display of pins and selected a jade spider in a silver web. "We ought to buy some little thing. This is nice."

"I should dye my hair red. Flame red. I'm so tired of platinum-blonde. Aren't you?" The artist glanced in a three-way mirror and wrinkled her nose. "It's so severe. I'm surprised you haven't said anything by now."

Yoyo brushed the bangs of Zannika's pageboy cut with his finger-tips. "Your hair is gorgeous. You're the only woman I know who could get away with brown hair. An *earth tone,* for Christ's sake."

"That was years ago. Back then I'd try *anything* once."

A pencil-thin boy carrying a silver tray entered the shop from a back room. On the tray were two small glasses filled with blue liqueur; the rim of each glass was coated with white powder. Yoyo and Zannika downed their drinks and licked the rims clean.

"Buy your little spider so we can go," the artist whispered in her manager's ear. "It's time for some serious shopping."

* * * *

It was a vile, ripe, impossible day. Heatwaves writhed up from the sidewalk like translucent tentacles. The heat stifled most of the shoppers but curiously, vitalized the streetpeople. Bag-ladies and hard-eyed fun-boys held sway on such a day, second only to the likes of Zannika. She did not perspire or even glow. Her pale skin was always dry and cool.

Zannika was a graceful, elongated creature: her hands and arms and legs were long yet elegantly, perfectly curved. She loved to look at her-self in the mirror. Sometimes she wondered what she would look like with a penis. Penises were usually lumpy, ghastly-yet-comic things. If, through some unlikely miracle, she should ever sprout a fleshy spout, she knew it would be the absolute best: a sculpted alabaster masterpiece.

Their next stop was The Long Look. Within the next half-hour, Zannika spent more than eight hundred dollars on gloves, hats, perfumes, and hair toys.

"Oh, Yoyo." She brushed her fingertips lazily over her manager's rump as he bent over a display of brooches. "I would ask what Mr. Soap Opera's got that I haven't, but I'm afraid I already know."

"That's the one thing I hate about being on the road with you. I can't keep an eye on Andros." Yoyo pouted. "I was on the phone with him and he kept going on about that cow Pauline. He says they're only friends, but I've been watching the show and he's always got his hands all over her. I know it's just acting, but *still…*"

"Andros is a common sort of man. That sort is notoriously indiscriminate. Why do you even put up with him?" Zannika poked her manager in the side with a pinky finger. "It's a miracle you can be so urbane with all those awful male hormones brewing inside of you."

Yoyo smiled. "It's the cross I must bear."

A young black-haired woman in a leather jacket came up to Zannika. "I know you! You're playing at The Black Box. I just love your show."

"That doesn't mean you know me." The artist crossed to the makeup counter and began to examine the mascaras, the lipsticks — anything so she wouldn't have to make eye contact with a fan.

The woman followed close behind. "I've been telling my friends, 'Go see *Meat for Daddy*. It's so unreal!'" The fan glanced at the lipsticks. "Try the deep purple."

At last Yoyo came to Zannika's rescue. "Ms. Taint does not feel comfortable talking with her fans," he said, taking the woman by the arm and turning her in another direction. "Her act is so very personal. You understand."

"Oh, I'm sorry. I didn't mean any harm." The woman turned toward Zannika. "Really, I didn't."

"That's fine, dear," Yoyo said. "Ms. Taint understands. Deep down she loves all of her fans." He gently pushed her away. "Bye bye, now. And thank you."

* * * *

"Why in the world am I carrying these?" Outside of The Long Look, Zannika handed her shopping bags to Yoyo. "A day of lugging these around and I'll turn into one of those awful muscle-women. Where now?"

Yoyo squinted down the street, past storefronts of faux marble and metal. "There. The Snake Pit." He pointed to a small boutique a block and a half away. The display case was filled with what appeared to be mannequins twined in telephone cord.

"It's not too Goth, is it?" Zannika's heels shot sparks as they hit the sidewalk. "I don't do retro." As they drew closer to the shop, she realized that the dummies were in fact wrapped in barbed wire.

Inside, the store was in fashionable disarray. Jewelry and scarves and boots were strewn on the steps of silver stepladders and hung from thin silver chains. Scattered on small tables were glowing spheres of blue glass. The walls were splashed with thick, shiny clots of black and red paint. The high ceiling seemed to be covered with dark lace or netting. No clerks or customers were in sight. Beside a bell on the counter stood a small engraved sign — WE LIVE TO SERVE.

Zannika tried on blue metal earrings shaped like fingers. "These are darling. I could wear them during my act. And look at this belt." She removed a long strip of shiny pinkness from a chain. "What do you think it's made of?"

An obese, perfumed shopboy appeared so quickly at her side that she gasped in surprise. "That belt," he breathed in a hollow tone, "is made from the sun-dried small intestine of a crocodile." His silver contacts rode his bulging orbs uneasily, occasionally flashing slivers of his dark brown irises. "Isn't it extraordinary?"

Yoyo picked up a small stone statue from one of the tables. "This little fellow. Is that a tail, or is a snake crawling up his ass?"

"A snake: but look closer. It's on the way out, not in." The shopboy grinned, revealing very small, very yellow teeth. "That figurine depicts the Egyptian god of insanity. He arrived this morning — isn't he delight-ful? The syllables of his name

happen to create a riotously obscene phrase in English. Since I do not wish to offend, I shall call him 'He-Who-Devours-Wounded-Moths.' More than anything else, ancient Egypt is an attitude, don't you think?"

Zannika noticed the woman in the leather jacket talking with a group of young people outside of the display window. She watched them out of the corner of her eye, hoping they wouldn't enter the store. Thankfully, they moved on.

"I happened to overhear mention of an act." The shopboy lowered his eyes. "Are you performers?"

"Ms. Taint is." Yoyo took Zannika by the hand. "She is a perfor-mance artist. There's a show tonight at The Black Box. Her act is the most—"

She dug her nails into his palm. "We mustn't take up the nice young man's time. He must have a trillion things to do."

A phone shrilled at the counter and the shopboy went to answer it.

"You know I hate to talk about my act," the artist said. "Why, why, *why* did you even bring it up?"

"I just answered his question." Yoyo rubbed his sore hand. "Besides, he might tell some of the other store patrons. A little word of mouth goes a long way in this set."

"This set? The place is as empty as a tomb."

"You might try being just a hair *friendlier* with fans and fans-to-be," Yoyo said. "They're your livelihood. At least give them a little smile."

"I'd rather give them lobotomies." Zannika rubbed her temples. "I'm not feeling very well. I'm getting a headache."

"Dr. Yoyo has just the thing." He reached into his breast pocket and pulled out a small cigarette case, but before he could open it, the shopboy returned. He held a long grey pipe which appeared to be carved from some sort of animal bone.

"You are not feeling well? Beautiful people should feel beautiful." The boy cocked his head to one side. "Might I suggest a headache remedy dating back to the days of our little friend, the eater of moths?"

Zannika looked into the pipe's bowl. It appeared to be filled with dried flower petals and bits of crystal. The shopboy lit the mixture with a silver cigarette lighter and took a puff himself. "Very pleasant," he said. "Very soothing."

The artist began to suck at the pipe. The mixture was spicy—like clove cigarettes, except sharper. She detected a faint blue glow around the shopboy; perhaps the petals were mildly hallucinogenic. Yoyo had a green aura that clashed with his suit.

A soft, sweet humming filled her head. She held up her hand and marveled at the coils of coral and deepest purple that swirled between her fingers. She felt so much better now. Perhaps someday she would come back to this shop and— What? Have sex with the shopboy? No, he was kind, but an awful eyesore. At any rate, he probably favored some oblique erotic predilection. Get more of the pipe mixture? She could probably ask for a shopping-bagful. The Snake Pit, she discerned, was an obliging establishment.

"I think Ms. Taint has had enough, Minty," Yoyo said as he took the pipe from Zannika and returned it to the shopboy. "We still have a few more stops to make." The shopboy merged with the shadows of the boutique.

"How did you know his name?" Zannika said. "He didn't tell us. He wasn't wearing one of those tacky name tags."

"I've been here before. Do you think I would take you to a complete-ly unfamiliar shop?" Yoyo shook his head. "I prepare for these outings. I want our time together to be perfect. Because you are perfect. No, I take that back: perfection does not allow for potential, and you have worlds and worlds of potential."

* * * *

It seemed a mistake to return to the street, Zannika thought, and yet what could she do? She couldn't stay in The Snake Pit forever. She had to prepare for her show. The humming in her head, at first so comforting, was beginning to bother her, and the sharp red and orange auras of the pedestrians hurt her eyes.

She looked down at herself. Her entire body crawled with glowing coral and

purple snakes. Pythons. People always told her she was special, but she never really believed them. She assumed (often rightly) that they merely wanted something. Now, here was visual proof that she was dif-ferent. Others wore their auras like tacky raincoats. Hers was vibrantly alive.

She plucked at Yoyo's blazer, begging for him to walk slowly. He recommended a few more boutiques, but she was no longer in the mood for shopping. She felt a little better by the time they reached the hotel. "I'm going to take a nap," she said. "Would you be a dear and piece together some sort of outfit for the show? I wish I could do it myself but I'm dead to the world. Dead, dead, dead."

Zannika stumbled into the bedroom, slipped out of her dress and threw herself on the bed. Though her body came to rest on the sheets, her mind did not. That part of her floated down through the fabric and springs of the mattress. In the distance she heard Yoyo on the phone: "Meet you there, lover." Poor Andros, the cuckolded soap stud. Her mind sank through metal and concrete, floor after floor, faster and faster, down through stone, stone, stone. She felt squeezed by the stone, the way Daddy used to squeeze her.

She had erased Daddy's face from her memory. All she remembered of him was his horrible desire. He had been an awful man, and she was living her revenge—telling the whole world about wicked Daddy through her art. She lived to communicate her feelings: not to any one person, but to the masses. Yoyo was the only exception. His shallowness made him a treasured confidant.

At last she passed through the stone into a fiery river of magma. And in this fierce fluid state she felt strangely aroused. The earth's hot blood washed lasciviously over her presence, searing away all of her cares, all of her limitations, leaving only passion and insatiable hunger.

Aeons passed, liquid stone boiled and churned, roiled and burned, and still Zannika flowed with the heat, even after the creature in yellow roused her and covered her with a second skin of shining rags.

She allowed the creature in yellow to lead her through the foolishly angled structure until they emerged into a great space of towering slabs dotted with brightness and a great looming void beyond. Chattering creatures pushed at her as they hurried along. The creature in yellow pushed her into the open belly of a large beast of metal.

She wished to drink the hot living fluids of the creature in yellow, to drain him utterly dry, to reduce him and all the chattering creatures to dust. Inside the metal beast, the creature in yellow poured a clear liquid into her throat that helped to ease her thirst. The creature made her consume tiny roundnesses of white and pink.

Zannika turned her eyes toward the creature's face and suddenly found herself wondering if they were going to be late for The Black Box and if they had enough cash on hand for the taxi.

Yoyo put the flask of vodka and pill case back in Zannika's purse. "I hope you like that outfit. I thought a metallic look would be just the thing."

"I'm hungry," she said. "When can we eat?"

"Miss One-Meal-a-Day? Miss Salad-Bar-and-Mineral-Water? The club can scrounge up something for you." Yoyo patted her hand. "At least you're talking. Do you need another pill? We have a special audience tonight, you know."

"No, I don't know. Some little art league?" She looked out at the stars. How could fire look so cold? "I'm still hungry. The stars are confusing me. Are we there yet?"

* * * *

At The Black Box, Yoyo went off to talk to the stage manager. In her dressing room, Zannika wolfed down a steak, two baked potatoes, and a slice of chocolate cake. She decided never to return to The Snake Pit. The mixture in the pipe had reduced her comprehension of the world to a primal state. True, the effect had worn off, but it still frightened her. She was an artist: communication was essential to her.

She was deafened by applause as she strolled onstage. The club was choked with swirling smoke. She picked up a remote control from on top of a large metal box in the center of the stage. With the press of a button, she activated the wall of televisions that served as the background for her performance.

Scenes from obscure, fetish-oriented porno movies sprang up on the screens. Zannika set down the remote control and opened the metal box.

"Meat for Daddy!" she cried, pulling out a raw chunk of beef brisket. She slapped it on the floor and against the wall of televisions. On one screen, a tall blonde with wrinkled lips sneered as she picked up a handful of clothespins.

"Daddy loves meat!" Zannika screamed. "Daddy, Daddy, Daddy! Feed me meat, Daddy! Show me that you care!"

The smoke coiling up from the audience had a spicy, familiar smell. Zannika pulled a raw chicken out of the box, selected a screen, and smeared the carcass against an especially exuberant close-up. She glanced out over the audience and blinked with surprise: she could detect auras of red and orange among the audience members. Offstage, she saw Yoyo laughing with a short, fat figure with a blue aura.

"Meat! Meat! Meat! Daddy's meat is so complete!" The artist reached again into the box and began to toss chunks of ground chuck against the screens. "Daddy likes cow meat! Pig meat! Woman meat!" As she screamed her litany, she suddenly realized that the audience was chanting along with her. "Red meat! White meat! Daddy wants all the meat!"

In the front row, the woman with the leather jacket stood on her seat, screaming, "I love you, Zannika!" Angered, the artist threw a heavy slab of meat in her face. The woman sank her teeth into the prize.

The glistening flesh on the screens also took on auras. Red, orange, magenta. Zannika suddenly began to feel hot. As hot as magma, as hot as the earth's core. And she was hungry again.

The black-haired woman removed her jacket, her tank top, her pants. Several other members of the audience also began to disrobe. Zannika felt drool streaming down her chin. She glanced back at the televisions and saw they had all been turned off.

Holding hands, Yoyo and the fat shopboy walked onto the stage. "Adore Her," they cried out in unison. Then her manager shouted, "She-Who-Hungers shall feast tonight. Worship Her, for She-Who-Hungers shall lead us into the Beyond. She-Who-Hungers desires all. Knows all. Reveals all."

"I'm not—" As the heat within her rose, Zannika found it difficult to speak. "Don't—don't—" Don't what? She stared at the audience. What were they doing to her?

This time, the heat did not stop with her mind. Her body turned feverish and began to expand. The metallic dress ripped and fell away as she billowed into an enormous, spongy mass, dripping with hot digestive acids. Purple and coral pythons of living power squirmed across her bulk.

Several members of her frenzied audience climbed on stage, and she writhed with pain and delight as they thrust themselves into her: first little parts, then limbs, then entire bodies. She engulfed them with tingling ecstasy. For a moment, she considered sparing Yoyo... Then a pang of ravenous *need* coursed through her. She thrust out a fat ribbon of tissue and wrapped it around her manager's throat. Another length of pink fiber shot forth to embrace the shopboy.

Why, she wondered, had they turned off her videos? Her act wasn't done yet! She stared sadly, longingly at the wall of televisions. Then she caught sight of a reflected image, segmented across all the dark, shiny rectangles of glass. An image of—

Herself.

She stared and stared, dumbfounded. She was now one big *face*... but not just any face. Big black ovals for eyes and a wide, curved slash of a mouth, set in an expression of banal idiocy.

An enormous, luridly enflamed, have-a-nice-day Smiley Face.

People from the audience were still climbing onstage and thrusting themselves into her, allowing themselves to be instantly consumed. She wanted to tell the people about desire, about meat, and as always, about Daddy. But her mind refused to focus on the task. She could feel her red-hot appetite sizzling away her intellect.

Zannika tried desperately to cling to her power of speech. The struggle, however, was futile. Every time she opened her mouth to say something, a cluster of fans crawled inside.

NIGHTMARES ONE THROUGH FIVE, AND WHAT COMES AFTER

NIGHTMARE NO. 1: SEX

Smell of coffee and roses in the air and you have tiger paws (where did you get tiger paws?) and bloodstained, thread-dangling clouds smother the sun and hey, these things happen, and a figure sweeps toward you through the red twilight (long, ragged black hair hides the face) and far more than two incredibly strong, thickly veined hands grab you here and there and there, too and soon the thrusting begins and you know, these things happen, and very soon you realize that you can feel the thrusting well up into your ribcage (harder, longer, wider) and only when it reaches your throat from the inside does the feeling, the heat, the delicious swooning reeeeeally begin and yes, yes, oooooooh YES in no time at all you are little more than a layer of elastic flesh wrapped tightly, SO TIGHTLY around this massive pulsing cylinder and you say to yourself as the high-pressure jets of oily blue-green climax burst you to ragged/ ecstatic/still-SO-VERY-EAGER shreds: ah well, these things happen

NIGHTMARE NO. 2: MONEY

You dropped your wallet YOUR WALLET! it had your credit cards in it AND NOW: someone incredibly ugly (with pimples at the corners of his mouth) is using all your pretty green money to have sex with glamorous prostitutes who can hardly WAIT, while you—so cold, so pitiful—beg in the streets you pick up dirty pennies with your long, yellowed nails OH PLEASE, MISTER, I used to have a lot of money but then I LOST MY WALLET won't you please help? and the man before you spits at you, says BEAT IT, YOU STUPID, DISEASED HOMELESS PERSON and then you realize that sure, he has boyish good looks but really, he's the ugly guy who STOLE YOUR WALLET and he used the money to buy a new face, soft and free of blemishes, so you throw yourself at him you tear off his face with your filthy nails and as that wet leathery handful turns into a BRAND-NEW WALLET you smile with your pretty green teeth and scratch at the corners of your mouth

NIGHTMARE NO. 3: HOME

Lock the doors (even the basement door) and pull the shades because the workday's done and you are HOME and its time to do what you do best: have a little drinky a big drinky THE WHOLE FUCKING BOTTLE and yeah, there's a thought, slip that bottle right in and then hey, slip a porno movie into the slot—not any machine's slot, but rather, your own slot, your own secret slot (the one under your arm) and hit PLAY and goodness, you surely love to play (you're HOME!) and just as you're getting into the game, with all its lovely toys, you see that the blinds have shot up, the door has blown wide open and all your heavyset, balding (no matter their gender) and so-very-pungent coworkers are standing there, watching you, laughing and whispering to each other, and someone mentions a pink slip—the cretins! can't they see how special you are?—and you know, perhaps they CAN because then they rush you, wrestle you to the ground and the many too-soft, too-long things they slip into you are indeed quite pink

NIGHTMARE NO. 4: FAMILY

Mommy (you cry) Why was I born SO FUCKING UGLY? Why does my forehead slant SO FAR BACK? Why do my eyes bug out and why are they SO YELLOW? O Mommy (you whisper) Can't I just crawl back inside your wet warm tummy-wummy? I wasn't done yet. And then you hear a wet stomping behind you and suddenly Daddy picks you up and SAYS—actually, Daddy says nothing; he never does; he simply picks you up and pushes your tiny mouth toward the larger of his swollen, hairy, booze-filled breasts, while Mommy smokes another cigarette, applies another fuming layer of makeup, and informs you, quite calmly, that your real parents were a home-ec teacher and a baseball player

NIGHTMARE NO. 5: FACE

Men and women think you are simply gorgeous, and you are: and gazing into your vanity mirror, you suddenly realize that you're not sure of your gender; but with a face this stunning, who cares? Lavender eyes, high cheekbones, square white teeth, thick black hair, golden skin that shines. You open your robe of green silk and begin to manipulate the subtle folds and tubes and corrugations that meet your fingers. No other living creature would know what to do with the maze of flesh that is your body: and even now, the utter pleasure has coaxed hundreds of thin chitinous needles to extend from your body; they pierce and suck at your own hands (hands as pale and as white and as damp as fish-bellies); but no matter: you still have that FACE

WHAT COMES AFTER:

Five nights of vile dreams, or perhaps one especially vicious quintet of nightmares: it doesn't matter. Love, security, and identity mean nothing to you now. And that's the way it should be. You find Fear tiresome; baneful knowledge has turned the world with all its woes into the dreariness sort of amateur theatre production. But you must persist: eat, drink, breathe, make love, go to work. You picture yourself as yet another robot filled with twisted springs and blackened, greasy gears—but oh, you know better. You try to cheer yourself: perhaps you shall pass a car-wreck on the way to the office. Complete your tasks, smile at everyone you meet, and go home. Sit in your easy chair by the window all night (Sleep? What's that?) and wait: it may take months, years, decades, or maybe just a few minutes, but sure enough, there will come a muffled giggling, followed by a tiny tapping at the glass. At this summons, your skin will split wide open: and hopefully, that part of you which emerges will take just a moment to give a Miss America wave (simply out of courtesy) to this spinning ball of mud and fire

THE ODOUR OUT OF THE
TERRIBLE OLD MAN

Take the Pickman Turnpike three miles past the billboard for Squamous &Rugose, Attorneys at Law, then turn left at the Shunned House (the blood-red one where Izakiah Whateley died screaming on that ill-fated Candlemas Night, not the baby-blue one with the cutesy hedgehog lawn ornaments) and follow Highway 8 until you see a little store that sells apple cider—*but don't stop there!* Go another half-mile and you will see, on your left, a dark and sinister shack where, during lunar eclipses, mad women have been known to dance madly to the fluting of lurid panpipes from beyond the stars. Drive past all that and turn right at the old stump, onto a little gravel road. Follow that into town and park next to the Civil War cannon with the broken wheel, outside the fire station.

That's where I work.

Well do I remember a certain lightning-streaked, eldritch and mystery-strewn Thursday night. Skoglund, Cheswick and I were sitting around playing Old Maid when we received the call from the house of the Terrible Old Man. I was the one who answered the phone.

"You must come quickly," he sputtered. "I am desperately in need of immediate and confidential medical assistance."

"Have no fear: we'll be right there," I said. I hung up and returned to the game. Half an hour later, we were on our way.

The gambrel-roofed residence of the Terrible Old Man sits on top of Sentinel Hill like, well, a sentinel of some sort. When we arrived, the elderly albino housekeeper, Florence, showed us into the sitting room— but our host was not seated.

The Terrible Old Man, wearing nothing but a pink paisley bathrobe and purple bunny slippers, rested bellyside-down on an overstuffed yellow sofa with dusty lace doilies on the arms (of the sofa, not the Terrible Old Man).

I noticed that the nearest doily had a greasy stain on it. "Remove that filthy antimacassar," I said to Cheswick. He responded by shoving Florence out the door.

"I am glad you are here," whispered the Terrible Old Man in a voice like autumn leaves being arranged into a festive holiday centerpiece. "It would seem that I have had a bit of an accident. Earlier this evening, shards of hell-wrought green lightning tore the skies asunder, and a curious and singular intergalactic anomaly—a meteorite, if you will—plunged out of the night's yawning abyss and into my backyard."

He shifted uneasily, perhaps trying to find a more comfortable position, before continuing. "I instructed Florence to bring this extra-dimensional souvenir into the house," he said, "so that I might examine it. Upon inspection, it proved to be tube-shaped, of a roseate hue, warm to the touch, and pretty hefty, too. Whether it was a product of nature, or instead forged in some forbidden kiln of strange lore and otherworldly technology, is pretty much up for grabs. As I examined the lengthy alien cylinder, I turned to fetch something really scientific from a low shelf. It was then that I slipped and fell, and—" Here the old man blushed. "I just happened to fall in such a manner that the meteorite was lodged, once again, in my backyard. So to speak."

I nodded sagely, and with trembling hands, lifted the hem of that accursed paisley robe, so that we might view the scene of the Terrible Old Man's misfortune.

From between his withered and lugubrious nether-cheeks protruded a pink extrusion of prodigious girth. Skoglund, Cheswick and I, in turns, tried first with gingerly caution, then with steadfast insistence, finally with workmanlike vigor, to remove the meteorite. All without success. During our efforts, the Terrible Old Man simply smiled in a disturbing, insidiously *pleased* fashion.

Finally, I grabbed the protuberance and, instructing Skoglund and Cheswick to each take hold of my elbows, we gave that stubborn obstruction a mighty tug.

It was *then*—God help us!—that the meteorite, with a loud and resounding SMACK!—popped out of its fleshy mooring.

I stared horrorstruck at the vision before me. Between the Old Man's bony mounds gaped a pink-rimmed orifice that opened into a nightmare vortex of swirling mists. Skoglund fainted dead away. Cheswick shrieked like a little girl and cried out not only for his Mommy, but also for someone or something named Mr. Boo-Boo Bear.

And then—merciful heavens!—SOMETHING oozed forth from out of the depths of that Terrible Old Man: a writhing conglomerate of oleaginous, rainbow-hued bubbles, twisted neon-blue tentacles, snapping squid-beaks, three-lobed burning eyes and flexing monkey-tails. The creature worked to squirm free of its rectal receptacle, and as it did, it began to grow, and to release an odour…the likes of which no human nose should ever be forced to endure.

This ripe, loathsome stench brought to mind a bubbling cauldron of gangrenous corruption—a sickening stew made from motor oil, rancid bacon, three-month-old cottage cheese, cat piss and a week's worth of diapers from a colicky baby that had been allowed to eat guacamole.

Suddenly that stinking monstrosity from beyond that enflamed colon of terrors REACHED TOWARD ME with a pustulent, obscenely engorged tentacle, dripping with the digested remains of the Terrible Old Man's last several meals. I surmised that the Old Man was especially fond of broccoli. The tentacle glowed from within with a hellish sort of light, of a colour I had never seen before—but it reminded me of certain fumes I had peripherally perceived floating up from the toilet bowls of ill-rumored truck-stop men's-rooms along the Pickman Turnpike.

I looked around the room for something, anything to use to fight off this ghastly intestinal interloper. But what? All I could see were shelves and shelves of books—self-help books, how-to gardening guides, tips of redecorating, bound volumes of carpet samples, and a really big, medieval-looking leathery thing with the title *Necronomicon*. I thought perhaps I could hit the creature with that, so I reached out for it.

"No! Stop!" cried the Terrible Old Man, who was watching me from over his shoulder. Florence, who had crept back into the room, began to fling thick paperback romance novels at me, and Cheswick latched onto my leg, screaming "Make it better, Mr. Boo-Boo Bear!" in the sort of high-pitched voice one usually associates with circus clowns addicted to crack.

I dodged Florence's barrage of bodice-buster bestsellers, but one hit Cheswick in the temple and he fell to the floor, out cold.

I lunged forward, grabbed the leather-bound tome from its shelf, and turned to do battle with the rectum-spawned abomination.

The monstrosity's grizzled eyebrows shot up. "Ooooh! Can I have a look at that?" it gurgled. "Yog-Sothoth told me my picture's in there."

So the Terrible Old Man made room on the couch, and those of us who were still conscious gathered around the book, turning pages, looking for the vile, unholy creature's picture.

We found it on pg. 387. It was a group shot—the colon-fiend, Cthulhu, and some Lemurian serpent-priests at the annual temple barbeque. The monster said it looked fat because of bad lighting, but I said that it looked fine. Still, it wasn't convinced. With a disappointed sigh, the repugnant creature returned (with a little cooperation from the Terrible Old Man) whence it came.

Finally Skoglund woke up from his faint. With a trembling hand, he pointed to a small, slime-streaked pile on the floor—an unspeakable token of soul-shredding horror left behind by that grotesque fecal daemon.

"Hey, my car keys!" Florence said. "I've been looking for those."

SHE'S GOT THE LOOK

"Something new…something *fresh*…" Hopelessly adrift in a sea of fashion magazines, Pretzel flipped nervously through high-gloss stacks of *Mademoiselle, Glamour, Harper's Bazaar,* French *Vogue, Miss Vogue* for teens, *Marie Claire, Sky,* and a half-dozen foreign editions of *Elle.* She glanced at Jasmine, who was still trying to squeeze her way into a brown-velvet Vivienne Westwood cat-suit. "It's not going to happen, you know."

"Pee pills." Jasmine began rolling the leggings down. "Just a few pee pills away."

"And an extra kidney. Where's my Japanese *Elle*? The one with Magda on the cover."

"She looks like a whore." Jasmine brushed a long curly lock of magenta hair off of her round face. "An enormous whore. *Massive.* Her left tit is bigger than my head."

Pretzel found the magazine and held it at arm's length. "My God, you're absolutely right. Gaultier must have discovered her—he's adores big freak girls. The woman is a *horse.* A horse on its hindlegs."

"With gigantic tits."

Pretzel was not to be outdone. "A *Clydesdale* with obscene mutant *cow* tits. Somebody should fly her to one of those needy countries and have her nurse all those skinny little babies."

"Not much nourishment in silicone, darling." Jasmine laughed as she threw the cat-suit back onto the pile of clothes on the couch. She poured herself her fourth glass of Dom Perignon that morning. "But seriously. Are you making any progress at all?"

"None. I can't believe I got roped into all this." Pretzel tossed an armful of magazines into the air. "Stupidest fucking idea in the world. Starving models raising money to feed starving children? Who could possibly tell them apart?" Her eyes widened. "Definitely *no* Kate Moss. She can't be more than—what? 85 pounds? The press would tear the whole thing to shreds. Maybe I should get that Magda cow after all."

"Good God, no—she's *too* big. You might as well throw Liz Taylor or a Russian tractor up on the catwalk."

Pretzel crossed to her work table, shooting a look at her reflection in the mirror above it. She still looked fantastic—to-die-for cheekbones, silver pageboy cut, Acapulco tan. A fashion journalist had to look her best to be taken seriously. And she was hot now: all eyes were upon her.

Her first novel, *Strapless,* was No. 3 on the *New York Times* bestseller list, and publishers were still bidding on her next book, *Catwalk Days, Doggy-Style Nights.*

But she had to face it: she was picking up weight from stress-eating and too damn many hors d'oeuvres. In another month she'd be as big as Jasmine, if she didn't do something about it. She opened her purse and found her Gucci pillbox. She picked out two yellows, then debated between blue and green before finally selecting a yummy pink one. Jasmine brought her a glass of champagne to wash them down.

"Darling, what's this?" Jasmine slid a maroon faux-leather valise out from under some catalogues. "This would go with that jacket I bought last week."

"Another stupid idea. I'm supposed to be judging the Miss Fresh Face contest for *Sizzle.* These are the finalists. Snotty little rich girls from all over America."

Jasmine gave her a small smile. "I was once a Miss Fresh Face, you know."

Pretzel studied her friend's plump, still pretty face. "We could get you up on that catwalk again, you know. I know this darling French doctor—liposuction, a little nip and tuck, injections of monkey gland extract—"

Jasmine shook her head. "I shouldn't even *think* of losing weight. It's impossible around Farouk. Every time I lose an ounce he buys a dozen cheesecakes. He's into big hips. Literally."

The women refreshed their champagne glasses and found some smoked salmon in the mini-fridge. During their snack, Jasmine handed Pretzel the maroon valise. "You said you were looking for fresh. Maybe you should use some of these girls. Just a thought."

"You might have something there." Pretzel opened the valise over the work table and scattered the pictures, to see which ones popped out at her. "Bimbo," she said, tossing one off the table. "Bimbo. Bimbo. Slut." Three more pictures hit the floor. Suddenly she gasped.

"What are you looking at?" Jasmine said, examining the seven pictures left. "Which—"

Then she, too, saw the photo. Saw…*her.*

A pale, luminous face. Thin, but not too thin, with full, pouting lips and an elfin chin. The cheekbones were wide, generously sculpted. Her forehead was high and narrow. And those *eyes*—huge, soulful, a little sad, extremely wise. Haunting, timeless eyes.

"Who is she?" Jasmine whispered.

Pretzel picked up the photo and looked at the information written on the back. "Veronica Gilman. From a place called Innsmouth."

* * * *

The next week, Pretzel had Veronica Gilman flown in.

She met the girl at the airport and was instantly charmed. Veronica was tall and willowy, with a throaty purr of a voice. She wore a black dress trimmed with white lace and carried a white umbrella trimmed with black lace. She also wore black silk gloves with the fingertips cut off. They had lunch in a sushi bar, where the girl ordered double portions of tuna, shrimp and octopus.

"You certainly have a healthy appetite," Pretzel said cautiously.

Veronica smiled, revealing a bright expanse of small, even teeth. "I simply *adore* seafood. Don't you? It's low-fat and *extreeemely* nutritious. A person hardly needs to eat anything else."

Pretzel watched the girl nibble daintily at her fishbits. "Those gloves are fabulous." She looked closer. "Oooh, they're studded with little pearls. I love the whole black-and-white look. Very Audrey Hepburn, with a touch of Goth-grrrrl. Tell me about this town you're from. This Innsmouth."

"There's not much *to* tell. New England. Old money. A lazy, crazy seaside town: lots of eccentrics. Punks and hermits and maiden aunts. Everybody knows everybody, for better or worse. *Steeped* in tradition, like a soggy old teabag!" Veronica laughed—a high, jubilantly warbling giggle. Pretzel was vaguely reminded of a show on dolphins she'd once seen on public TV.

A short blond waiter stopped by their table. "Can I bring you anything else?"

Veronica flashed her huge eyes at him. "Mmmmm. More octopus, please." She turned back to Pretzel. "So. I can hardly *wait* to hear about this fundraiser. It sounds *tremendously* exciting, It's a terrible thing, world hunger and what-not. I'm flattered you think I'd be able to help."

Pretzel reached out and squeezed the girl's hand. She was surprised by how muscular it felt. "This event needs a fresh face, Ronny—can I call you Ronny? A fresh face and a new look. That new look is *you,* my dear. A classic look with a modern edge: Old World meets New Wave. The Ronny Look. The Innsmouth Look."

Again, Veronica let loose with that high, warbling laugh.

* * * *

That evening, Pretzel, Jasmine and Veronica converged at the Hot-Box, a dance club that Jasmine suggested. The club was lucky for the former model—it was where she'd met her meal-ticket/millionaire/chubby-chaser Farouk.

Pretzel wore a black leather mini and bustier from the Gaultier collection. Jasmine wore her old figure-shrouding favorite: slightly baggy, red-velvet hip-hop bib overalls with matching pumps. Veronica wore black lipstick, her gloves, a black lace evening gown with fishnet shawl, and black stiletto heels.

"You be looking so fine," Jasmine said to Veronica in what was possibly the world's worse possible approximation of homegirl lingo. Her wits weren't entirely about her: she had just done a line of coke in the ladies' room with a Hispanic transvestite named Caliente.

"You're *too* kind," the Innsmouth girl purred, absent-mindedly running the fingertips of one hand over the pearls of the other's glove. She turned to Pretzel. "Any celebrities here tonight? I thought I saw Cher a moment ago."

Jasmine shook her head. "That was Caliente."

Pretzel popped a pink pill and a couple baby-blues. "There's Rod Plunge over by the flamingo ice-sculpture. Gay porn star. Should I ask him to do the hunger thing? Get him on the catwalk? I mean, just because he's a porn star doesn't mean he's not worrying about starving babies. The press would absolutely eat it up." She looked around, slightly dazed. The pills were beginning to kick in. "Where did Ronny go?"

Jasmine nodded toward the dance floor. "Over there. Doing the Petit Mal with Johnnie Depp."

Pretzel watched as the Innsmouth girl twitched and jerked ecstatically among all the giddy clubhoppers. Green and blue flashes from the swirling disco ball overhead gave the dance floor a sort of manic underwater effect, and for one freakish moment Pretzel felt that she was watching some sort of nightmare nature documentary. Behold the slinky, murder-mouthed moray eel: see how it gracefully weaves among all the mindless little prettyfish, sizing them up, biding its time, flexing its jagged jaws, waiting to *bite bite bite*—

Hot pain in the side of her face brought her to her senses. It took her a moment to realize that Jasmine had slapped her.

"What is *wrong* with you?" Jasmine was looking at her with utter incredulity. "You were whimpering like a scared puppy. Right in front of Barbra Streisand's personal shopper. I told him you had asthma." The plump woman handed her a gin & tonic.

Pretzel sipped at the drink, savoring its faint tang of pine. "I'm fine now. A little anxiety attack, that's all." She looked back at Veronica, still dancing, this time with a TV sitcom prettyboy. A lovely girl. Fabulous. A superstar in the making. Nothing to fear, nothing at all.

And yet...It suddenly dawned on her that there was something vaguely disturbing about the girl. Those pouting lips...those huge eyes, haunting and more than a little wide-set...

She turned to Jasmine. "Is it my imagination, or does Veronica look like...in this light, mind you..." She cocked her head to one side. "A carp?"

The plump woman considered this for a moment. "Yes, but a very pretty carp. Like one of those darling two-color Koi. Farouk has a whole pond full of them." She tapped her chin thoughtfully as she watched Veronica bump bottoms with a tanned soap-opera hunk. "We should play it up! Sea-green eye-shadow. Big flaming orchids in her hair. Silver lamé and a seaweed boa. An island look. Primitive. Exotic. Powerful."

"And *very* Third World." Pretzel raised an eyebrow. "*I love it.*"

* * * *

The next month flew by in a mad blur. After considering dozens of designers, Pretzel and Jasmine commissioned Cosmo Sarkazien, a Versace protégé, to whip together some super-slinky variations on the tropical theme: sharkskin micro-minis, kicky cyberpunk/hula girl couture, black fishnet body stockings, and more, more, more. They asked Naomi Campbell and Linda Evangelista to tutor Veronica on catwalk poise. But it turned out she needed very little instruction; the girl was an absolute natural.

At first Pretzel and Jasmine had wanted to hold the fundraiser at a New York homeless shelter, but at Veronica's suggestion, they moved it to an abandoned church on Easter Island. The girl's family owned a beach house there—that was where they went when winter hit Innsmouth hard. The tag on Veronica's keychain was an actual chunk from one of those enormous heads.

A week before the big event, Jasmine, Pretzel, and Veronica flew down to the island with Cosmo and his boyfriend, a Las Vegas magician with an impossibly golden tan named Johnny LaRock. Pretzel was hugely impressed with the beach house—it had the biggest hot tub she'd ever seen in her life. For the most part, the place was decorated with pirate goodies, nautical oddities, and quirky little statues of what looked like scrawny dogs with scales and batwings.

She told Veronica to fire up the hot tub and then headed for the bar in the living room. The Gilmans kept an enormous supply of liquor on hand, including some odd green bottles shaped like conch shells and seahorses. She opened one of the conch shell bottles and took a sip: some sort of dark beer, it seemed. Rather sweet, with no bitterness at all. She drank half of the glass sea-horse's contents in three swallows. Bottle in hand, she went to see how the tub was coming along.

Veronica was already lounging in the bubbling water. "I see you found the Essence of Anemone," she said. "Come on in. The water is perfectly lovely. Just strip down and jump in."

Pretzel was beginning to feel lightheaded. "Essence of what? Anne who?" She finished the bottle and slipped it into the water to let it swim. As she removed her top, a button came off in her hand and she realized, with a giggle, that she didn't care. She couldn't even remember who the designer was, or why it even mattered. Before she knew it, she was as naked as a coffee bean and brewing in the big yummy cup with Veronica.

Jasmine entered the room leading a handsome, olive-skinned middle-aged man. "Pretz! Ronny! Look who showed up!"

Pretzel smiled at him. "Ali Baba?"

"Veronica," Jasmine said, "I'd like you to meet my gentleman friend, Farouk Alhazred. Farouk, this is my friend Veronica Gilman, from Innsmouth. It's in New England somewhere—"

"I am familiar with Innsmouth." Farouk's upper lip curled into a sneer. "And with the Gilman name."

Veronica's huge eyes narrowed to slits. "Hello, Mr. Alhazred. Read any good books lately?"

Jasmine put her hands on her hips. "Do you two know each other?"

Farouk turned to her. "Do you recall, my precious lamb, my telling you of an extraordinary book written many centuries ago by one of my kinsmen? The *Necronomicon*?"

"Vaguely. Has it come out in paperback yet?"

The Arab simply stared at her.

"When it does," she said, "tell them to put Fabio on the cover."

"The *Necronomicon* is a book of ancient wisdom, of secrets from beyond the stars and beneath the sea. It tells of evil beings who long to degrade, to torment, and ultimately, to destroy all of humanity." Farouk turned his stare toward the Innsmouth girl. "I am leaving now, but I shall return. And I expect you to be gone, Daughter of Dagon. Return to the black mud of the ocean floor. That is the only home this world can offer for you and your filthy kin."

Pretzel laughed nervously. "Farouk *darling,* please ease up on the girl. Veronica is going to be very big. She's having lunch with Giorgio Armani next week. That's one of his suits you're wearing."

He placed his firm, tanned hand along the blonde woman's jaw, cradling her face. "Pretzel, you are a child, a lovely spoiled child, and you are playing with a serpent that has crawled out of the depths." He brought his lips close to her ear. "She wears those gloves all the time, yes?"

Pretzel thought for a moment. She still felt extremely groggy from her sea-horse cocktail—it was difficult to gather her thoughts. But yes, Veronica *always* wore those gloves, those black gloves with the fingers cut out. She looked up and realized with a jolt that the girl was *still* wearing them.

In the hot tub.

Farouk bowed toward Jasmine. "When I return, you can expect a gift of jewelry. A traditional necklace of soapstone stars. It has powers to protect the wearer from evil."

The Arab left the room. Jasmine waited to be sure he was out of earshot before she turned toward Veronica. "You'll have to excuse Farouk. I've never known him to be superstitious or—well, so *B-movie.* He must have had you mixed up with somebody else. I'll go have a talk with him." She smiled apologetically and then followed her boyfriend.

Veronica moved with an eel's grace to Pretzel's side. "And what do you think, my salty, twisted friend? Do *you* think I am some sort of naughty sea serpent?"

"That's depends." Pretzel took the girl by the hand. Then she quickly grabbed her glove by the cuff and pulled it off.

Between each finger stretched a half-inch of translucent, lightly veined webbing.

"I think I'm going to be sick," Pretzel whispered.

Veronica edged closer, smiling. "Not feeling well? Nurse Ronny knows what to do. You'll love it—better than a B-12 shot." She opened her mouth wide. Two thin, flexible pink spines lanced out from under her tongue, embedding themselves in the soft flesh above Pretzel's left breast. The blonde woman passed out a moment after the hot fluid began to pulse into her body.

* * * *

Pretzel spent the next two days in bed with a high fever. Every now and then she stumbled to the bathroom to throw up, or gulp down glass after glass of cold water. She found it impossible to rest. Whenever she did manage to fall asleep, she would soon find herself having nightmares about horrible, nauseating things—worm-riddled sailor corpses, babies with tentacles, giant yapping clams with eyeball-covered tongues. She also dreamed of a super-old stone building that seemed somehow to be inside-out and backwards. Frog-faced fishpeople swarmed in and out of the place, laughing and plotting and singing froggy songs. Somewhere inside slept a giant snot-covered bat-lizard-monkey-devil, a snake-bearded boogeyman that called out to her in a voice like poisonous syrup. It told her that it loved her, and that she would soon be more beautiful than she could ever imagine, and that she would have luxury and pleasure and power forever and ever. Then it told her to find Dagon. Yes, Dagon would know what to do…

At one point, Jasmine came to her room to check on her. Pretzel noticed that she was wearing a necklace of stone stars. She found it unspeakably repulsive and screamed that it was tacky, hideous, a piece of trash. Furious, Jasmine stormed out of the room.

At last the fever passed, and Pretzel felt better. Better than ever, really. Jasmine went out of her way to avoid her, but that was fine, perfectly fine, so long as the plump woman wore that ghastly necklace.

* * * *

"There you are." Carrying a sketch pad and several notebooks, Cosmo Sarkazein crossed to the kitchen counter next to Pretzel. He was a slim, elfin man with short red hair and seven small gold hoops in each ear. "I've been looking all over for you. I had to get away from Johnny. He's driving me crazy, bitching and moaning just because we left his conditioner behind. Anyway, do we have a final line-up—a *definitive* line-up—for the big event? I hope we've got Yasmin Le Bon. She's super-nice, she really is. Why'd she ever marry that huge prick Simon?"

"I think you answered your own question, darling." Pretzel opened a drawer and after a moment's searching, pulled out a melon baller. "Jasmine used to look like Yasmin, you know. People thought they were sisters. But then Jasmine discovered food. As for the line-up: big names. All the big names, except big fat Magda and tiny little Kate. Oh, and no Yasmin—she's got a sick kid. I told her to give the brat an aspirin and she hung up. We've got Naomi. Niki. Brandi. Cindy. Eva. Linda. Claudia. Nadja. Irina. Tatjana. Saffron. Shalom. And of course, Veronica, lovely Veronica at the center of it all."

Cosmo examined her face. "You know, I never noticed before, but you kind of look like Veronica. Around the eyes, I think." He then looked down at what she was doing. "Oh. My. This is interesting. Are you making sushi? Are those even fish?"

"Veronica had these delivered. A pretty island boy brought them by. You'd have loved him." Pretzel dug her fingers into the mass of chopped sea-life on the marble countertop. "There's something about all this fresh salt air that makes me feel so alive. And so hungry." She dug out a few green and red strands and thrust them into her mouth. Then she began to gnaw on a large, juicy, dark-orange egg sac. "Want some?"

Johnny LaRock popped his golden-maned head into the room. "I thought I heard voices in here. What are we having for dinner?"

Cosmo turned toward him, his hand over his mouth. "I'm never eating again," he muttered from between his fingers. He rushed past Johnny, away from Pretzel and her sea-feast.

The tall, tanned magician moved toward the blonde woman, studying the array of minced goodies before her. "That's quite a spread you've got there. Are those local delicacies?"

Her slime-streaked lips stretched into a smile. "I take it you're not as squeamish as our Mr. Sarkazien."

The magician checked his reflection in a silver soup ladle he'd found in the sink. "Cosmo's a very sheltered person. He hasn't seen that much of the world." He wiped her mouth with his thumb and forefinger, then licked the juice from his hand. "I've seen a lot more of it. I get around." He gave her a wink and pointed his finger like a gun-barrel at her. "I'm Johnny LaRock. The name says it all."

"We haven't known each other very long," Pretzel said, "but I think it's safe to say that you're a complete bastard. A vain simpleton with more hair than brains. More tan than tact. And by the way, Mr. Magic: I predict that you're going to say 'ouch' in the very near future."

The magician smoothed his eyebrow with his left pinky, which sported a ruby ring that once belonged to Liberace. "That's ridiculous. Why would I say —"

Pretzel grabbed his elbow in a grip of iron and pulled down, so their faces were at about the same level. She opened her mouth, aiming for the base of his throat.

* * * *

"I'm worried," Jasmine said.

Pretzel looked up. She was sunning herself on a huge beach towel— the fundraiser was only two days away, and she wanted to be rested so that the event wouldn't tire her out. Not that she was feeling the least bit tired since her recovery from the fever. "Is that a fact? Well, I'm worried, too. Worried that your sense of style has completely evaporated." She pointed to the necklace. "What next: earth shoes?"

"Farouk made me promise to keep it on. Humor me." Jasmine sat down in the sand and sighed. "Everything's going wrong. First Farouk went weird on me. Then you were sick, then Johnny and Cosmo got sick…then you and Veronica started treating me like utter crap. The models arrived a few days ago and now most of *them* are throwing up— at least, more than they usually do. I hired a private nurse and sent her to their hotel to look after them. I'm beginning to think this whole Easter Island idea was a complete mistake."

"Well, of course you think that." Pretzel stood up and gathered her beach towel. "Because it was Veronica's idea. A fabulous idea. This stomach-flu thing is *nothing*. A bug that's going around, that's all. Face it, sweety: you're as jealous as hell. Jealous because she's thin and in, and you are stout and *out*."

"I can't believe you're saying all this. I've always been nice to Veronica, and I've been working my ass off for this fundraiser. You haven't even noticed. All you can talk about is Ronny, Ronny, Ronny. Good God, you're even starting to look like her." She got to her feet. "We *are* friends, no matter what you say. We've known each other for *years*. You're just mad at my silly old Farouk and taking it out on me. Talk to him when he comes back." She stepped forward to give Pretzel a hug, but the blonde woman moved away from her.

"Farouk? I'd thought he'd left for good after he dropped off that—" Pretzel waved her hand at the necklace. "—that rubbish."

"He wants to be here for the fundraiser. He thinks something is going to happen because it's on May first. Beltane."

"What's that? Some quaint Middle-Eastern holiday? The day they pray to Allah to send more fat chicks?"

"Now you're being cruel. Beltane is an ancient fertility holiday. He told me all about it. Sacrifices. Orgies. Fucking in the fields."

Pretzel walked away from Jasmine. "Your precious Farouk has gone insane. Just keep him away from me."

Once she'd returned to the house, Pretzel chopped up some sea urchins and jellyfish and had lunch. Then she went straight to Veronica's room.

She found the Innsmouth girl and Cosmo sitting on the edge of her bed, drinking Essence of Anemone and studying a chart drawn in his sketch pad. "Progress report?" she said, lounging on the bed behind them.

"Things are coming along *swimmingly*," Veronica said. "I've taken care of Naomi and Linda, and I'll be seeing Claudia this afternoon. Cosmo has worked his magic on Nadja, Niki and Saffron." She consulted the chart. "You handled Eva and Irina, yes? Johnny is making himself useful—he's already tended to Tatjana, Shalom and Brandi, and he'll finish up with Cindy later today. All with time to spare. I love it when a plan comes together." She poured a glass of the liqueur and handed it to the blonde woman.

"I'm really learning to like this stuff," Pretzel said. "By the way, I talked to Jasmine before lunch."

"Life would be so much easier if she would just take off that necklace," Veronica said.

"Can't we just kill her and be done with it?" Cosmo said. "We could shoot her, or poison her."

Veronica nodded. "Yes, and then chop her up and throw the bits into the sea. She'd be quite a chum then! Wouldn't take more than a minute."

"Well, if you think that would—" The blonde woman stopped and shook her head. A frantic little voice—*what are you THINKing?*—echoed through the oily black abyss of her mind. "No, no, no. Of course not. She's no danger to us. She doesn't know a thing. Besides, I can make her change. I *know* it. I've done it before. She used to be bulimic, and I fixed *that*. Too well! The real problem is Farouk. Jasmine said he'll be returning for the fundraiser. Should we be alarmed?"

The Innsmouth girl crossed to the window and looked out over the ocean. "Forewarned is forearmed. I am not worried about this mad Arab." A slow smile crept over her full lips. "He is a big man, and his complexion is like rich coffee with a dollop of cream. I shall have his skin made into a bolero jacket and some kicky capri pants."

* * * *

On the day of the fundraiser, the skies over Easter Island were filled with private jets and helicopters. Everybody who was anybody was at the church, along with swarms of pop stars, paparazzi, high-class pushers, callgirls, partyboys, hangers-on, has-beens and wannabes. The pews had been removed from the nave, replaced by director's chairs sprayed gold metallic.

Johnny LaRock studied the crowd over the edge of his glass as he sucked down his Manhattan. Like Veronica, he now wore black gloves without fingertips. He turned toward Pretzel and smiled. "I can't believe this crowd. Wall-to-wall movie stars and socialites."

"An army of aging rich-bitches," she said. After much deliberation, she had finally decided on Chanel couture for herself: something tailored and powerful. To suit the theme of the event, she'd pinned a gold seahorse on the jacket. She watched as the magician moved through the crowd and sidled up to a chubby old salt-and-pepper brunette dripping with emeralds.

Pretzel tried to find Jasmine in the room, but she was nowhere to be seen. Where was she? And more to the point, where was that troublesome bastard Farouk? A waiter with a food tray passed by, and she snatched up some morsels of sushi with a gloved hand.

In the ladies room, she watched as a world-famous newswoman, a lesbian tennis star and an upscale hooker from Brazil snorted up lines of coke as they gossiped. She joined the group and invited them to try a sea-green powder that Veronica had given her the day before. Before long, the three women were writhing happily on the floor. Pretzel locked the door and gave each a dose of her venom—the Kiss of Dagon, as Veronica called it.

When she returned to the nave, the fashion show was already underway, and Veronica and Naomi Campbell were sauntering down the catwalk in fishnet and black lace evening gowns. Waitresses in gold metallic bikinis offered the guests fluted glasses of Essence of Anemone. Some bouncy Euro-disco dance mix was blasting over the sound system. Suspended from the ceiling by gold chains were video monitors, continuously running underwater scenes of sharks feeding, lobsters fighting, octopi lazily gliding over the ocean floor.

Pretzel slipped backstage, where Cosmo was frantically primping the girls preparing to go on. "Have you seen Jasmine?" she said.

"I don't have time to worry about your fat friend." He sighed hugely. "This church is a nightmare. It's too damp! Claudia's hair is all frizzy! The whole place smells like cheese!"

One of the girls tapped Pretzel's shoulder. "Jasmine's on the phone in one of the dressing rooms."

Pretzel found her planted in front of a tray of hors d'oeuvres, alternately shouting into the phone and cramming her face with calamari. She noticed with exasperation that her friend was still wearing the star stone necklace.

"Please, just *stay away.* I mean it!," Jasmine cried. "It's only a fashion show, for Christ's sake, not some crazy cult conspiracy! If you and your—Farouk? *Farouk?*" She hung up and flung the tray to the floor. "Stupid bastard! He's going to ruin *everything!*"

Pretzel could feel a jumbo-migraine coming on. *Calm down,* she told herself, *nothing's as bad as it seems.* "What's he going to do?"

Jasmine rolled her eyes. "He's on his way here with some stupid freaked-out holy soldiers and they're going to take the place by storm."

Pretzel shook her head. *I stand corrected.* "We've got to tell Veronica. And the bouncers. But first we've got to get you out of here."

"*Me?*" Jasmine put her hand to her chest. "I'm the only one Farouk will listen to. Why in the world would you want me to leave?"

The blonde woman sighed. "Because Farouk is right. There *is* a cult conspiracy. You're the only one who's not in on it. And if you're not one of us, you're fish food."

"Oh my God! *You're all*—" Jasmine stared into space for a moment. "I guess I don't know. What *are* all of you?"

Pretzel took a deep breath. "We worship the power of the sea and its Dark Lords."

"But that sounds fun! Why didn't you invite me?" Jasmine pouted. "Is it because of my weight?"

"You want to join us? Oh, Jasmine, that's fabulous! I guess we thought—well, what with Farouk being our enemy and your boyfriend, too—"

"But darling, he's just a man. A really, really *rich* man, but still, just a man. If the Dark Lords of the sea are good enough for you, they're good enough for me. Where do I sign?"

"Well first, throw away that awful necklace! It's like garlic to Dracula."

Jasmine took off the necklace, and in her excitement, accidentally snapped the cord, scattering the star-shaped stones. She kicked away the ones that had fallen at her feet. "Do we get to be vampires?"

Pretzel drew closer to her. "Something even better."

She was about to give Jasmine the Kiss of Dagon when a colossal explosion shook the building. "That can't be Farouk already!" she screamed.

Jasmine winced. "He was calling from his car. They were on their way here."

Pretzel took her friend's hand and together they raced to the fashion show. There, they found that the front doors had been blown to bits, along with much of the surrounding walls. Farouk marched through the rubble. He wore a khaki jumpsuit with various black holsters containing a mini-arsenal of weaponry. Several other similarly dressed soldiers marched behind him.

"Really, Farouk!" Jasmine said. "Those doors weren't even locked."

The Arab stopped and stared at her. "I am here to save the world."

She nodded. "I'm sure you are. But while this is all very macho and it has me terribly excited, you must understand that it upsets me when you interfere with my career. I'm a working girl, and unless you're ready to put a ring on my finger or at least set me up in a Park Avenue penthouse, I'm going to have to keep on working."

Farouk blinked, speechless. Finally he said, "My darling, you are dealing with a virulent evil from beyond the boundaries of time and space. This isn't a relationship issue."

"Oh, so *you* get to say what is or isn't a relationship issue? I should be allowed to do my work, pick my own friends and have a good time without you blowing the doors off a church on Easter Island during a fashion show." Jasmine put her hands on her hips. "That isn't too much to ask."

One of the soldiers tapped Farouk on the shoulder. "Sir, are we still going to destroy the ancient evil today? If now's not a good time…"

"Now is a *very* good time!" Farouk turned back to Jasmine. "You're just going to have to trust me on this." He then fired a pistol into the air. "*Attack!*"

Jasmine and Pretzel crept along the wall to the bar, where each grabbed a champagne bottle. They then hid behind some ferns, drinking straight from the bottles as they watched the battle. For fifteen minutes, Farouk and the soldiers fought the venomous models and various other glitterati. Johnny LaRock was the first to go, disemboweled by a soldier's bayonet. As he writhed on the floor, bleeding to death, he took a moment to check his reflection in his attacker's shiny black boots.

Some of the models sprouted barbed tentacles, which they used to whip at the eyes and groins of the soldiers.

"Can you do that?" Jasmine said.

Pretzel shrugged. "Probably. I'd rather not." She looked around the church. "I don't see Ronny. This whole thing was her idea. The first scuffle in our war to take over the world, and she's nowhere to be seen. That *is* disappointing."

Naomi's severed head rolled to their feet, venom dripping from her dead lips.

"Well, that tears it," Pretzel said. "If Ronny can't be bothered to fight alongside her own army of evil super-models, then I'm leaving. Come on, let's get out of here."

"I'm with you. I am completely feed up with Farouk." So saying, Jasmine zipped back to the bar and grabbed a couple fresh bottles. Then the girls slipped out of the church.

Farouk's limousine was parked right outside. "They left the motor running!" Pretzel said. "Cocky bastards. They must have thought this whole thing would take two minutes. I need a drink. Hand me one of those bottles, darling."

Jasmine took the wheel and they headed down the road. A few minutes later, Pretzel said, "Say, there's someone naked on the beach over there. Isn't that Ronny? Stop the car."

They got out of the car and sat on the hood. Yes, the nude figure was indeed Ronny. She appeared to be chanting and dancing around one of those enormous stone heads. This one had gill-like grooves carved into its cheeks. The eyes seemed buggier, too.

Jasmine pointed out to sea. "Look at all those bubbles. What's the deal there?" A huge frothing patch of turbulence churned violently. "Maybe we should just drive on."

Pretzel shook her head. "I know what that is, and driving away won't do any good. The world isn't big enough to escape—that."

Suddenly Ronny spotted them and began walking their way. As she approached, it soon became obvious that Veronica Gilman was not like other women. She was still extraordinarily beautiful, yes, but in the short time since they'd last seen her, Ronny had grown iridescent scales all over her body. And she had another addition: flapping gill-slits on her cheeks, neck and under her breasts.

"You're just in time, ladies," Ronny said. "I have only to recite one more incantation to awaken Dagon from his timeless slumber beneath the waves. Even now the Deep Ones are throwing open the doors of his sunken temple. Dagon will in turn awaken Cthulhu, Master of the Ocean Depths, and that will spell the beginning of the end for humanity."

Jasmine raised an eyebrow. "All this work just to wake up some old fish? Somebody should buy him an alarm clock for his birthday." She ran her hands through her hair. "What's this—?" she said, but then stopped.

Ronny advanced on Pretzel and put her webbed hands on her shoulders. Poisonous claws shot out of her fingertips. This new dose of venom brought up patches of scales on Pretzel's slender arms.

"Join me in the final chant, sister," Ronny hissed. "Then we will sacrifice this fat land-hog—" She nodded toward Jasmine. "—to our new masters."

"Don't do it!" Jasmine said.

"Dagon k'hra! Cthulhu ph'galla m'nak!" Ronny and Pretzel intoned together. "M'hraa gl'gra ph'thaka! M'baga Dagon blaggog! Cthulhu blaggog!"

As they intoned, a fresh surge of furious bubbles rose up from the ocean floor. Then a claw, mud-streaked and as huge as a house, broke the surface, followed by a muscular, scaled arm. Deep-sea fish and octopi flopped and tumbled in the ooze that slithered down its length.

As Ronny and Pretzel continued to chant, Jasmine brought forth the item she had found tangled in her hair—a star stone from the broken necklace.

I believe it's time," Jasmine said, "for you to get stoned, Ronny." She bounced up to the Innsmouth girl and popped the stone into a gill-slit beneath her left breast.

With a shrill cry of hellish pain, Ronny fell writhing to the sand. Black blood poured from her lips and gills, followed by gouts of thick, greenish slime. This outpouring, thankfully, did not wash out the offending stone. Her flesh began to blister around her scales, until she looked like a huge trout that had been attacked by a swarm of bees. Her eyes—so big, so lovely—popped like two huge pimples, spraying goo across the sand. She continued to bubble and seethe until all that remained was a pile of bones mired in a multi-colored paste of ruined flesh and ruptured organs.

Pretzel and Jasmine looked out to sea.

The claw clenched into a fist as it sank back down beneath the roiling water.

Pretzel, however, still had her new scales.

"Oh, dear," Jasmine said. "I was hoping that little skin condition would clear up after I finished off Ronny. Well, we've saved the earth."

Her friend nodded. "Actually you did, but at least I didn't stop you. So what now? Should I turn you into a sea-creature, like we talked about earlier? That might be fun. Swimming around with the dolphins all day. They're supposed to be very smart."

Jasmine thought for a moment. "I think we're forgetting something. The only thing we'd be able to drink underwater—is water."

Pretzel gasped. "*Nightmare!* Yes, let's stay up here on land. I can always wear long sleeves. Speaking of drinks, let's go to the beach house."

They returned to Farouk's limousine and headed down the road.

"Next week," Pretzel said, "I was supposed to go with Ronny to a big to-do in New England. A birthday party for some Miskatonic University girl named Wilma Whateley. From some place called Dunwich. Her family is fairly established—old money and all that. Since Ronny's out of the picture, do you want to go with me? I'd hate to go alone."

Jasmine shook her head. "Tell little Miss Whateley you can't make it. We'll go shopping in London instead. Forget about small-town girls. They're nothing but trouble."

"Yes, of course you're right. What was I thinking?" The blonde said. "She's probably some slutty coed who'd give us just as much grief as Ronny. We certainly don't have time for the Dunwich Whore!"

THE BROUHAHA OF CAT-HULA

Truly it is a merciful fact that humankind has abundant difficulty in discerning its fecal egress orifice from a perforation in the surface of the earth's crust. For if us mammalian bipedal units were even just a shade more clever, the true facts concerning the state of the Universe, and our true place in said piece of real estate, would hurl us into a planet-wide hissy-fit of mind-boggling proportions. Yes, if we could decipher even the weensiest rune of some of the noisome mysteries to be found certain Forbidden-Book-Of-The-Month Club selections, humanity in general would endure a mind-boggling freak-out of such duration that the world's underwear would be ere long filled with fear-pinched crap-logs of madness.

I am Wilbur Tillinghast McAzathoth IV. My awareness of the events, circumstances and memos entailed in this narrative began with the sudden and irreversible death of my nephew's father, Zebediah LaMambo in the year 2——, in the month of J——on the day of 2—, at the time of about 6:3—p.m. He had been a renowned go-go dancer and part-time man-pussy at the Spotted Rakshasa Gentlemen's Club in southern North Dakota. As his only living relative (the rest of the family had perished years earlier in a freak barbecue accident), his every dossier, diary, notepad and feather boa went to me.

In the homey comfort of my own well-appointed masturbatorium, I opened the first packet of journals and letters, and—Great Gurgling Shoggoths!—I received a paper-cut that really hurt, especially since I was a little sweaty and some sweat got in the cut. Would that I had stopped there! Would that I had taken that paper-pushing epidermal misfortune as a clear omen of worse extra-dimensional tidings to come. Would that I had never inherited that bloatsome and lugubrious legacy. But alas, terror was the order of the day, served with a side salad of wild greens and despair.

Fool that I was, I willingly studied the fear-wizened legacy of Zebediah LaMambo. It appeared that Zebediah had been embroiled in various esoteric studies at the time of his demise...In retrospect, how strange it was that the statue of an ancient sea-daemon should fall on him not once, but in fact, fourteen times at a dock bordered by not two, but seven disreputable houses of pagan worship. Hula-hoops seemed to be a major preoccupation of Zebediah's, as well as their oblique connection with especially large cats from a certain fear-beshrouded island.

References were made in his notes to corrupted spellings of cryptic terms: "Cat-Hula? Kathooloo? Kt'hu'lu, or who knows, maybe even *Cthulhu?* It's hard to say." These terms, it was revealed, had some sort of connection to "the Kat-Hooloo Cult of the volcanic island of Tikki-Takki-Toa," which was in fact only a branch office of a larger cult base— on Asparagus Island.

One hastily scribbled entry read: "Why do the cats of Asparagus Island begin to walk on their hindlegs mere moments after they are weaned from the soggy teats of their mothers? A cat on its hindlegs—signs of *Hula Worship?* Who do these cats hope to summon, or what, and where, and when and why? And in what manner?"

Impromptu sketches suggested that the cats of Asparagus Island were not only larger than most, but also had rounder, fuller hips. "For more insidious hula action?" wondered one note in the margin of an especially disturbing pen-and-ink sketch.

Zebediah also feared the coming of some great and cataclysmic event known as The Brouhaha. The notes stated: "Ten-thousand monkeys on ten-thousand typewriters can recreate Shakespeare, so there's no telling what The Brouhaha will bring forth—I fear that—" and here the ink— curse him for using a fountain pen instead of a ballpoint!—had been blurred into incoherency by a stream of some yellowish liquid which stank—God help us!—of the musky excesses of a ripe cat-box.

Other miscellaneous notes only served to deepen, obfuscate and murkify the mystery:

"Hula-hoops—plastic? Can certain rotating polymers warp the space/time continuum? Maybe!

"Cats—devolved descendants of an ancient, alien race that crash-landed on Earth, eons ago? Perhaps!

"The Brouhaha—'Brou' as in 'brew,' as in 'beer'? 'Haha' as in 'ha-ha,' as in 'laughing'? The drunken laughter of an unimaginably vile deity about to be unleashed on an unsuspecting cosmos? Sounds about right to me!

"Must remember to take the Scarlet Acolyte of Horror his dry-clean-ing—and ask him to explain everything, since he holds all the answers."

This last entry was followed by a street address, phone and fax num-bers, and three e-mail accounts. Curse Zebediah for being so damnably vague! If only he had left me some blessed clue toward the decipherance of this unholy enigma!

I then noticed a book among Zebediah's belongings—a leather-bound tome entitled SECRETS OF THE CAT-HULA CULT REVEALED. A sticker on the inside cover indicated that the book was 'From the Library

Of' an individual known as 'The Scarlet Acolyte of Horror.' A coincidence indeed.

I called the Acolyte that very minute. "Hello, you don't know me, but I am the last remaining relative of the late, deceased Zebediah La-Mambo, who has passed away and is in fact dead. I see that he expired with a book of yours in his possession. Could you stop by and get it one of these days? I'm too busy investigating the mysterious circumstances of Zebediah's death to bring or even ship it to you."

The Acolyte had a voice like dried leaves blowing across a time-forgotten Lemurian tomb. I think he had a cold, or maybe he smoked. "Yes, I gave him the book so that he could at last figure out—"

I was bored by the Acolyte's incessant prattling, so I ignored him and turned on the TV. A documentary sprang to life on the screen—the title EVERYTHING YOU COULD EVER POSSIBLY WANT TO KNOW ABOUT THE CAT-HULA CULT appeared, emblazoned across a scene of lush island scenery.

"I'm going to have to hang up," I said, interrupting him—he was in the middle of a tedious explanation of some sort. "I think, Mr. Acolyte, that the answers to my enquiries can be found on a news program which has just started on the Eldritch Mystery Channel."

"Yes, I researched, wrote, directed and produced that show," the Acolyte said.

"I have no time for your vainglorious boasting!" I cried, slamming down the phone.

I listened intently as Niles Lathotep, the program's smiling host, explained the goings-on at Asparagus Island.

"This pleasant, breezy, delightful tropical paradise," he said, "does in fact hide a curse-ridden secret that threatens to destroy not only the Earth and the entire Solar System, but also humanity."

I shuddered with dread, and also because the room was a little drafty.

Niles continued. "Asparagus Island is famous for being the home of an indigenous species of domestic cat that can walk on its hindlegs. In recent weeks, island homeowners with cats have been receiving mysterious packages addressed to the afore-mentioned felines. These packages have contained rings of plastic, about eighteen inches in diameter. The rings look much like hula-hoops, except they are far too small for human hips. A small animal walking on its hindlegs might be able to use a hula-hoop of this size—but what sort of animal? And, why would anyone bother to send such hoops to the cats of Asparagus Island? And most importantly, why have these mysterious hoops—*and* the hindleg-walking cats—suddenly disappeared at the same time?

"We've asked the islanders, but all they can do is look to the east and scream. This behavior is especially inexplicable, since the eastern half of the island is the forbidden half, where it is rumored that a valley can be found that is sacred to an ancient deity named Cat-Hula, or Kathooloo, or Kt'hu'lu or maybe—and this is a long-shot—*Cthulhu*. Legends state that if some act—we're not sure what—is performed by ten-thousand animals—we're not sure which kind—at the same time, then that unspeakable deity will rise up from its forbidden tomb, sunk beneath the waves just off the coast of Asparagus Island. And *then—*"

I'd heard enough. It was clear what I had to do.

I turned off the television and called my travel agent, but his prices seemed a little steep, so I called a different travel agent but he wasn't any better. So then I went on the internet, found some reasonable ticket prices for a round-trip flight to Asparagus Island, and made my arrangements online. I then went to the bedroom, opened my closet, picked out some nice outfits, and called some friends until I found one who was willing to come by and water my plants for a few days. Then I crammed some odds and ends in my overcoat pockets, since you never know what you'll need on a long trip (especially if you're making your plans at the last minute). Suitcase in hand, I ran to the car, then remembered I hadn't turned off the computer so I went back and did that, put some more stuff in my coat pockets and then went back out to the car and was soon heading down the road. Next I stopped for gas, and then remembered I had to drop off my key at my friend's house or else he'd never be able to get in to water my plants. When I got to the airport I had a little trouble getting my ticket order straightened out—that particular online service still has some bugs to work out, or so they told me at the airport. But before long, I was on a plane to Asparagus Island, and the in-flight movie was *Footloose II,* which I liked, but then, I really liked the first *Footloose* and I was pleasantly surprised that Hollywood had finally gotten around to making a sequel.

"I can hardly wait until we land," said the kindly old grandmother in the seat next to me. "I have family members on Asparagus Island who I haven't seen in thirty years. Plus, I'll get to see my six grandchildren for the first time. Why are you going?"

"Oh, I'm tracking an ancient abomination and its current repercussions, and if I can't stop the madness in time," I said, "we'll all end up dead. Unfortunately, I haven't really figured out the entire puzzle, so there's a good chance the whole thing will just blow up in my face, plunging the world into a nightmare of endless horror."

The old woman said nothing but only shifted in her seat, obviously nervous and perturbed. Maybe she had hemorrhoids.

When at last we landed, I quickly checked into the nearest hotel. I then took a bath, put on some fresh clothes, and then went to the lobby restaurant for some chicken fajitas. The chicken meat was a little dry.

Outside the hotel, I asked a young man in a red suit—I figured this was a native costume—for directions to the forbidden east end of the island.

"Well," the young man said, "this is the west end…the part that isn't forbidden…so I suppose your best bet would be to walk east."

"So I see," I replied. "You are trying to confuse me with your island witch-doctor voodoo mumbo-jumbo."

"Actually, the people of Asparagus Island are descended from French colonists." He shrugged. "I'm not even from around here. I was on the flight in the seat behind you. You know, your voice sounds awfully familiar. In fact, I think you called me. I'm the Scarlet Acolyte of Horror."

"Your book's still at my place," I said.

"I'm not worried about the book. I'm just here to stop an unspeakable calamity. Follow me. We'll walk and talk."

Half a block later, we met the old woman. "Oh, hello, boys," she said. "You were both on the plane." She turned to me. "Your mindless ramblings really got me thinking. So I went to the Asparagus Island Public Library and figured out this whole ancient menace thing. That reminds me—I should bring that nice librarian some cookies, since she was kind enough to translate all those passages from the *Necronomicon* for me. Anyway, I'm off to the east end of the island now."

"Oh, so are we," my companion said. "By the way, I am the Scarlet Acolyte of Horror."

"And I am Wilbur Tillinghast McAzathoth IV," I stated.

The old woman smiled. "I'm Doris. I was voted Miss Teen Baked-Goods of Rutherford County back when I was in high school."

The three of us continued walking toward the forbidden east end. "This whole eldritch conundrum should take us about ten minutes to fix, once we get there," the Acolyte said.

Doris seemed surprised. "Ten? I'd say five."

"Well, I guess you two are just the smartest people who ever drew breath!" I cried. "Would one of you care to explain these seemingly obvious developments to poor, stupid, pitiful *me?*"

"Just watch and learn," Doris said. Typical: just because she had once held a title, she still thought she was some sort of hot-shot. Those teen baked-goods competitions are all fixed anyway.

It was a pretty small island, and in no time, we arrived at the forbidden east end. Soon we were standing on a hill overlooking a grassy valley filled with—wonder of wonders! horror of horrors!—ten-thousand big-hipped cats standing on their hindlegs, spinning ten-thousand hula-hoops in unison. A high, mind-numbing *hummmm* filled the air. All around the hula-cats, a battalion of large, ferocious tom-cats stood guard to prevent any interference with the diabolical feline ritual.

"Just what I thought," Doris said.

"Yep. Same here," the Acolyte agreed. "I think it's the insidious frequency of the hum produced by the hula-hoops that will ultimately awaken the sleeping deity from its vile slumber."

"But how can we stop their malignant synchronized gyrations?" I whispered with dread.

The old woman reached into her purse as the Scarlet Acolyte put a hand in the pocket of his blazer. Each then held out—

A mouse. Doris had a white one and the Acolyte's was brown.

"Mice! Of course!" I said. "Once you release them, they'll scamper past the guard-cats and into the valley. Those silly cats will be scurrying to catch them and they'll soon forget all this hula-hoop nonsense."

"He's finally caught on," the old woman said.

"Even a blind squirrel finds the occasional nut," the Acolyte replied cryptically.

Each lowered their precious, furry, world-saving burden to the ground.

The mice moved toward each other and rubbed muzzles. As cute as buttons, they were! Together they looked toward the valley of ten-thousand cats.

Then they ran off in the other direction.

"We should have just tossed them down into the valley," the Acolyte said.

Doris sighed. "That would have been the thing to do." She pointed toward the sea. "Well, I guess we'd better start running."

On the horizon, a massive shadow, bat-winged and serpent-bearded, arose from the ocean depths. It stretched out its claws, lifted its head and released a howl of cosmic triumph. But *was* it a howl? Perhaps it was more of a laugh—the victorious laughter of a mad being, drunk with power. A regular *brouhaha.*

And so, I now sit in the hotel bar, hiding behind some potted ferns and writing this manuscript on all the napkins I can find. That horrendous, slime-spattered creature from the deep captured and ate Doris half an hour ago, and the only reason I escaped is because I tripped the Scarlet Acolyte and the monster slowed up a moment to chow down on him.

Outside, people are screaming and buildings are collapsing, and since I just saw Abraham Lincoln walk by, I guess that means the space/time continuum is starting to come apart.

The funny thing is, I just found a ball of yarn in my overcoat pocket—one of the things I'd grabbed on the way out of the apartment. You see, at the time I'd thought that if I washed my socks in the sink of my hotel room, the yarn might serve as a dandy makeshift clothesline.

If I'd thought to throw the ball down into the valley of ten-thousand cats, they'd have gone absolutely nuts over it. Cats can play for hours with a good yarn-ball.

Why, if I'd have done that, the world would still be safe and sound.

I could just kick myself.

NOW THE HEALING BEGINS: A GUIDE TO CHILDREN'S SERVICES AT ST. TOAD'S MEDICAL CENTER

WHEN BAD THINGS HAPPEN TO GOOD KIDS

Hi, my name's Brian! Last week, I got really sick, so Mommy and Daddy took me to Children's Services at St. Toad's Hospital. I'm sure glad they did. It's a super-neat place for kids who need extra-special care.

Kids need to visit Children's Services for lots of different reasons. Some kids come in for check-ups, to make sure they don't have any hidden problems, like the bowel slugs you can get from drinking tainted water. Some have health problems that won't go away—they're called 'chronic' diseases—and so they need extra-special care on a regular basis. For example, my sister Amy has sores on her arms and legs that get all weepy, and the nurse has to shine a special light on them to make them dry up. Some kids fall down and break their bones. Others get burned or attacked by mutants from the 'Blasted Zone.' The 'Blasted Zone' covers most of the surface of the Earth, which is why Children's Services at St. Toad's Hospital is safely located in the underground city of P'zogna.

Some kids need 'operations'—that's when doctors have to open up the body to fix stuff on the inside. That may sound scary, but don't worry, they always close up the body when they're done. And all the doctors at St. Toad's Hospital have been trained by other doctors with a lot more experience. Or, they've read old books from before the Great Invasion and have practiced on captured mutants or night-gaunts.

Operations can be small, like when kids need their tonsils taken out. Operations can also be big, like when a kid finds she has a baby shoggoth growing out of her back and it needs to be removed. When bad things happen to good kids, you can count on Children's Services at St. Toad's Hospital.

Back before the Great Invasion, life was pretty simple. Families worked and played in peace and enjoyed TV dinners and video games. But then the evil priests of the space-demon Nyarlathotep found out how to throw open the Great Gates of Doom, and boy, once those Gates were opened, life was sure different after that.

Now we all live in cities in big caves underground, or in towns under metal domes on the surface of the Earth. Those caves and domes are protected by magic, so Nyarlathotep and his bad friends can't get us. Nyarlathotep sure is mean! But someday, us humans will figure out the right spell to cast him back out into the icy depths of outer space, and then we'll all be happy.

These days, life is all about change, and St. Toad's Hospital is dedicated to helping families face the many health problems that come with living in a world threatened by cosmic evil.

I WAS SCARED

When Mommy and Daddy brought me to Children's Services at St. Toad's Hospital last week, I was scared, because I was feeling really sick and didn't know what was going on. But the nice people there soon made me feel happy again. Let me tell you what happened to me, so you won't be scared when you're feeling sick and need extra-special care.

One morning, after a really weird dream filled with fish and whales and other funny ocean creatures, I woke up all hot and sweaty. I was so wet, I thought I'd made pee in the bed, like a little baby. I looked at myself in the mirror over the dresser near my bed, and wow, was I shocked! I had a something long and slimy growing out of my chin. It was a 'tentacle'—that's a fancy word for a curly octopus arm.

Mommy put some cream on the tentacle, but that didn't do any good. Then Daddy tried to slice it off. Ouch! That really hurt. So Daddy stopped, and it's a good thing he did. Daddy's not a doctor, and people who aren't doctors shouldn't try to cut stuff off other folks.

More tentacles started popping out from under my chin, and a few coiled out of my armpits. That was when Mommy called Children's Services at St. Toad's Hospital. The nurse who answered the phone listened to Mommy describe what was wrong with me. Then she told Mommy to bring me over right away.

The nurse also told Mommy that since I'd be staying at the hospital for a few days, I could bring some of my favorite things from home. So I packed my blue pajamas, a few lucky amulets and my favorite toy car. Some kids take a teddy bear, a doll or a blanket.

When we arrived at Children's Services at St. Toad's Hospital, a nice lady called Nurse Flugg brought me a wheelchair and took me to my room. I found out I had a roommate. Oh, boy! A new friend—someone to talk to and play with during my stay! The bed in my room was really neat. The head and foot of the bed both went up and down, and if I needed a nurse's help, there was a big red button to press on my bedside table.

Nurse Flugg told Mommy and Daddy they could spend the night in the hospital, if they thought I'd want them near me. Wasn't that nice? Daddy told her I was a big boy and I'd be okay by myself, and that's true. I *am* a big boy. I've always been bigger than other kids my age, and the tentacle disease was making me even bigger. Tentacles were starting to sprout from funny new places on my body, but I wasn't worried. I was at the hospital, and I knew they'd make everything better.

Mommy and Daddy and Nurse Flugg went away to fill out some papers, and I got to talk to my roommate. His name was Zeke, and he was sick with a case of Creeping Rot. He'd been swimming in an underground river that connected to the sea, and a Deep One had tried to grab him. Zeke had escaped, but bad germs from the creature's slimy paw were making the skin on his right leg all puffy and green.

Soon Nurse Flugg came back and told me more about what to expect during my stay. She said I would eat breakfast, lunch and dinner in bed, just like a prince. She also showed me her 'thermometer'—that's a medical tool used to see if a kid's body is too hot or too cold. Mommy and Daddy had one at home, but it didn't beep like the one Nurse Flugg used.

Nurse Flugg explained that in a few hours, Dr. Gilman would run a few tests on me to find out what was wrong. She then suggested I take a little nap, since lots of sleep is an important part of staying healthy.

So I took a nap, and dreamed I was swimming at the bottom of the sea, around really old ruins and the bones of huge creatures that lived in the deeps, never knowing the light of day.

WHAT WAS WRONG WITH ME

When I woke up, I found myself chained to a huge metal table, surrounded by doctors, nurses and hospital 'security'—that's what you call the guards, who make sure everyone at the hospital is safe. I also felt very angry, and it seemed like I was looking at the world through an evil red mist of hate. I wanted to hurt all the nice people. I wanted to make bad things happen, which is not how I usually am. I'm a good boy.

Nurse Flugg explained to me that I'd growth four times bigger during my nap, and that I was transforming into one of the 'star spawn.' That's a fancy name for a creature that looks like a smaller version of Cthulhu, a giant space-demon who used to be trapped in a temple on the ocean floor. When the Great Gates of Doom opened, Cthulhu was released from his underwater prison, along with many of his alien followers, including some star spawn.

Standing next to Nurse Flugg was Dr. Gilman, a nice man around Daddy's age. He said Cthulhu can talk to people and touch them in their dreams, and it looked like Cthulhu had touched me. That bad touch was turning me into one of the star spawn. Oh no! It was also making me hate nice people and want to eat them. That was a 'symptom' of my illness—meaning, a clue there was something wrong with me.

THE ROAD TO RECOVERY

Dr. Gilman and Nurse Flugg ran some tests and decided to treat me with star-stone powder. Star-stones are like magical toys that can be used to scare off evil monsters, because they're etched with the Elder Sign, which is very powerful. Star-stones are neat! They added a little powder to some water and gave me an 'injection.' That means they put something to heal me inside my body through a hollow needle. It did hurt a little bit, but I'm a big boy—I didn't cry a single tear. But I did try to attack Dr. Gilman and Nurse Flugg with my tentacles. The urge to kill was a very bad symptom. I'm sure glad it went away.

Several nurses also circled my table and whispered holy 'incantations,' and those helped, too. 'Incantations' help to drive the forces of evil out of the body. Children's Services at St. Toad's Hospital uses the most up-to-date magic to help you get healthy again.

Next I was taken to a special 'recovery' room with star-stones attached to the walls in holy patterns. 'Recovery' means you're getting better. In that room, Nurse Flugg cried out more incantations and injected more star-stone water into my tentacles. Soon, the tentacles started shrinking and a few even dropped off. My body started shrinking, too. I was turning back into a kid again. Hurray! Soon the urge to kill was all gone.

I told Nurse Flugg I wanted to get back to my room and play some games with my new friend Zeke. She let me know that Children's Services at St. Toad's Hospital has a playroom where kids can have fun during their stay. If a kid is really sick and has to stay in his or her room, the nurses will bring plenty of toys and lucky amulets for the kid to play with.

A SPECIAL SERVICE, JUST FOR KIDS

Once all my tentacles had fallen off, I was able to go back to my room. There, I saw something that really made me sad. Zeke's bed was empty. Nurse Flugg told me he'd died from the Creeping Rot. But lucky for Zeke, 'Children's Services' has two meanings: not only does St. Toad's Hospital offer health services for kids, but they also offer 'funeral' services when kids have problems that are just too big to fix. A 'funeral' is a gathering where friends and family come to honor someone who has died.

Mommy and Daddy said I could go to Zeke's funeral, which was held in the special recovery room. Zeke's recover was very different from mine. Dr. Gilman screamed a special incantation to turn Zeke into a 'zombie'—that means, a dead person who can still move around and be useful. Dr. Gilman told us that Zombie-Zeke would soon be put to work, gathering things from the Blasted Zone.

The Blasted Zone has a lot of neat stuff in it, like metal and bricks. And the best way to go get that stuff is to send a zombie after it. A living person wouldn't last more than five minutes in the Blasted Zone, since it's so hot and full of strange gases. Dr. Gilman said Zombie-Zeke should be able to gather stuff for at least two or three weeks. And since he's not alive, the monsters that lurk there won't bother him.

Zombie-Zeke gave me a great big smile. I'm sure glad he'll be gathering stuff in the Blasted Zone, instead of me!

IT'S THE PLACE TO GO

Remember, everyone at Children's Services at St. Toad's Hospital wants to help. Keep in mind, it's always okay to ask questions if you don't understand what's happening. The treatment may hurt a little sometimes, but being sick or turning into a thing with tentacles is a lot worse.

Always talk to your family, your nurse and your doctor about how you feel. They don't want you to be afraid. Children's Services at St. Toad's Hospital is the place to go when you're sick or injured. If there's something wrong with a kid, they'll know just what to do next.

SUPER DIGITAL NEKRONOMI
PALS ARE ZING!

Bold adventurers Brott and Chayla marched happily down the road to Excitement City, where dreams come true if you are brave enough. Both carried backpacks filled with snacks, clothes, camping supplies, and Shining Dodecahedrons.

Brott was a stalwart, dark-haired young man with lively bright eyes, like those of a jaunty rooster. "I can hardly wait to get to Excitement City!" he said. "Tomorrow they will hold the Nekronomi Master Global Competition, and I shall be the victorious one, you bet!"

Chayla laughed. "Global? You want to win every competition in the universe!" She was a sweet-faced, slender woman with round blue eyes and pursed cherry-red lips. "You are very good, but many others have been Nekronomi Masters for so much longer. Do not be despaired if you are beaten."

"If they beat me, I will surely kill myself, plain and simple!" He put his hand to his heart. "But what have I to fear? My Super Digital Nekronomi Pals are Zing! They are the best in all of Computronea!"

The land of Computronea used to be ruled by a power-mad mega-computer known as the Continuum. To save the day, a noble warrior scientist had overloaded the evil machine with data on goodness, causing it to explode. The explosion released a great amount of the mysterious Zing Energy that powered the Continuum. All this unleashed power created a new race of beings known as Nekronomi Pals, composed of either digital goodness or evil, or sometimes an unpredictable mix of both.

Basically, there were four main types of Nekronomi Pals. The most common by far were the Tulus—loyal, doglike creatures with tentacled faces, bat wings, claws and scales. Brott's very favorite Pal was one of these, and his name was Peeka-Tulu. Most of the Tulus were friendly and relaxed. Their favorite pastime was taking long naps in dark, damp basement corners. But some could be quite snarly and ill-tempered, and their claws left awful scratches. Tulus contained high levels of Zing Energy.

Daggies resembled monkeys that had been crossed with goldfish. They had pale, lanky limbs, big fishy eyes and blubbery lips. They enjoyed swimming and splashing around in cool streams. Though electro-digital by nature, Nekronomi Pals could move about in water when in solid form—in fact, many enjoyed it. All the Pals had to eat and drink to nourish their solid bodies, just like real animals. Daggies loved water the most. Each Daggy was either all-the-way-good or all-the-way-evil.

Fungos had the appearance of hermit crabs, but instead of shells, they sported over-sized mushroom heads on their backs. Their stretchy eyestalks allowed them an expansive field of vision. They were aggressive fighters, with sharp, fast pincher-claws. Also, each type of Pal had its own special power—and the power of the Fungos was an especially formidable one. The other Pals certainly did not like to fight Fungos.

Shoggies were big, bouncy, rubbery Nekronomi Pals. They looked like juicy globs of gelatin with funny little wiggly bits suspended inside. These wigglies were their internal organs. Each Shoggy had two sturdy hearts and three pulsing brains, and so they were very industrious and intelligent. Their Zing Energy burned with a steady glow.

The people of Computronea accepted the presence of the Nekronomi Pals, and many would train them, trade them and engage them in competitions. The digital nature of the Pals allowed them to transform into raw Zing Energy, and they could travel through computer cables and phone lines. Owners of Pals could command their pets to download into handheld storage batteries known as Shining Dodecahedrons, which had metal sides and crystal faces.

"Let us rest," Brott said, "and allow our Nekronomi Pals to play for a spell in this meadow by the road. I wonder if they get bored inside their Dodecahedrons?"

"Oh, I think it's just a nice sleep for them. But yes, we ought to let them out. They might be hungry." Chayla opened her backpack and brought out her collection of five Dodecahedrons, while Brott unloaded all ten of his.

Chayla pressed the Zing Button on each of her digital pet carriers. "Zing-Time! Awaken, Mup-Tulu, Flap-Tulu, Snap-Daggy, Fin-Daggy and Foo-Fungo!"

"Power up!" cried Brott. "Harken to my command, Peeka-Tulu! Arise, Ruf-Tulu, Glub-Tulu, Zuk-Tulu, Turbo-Shoggy, Kika-Shoggy, Goo-Daggy, Bug-Daggy, Shub-Fungo and Prima-Fungo! Super Digital Nekronomi Pals are Zing!"

Sizzling zaps and bangs sounded as the creatures shot out of the glass faces of their Dodecahedrons. They shimmied and swirled—some of the showier ones even cascaded through the air as lively spark showers. And soon they materialized as lively, happy Nekronomi Pals. All fifteen began running, jumping and playing in the lush grass. The Pals gurgled and purred with delight.

A stream flowed through the meadow, and some began swimming and catching fish. Others found berries and tasty leaves to eat.

Peeka-Tulu carried a branch laden with plump berries to Brott. "Thank you, my digital friend!" the young man said. "Your wholesome goodness makes my heart sing."

Chayla pointed down the road. "Say, who is that coming this way? He looks familiar."

Brott scowled. "Why, it is that no-good Peetro. He and I had a furious Nekronomi Master face-off in Belt-Buckle City about a year ago. Remember? Peeka-Tulu whipped his awful Caca-Daggy into submission! His evil Pals all fight dirty."

"Oh yes, now I remember." Chayla crossed her arms. "His Pals have bad Zing Energy. He should not be allowed to join the competitions."

"What is this I see?" Peetro shouted. He had white hair, a black moustache and deep-set eyes. "Two steaming turds in the middle of a meadow! Yes, their smell is strong and ripe."

"You have a dirty mouth. It matches your mind!" Chayla stated angrily.

"Suck upon my pizzle, you demented whore!" Peetro suggested.

"You are even more rude and foul than I remembered, you scoundrel," Brott said. Then a breeze blew wildflower pollen in his face and he sneezed.

"Oh, are you ill? Bend over, my round-bottomed friend! I will take your temperature with my sturdy meat thermometer," Peetro offered. "Then I shall give you a bountiful protein injection. How generous I am!"

"That does it!" Brott raged. "I challenge you to a Nekronomi Master battle!"

"With pleasure," Peetro said. "If I win, I get to use the two of you to pleasure myself as I see fit."

"No way!" Brott ejaculated.

"Are you afraid you will lose? Then let us call off the battle, because I do not fight chicken-shit wussy-wimps," Peetro informed him. "You know, it astounds me that the both of you aren't always rumping and humping like crazed insane maniacs. Don't you know what sex is?"

"Brave adventurers have no need for that sort of thing!" Brott turned to Chayla. "Isn't that right?"

The girl shrugged. "If you say so."

Peetro laughed. "So what is your final answer?"

"Very well, I accept your challenge! Do not worry, Chayla—we shall not lose!"

Chayla studied Peetro, who, though evil, was actually rather handsome. "I am not so worried. You know, Brott, you do not want to tire yourself too much—we have much to do in Excitement City tomorrow. Maybe we should just give up and accept the consequences."

"Never!" Brott stared at his white-haired enemy. "Bring out your Nekronomi Pals. Let me see the creatures that serve such a deplorable master."

"I have rid myself of my old Tulus, Daggies, Shoggies and Fungos. They were so common and boring!" Peetro reached into his coat pockets and brought out a pair of black, not-at-all-Shiny Dodecahedrons. "I have only two Nekronomi Pals—but they are unique! Their Zing Energy is ominous! Believe me when I say: you cannot win!"

"We'd better just give up," Chayla said.

"Give up? Ha! Winning is the answer! Triumph is my legacy!" Brott enthused. "Peetro, let us see these so-special Nekronomi Pals of which you speak."

The villain smiled. "When the Continuum exploded, the most evil data on its hard drive recombined into two especially wicked Nekronomi Pals. And here they are!" He pressed the buttons on the Dodecahedrons. "by the black heart of Zing Energy, I summon you, Ultra-Nylotep and Mondo-Aztoth!"

Ultra-Nylotep was the most humanoid Nekronomi Pal that Brott and Chayla had ever seen. Like most of the Pals, he was about as big as a dog, but he walked on his hindlegs and looked like an elfin pharaoh. His wide, slanted eyes glowed bright magenta. Brott was shocked to see that unlike the other Pals, Ultra-Nylotep was endowed with genitalia—large, male, and abundantly engorged.

Mondo-Aztoth resembled a large cluster of oily, shiny bubbles. Among these bubbles rolled numerous bloodshot eyeballs and thickly veined testicles. The being exuded syrupy streams of yellow and green slime that wilted the grass it dripped upon. The reek of this Pal was like the mingled stenches of dead fish, burning plastic and a sick pig's diarrhea.

"These Pals are obscene," Brott said. "They are corrupt with bad Zing Energy. My good Nekronomi Pals will be able to defeat them easily!"

Peetro cocked his head to one side. "Indeed? I am so sure that Ultra-Nylotep and Mondo-Aztoth shall win, I will even allow all fifteen of those good Pals to fight mine at the same time."

"Truly you have sealed your own doom with your reckless boasting," Brott replied. "Let it be so. I do feel sorry that soon, your two freakish Pals will be moaning in bruised defeat."

"It is time to fight!" shrieked Ultra-Nylotep.

"Your Nekronomi Pal can talk!" Chayla said. "I've never seen one that could speak before."

"Well, now you've seen two," thundered Mondo-Aztoth in low, bubbly tones. "Let the fighting begin!"

By this time, all the Pals of Brott and Chayla had gathered behind their masters, curious about the strange evil Pals. Brott turned to the assembled digital pets. "I call upon all of you to use your special powers to conquer these vile beings. Fungos! Use your super-powerful freeze-beams! Shoggies! Fire your glue spray! Daggies! Hit them with your hypno-eyes! Tulus! Activate extra-fierce tentacle action! Super Digital Nekronomi Pals are Zing!"

For the next hour, the good and evil Pals tore up the meadow as they engaged in a ferocious battle. The Fungos fired their mighty freeze-beams, but the chilling rays of their special power just bounced off of Mondo-Aztoth and gave Ultra-Nylotep a slight itch. The two evil Pals drank deep of the thick Shoggy glue spray, and the hypno-eyes of the Daggies only made them laugh. The whipping face-tentacles of the Tulus gave the wicked Pals quite a challenge, but alas, even those sinewy appendages could not subdue so much concentrated bad Zing Energy. Peeka-Tulu fought long and hard, but in time the brave pet slumped to the ground, exhausted.

It was only after the fifteen good Pals had depleted their powers that the nasty ones began their own special attack.

Ultra-Nylotep held up his slender hands, revealing huge, rolling eyes in his palms. Magenta heat-rays shot out of these eyes, scorching and blistering all the sad, tired good Pals. Then Mondo-Aztoth floated overhead and began to gush glowing purple ichor on them, causing all the friendly Daggies, Tulus, Shoggies and Fungos to wail in agony.

"What is that horrible fluid?" Brott shouted.

"My specialty: Liquid Pain!" the evil, bubbly Pal roared.

"It is clear that you and your weak Pals are defeated," Peetro announced. "Their inability to succeed is a testament to my power. Now bend over, you two, and allow me to deal to you the penultimate degradation! Then, when I am done with you, Ultra-Nylotep will use you to demonstrate his erotic digital perversions! How he will relish the opportunity to ravish your tender human flesh!"

"Start with me!" Chayla urged, lowering her pants. "Do not worry, Brott. I will take the brunt of their sexual frenzy, and perhaps they will not have any stamina left for you."

Brott marched up to his exhausted Pals, who were huddled together in a quivering mass, crying and moaning.

"Do not accept this fate!" Brott cried. "Rally to the cause! Regain your strength and protect the virtue of Chayla! See how she squirms helplessly, skewered by the relentless Peetro! See how Ultra-Nylotep eagerly strokes himself to readiness! Such abominations cannot be tolerated! You have no time to nurse your wounds. You still have more courageous fighting to do! Serve! Strive! Protect! Super Digital Nekronomi Pals are Zing!"

It was then that Peeka-Tulu, the most cherished of the Pals, separated from the group and crept toward Brott. With a supreme effort, he managed to squeeze out of his throat the first words of his whole digital life....

"Oh, shut the fuck up."

Peeka-Tulu then stretched out his tentacles and strangled his master to death.

THE PECKER AT THE PASSAGEWAY

As he towed my car that crummy day,
the crazy, gap-toothed hick had this to say:
City boy, you'd have to be a fool
not to know that someday, birds shall rule.
We breed the fiends as food for finger-lickin'.
We're hatchin' our worst enemy, the chicken!
They've got a god, you know—a rooster-thing,
so huge and fat, it couldn't lift a wing.
Instead of feet, there's tentacles. The beak
is edged with fangs. That puffy feathered freak
dwells in a nest beyond the wall of time,
beside a river filled with livin' slime.
His name's Clukthulhu, Lord of All the Hens.
You won't find humans on his list of friends.
One day he found a passageway to Earth,
but could not pass because of his great girth.
Let's hope he can't peck into our dimension—
our fate would then be far too vile to mention.
But still, I fear that fowls shall rule someday.
They'll burst forth from the coops and spread dismay!
We'll all be torn to eensy-weensy bits.
Just thinkin' 'bout it sends me into fits.
Remember, circuses have no more geeks,
the kind that bite off chicken heads and beaks.
Without that geek protection, we are lost.
Into a giant stew-pot we'll be tossed!
Oh, how that rooster-god will cluck with glee,
as human bein's become a fricassee.
We will be the ones to scream and bleed
as families are pecked to chicken-feed.
The hens will sprout fierce tentacles and fangs
just like their god—those evil poultry gangs
will hunt down men and turn them into poop!
The White House will become their finest coop!
You think I'm crazy? Well, boy, that may be.
But 'crazy' does not necessarily
mean that I'm lyin'. One sure thing I know:

the dawn of doom begins with one loud crow!
Why'd the evil chicken cross the street?
To gorge itself on tasty human meat.
There's the shop—those guys can fix your car.
I know you have to travel pretty far.
At least you will not have to take the bus.
Just heed my words, my boy…for soon
the yolk will be on us.

THE SLITHERING QUIVER OF THE RIVER LIZARD'S TWISTED LIVER-BLISTERS

In the city of Phlemuria, three miles west of Ulthar in the Elder Dreamlands, folks had a saying: the god of Fate is no more than a capricious old pig-herder made cranky by an embarrassing rash. And who knows, perhaps there was some truth in that sage bit of gossip: for alas, Phlemuria is no more.

Phlemuria was once a fine and noble city, with cobbled streets, quaint thatched huts, and an interesting choice of religions. Folks could worship Krog-Kablog, the River Lizard of Unspeakable Death and second-cousin of Dagon, or perhaps the insect god Blaalador, whose priests were man-sized dung beetles in flowing brown robes. They could even worship the blacksmith's hermaphroditic man-daughter Sha-Boom—though really, Sha-Boom's worshippers were not exactly members of a religion. More of a dating service, really.

Know this: I, Qizami, was the High Priest of Krog-Kablog, and this is my tale, and my tail as well. For I am now inscribing my long tale upon my longer tail in letters as tiny as baby ants, with the indelible pigment one collects upon squeezing the bright scarlet protuberances of the p'narr frog.

Eventually Sha-Boom ran off with a demigod named Kyle. Kyle: such a disturbing, alien name—verily, it chills my blood. They'd met at a nightclub in Kyle's neighborhood on the semi-forbidden continent of Mu. So Sha-Boom's worshippers were left without a deity, and as we all know, municipal law states that to abide in Phlemuria, one must be a registered worshipper of someone or something. These faithless folks had to select between Blaalador and Krog-Kablog.

As High Priest of Krog-Kablog, it was my sacred duty to enlist the faithless to the worship of the River Lizard of Unspeakable Death. This was not as easy task, for although I was the earthly spokesperson for said deity, even I had to admit that he was not what one would call 'easy on the eyes.' So in a dimly lit cafe off the Avenue of the Seven Unlikely Torments, I sought out and chatted with Grohkma, former High-Priestess and Beauty Consultant to Sha-Boom, to see if I could purchase some council from her. After all, she was out of a job, so she probably needed the money.

"Before I got a hold of him—or her," Grohkma confided, "Sha-Boom looked like a long stretch of country road well-travelled by overfed donkeys with irritable bowel syndrome." She was a slender lass with long silver nails and an abundance of stylishly pointed teeth. "Sha-Boom was very large, you know. Her—or his—skin was of a texture reminiscent of that loose, watery white cheese made by cottage dwellers…Someday, someone should think of a name for that small- or large-curded comestible. Anyway, one day I took a good look at Sha-Boom and saw—potential. A whisper of bone structure. I worked with Sha-Boom for three weks solid. From that point on, he—or she—had worshippers lined up around the corner, down the street and a few paces into the valley. All because of me. And now that bitch—or bastard—is shacked up with Kyle in a temple of eldritch dread in Mu, and I'm out of a job. That's the thanks I get."

"Do you think you could do anything for Krog-Kablog?" I whispered. Then a thought came to mind, and I added, "Of course, I know it would really irritate Sha-Boom, so if you'd rather not…"

A terrible light sprang up in Grohkma's baby-blues. "You know, for a River Lizard of Unspeakable Death, Krog-Kablog ain't so bad. And he *is* second-cousin to Dagon. I mean, at least he walks on his hindlegs, and his forepaws have opposable thumbs. And really, his gills aren't so noticeable. With a lot of work—and plenty of gold pieces—I could make a real hotty out of him. Does he have any allergies?"

This term was new to me. "What, pray tell, are allergies?"

"Well, they've been around since life first sprang from the Bog of Eternity, but only just recently have they been given a name. An allergy is a harmful sensitivity to a particular substance. For example, humans like us are allergic to cyanide. It makes us die."

"Actually, I'm only half human," I said. "The other half is Skragdazian swamp-satyr."

"Well, I guess that explains the hooves. And that fishtail. Swamp-satyrs are also allergic to cyanide, so don't order it if you see it on a menu. Are there any foodstuffs, ointments or poultices that bring about an adverse reaction when fed, rubbed or applied to Krog-Kablog?"

I thought for a moment. "Well, he has never liked vegetables, but who does? Besides, of course, the uncouth Vegetable Eaters of Leng. If Krog-Kablog had his way, he'd just eat virgins from dawn to dusk."

"Who wouldn't? Well, Qizami, if you haven't noticed any disturbing reactions in the past, I guess there's nothing to worry about. He still lives in the Marsh of Glistening Horror, right next to that river of his, yes? Meet me there at cock's-crow tomorrow with twenty gold pieces and we'll get started."

I gave her a warm smile. "I look forward to working with you, and I will have your full payment ready for you in the morning."

Grohkma laughed. "Full payment? That's just to cover supplies and the first three hours of treatment. And even then I'm giving you a discount."

That evening, I visited Krog-Kablog in his marsh-cavern to tell him the news, and also to question him about this matter of allergies. I had to push through a small herd of goats—his dinner—to reach the side of his throne.

He thought for a moment, lazily scratching at his back-scales with a bloody goat femur. "Sometimes my stomach hurts if I eat too many wild boars from the Plateau of N'keeba. Is that what one would call an allergy?"

"No, that is just the result of an overly full belly."

Spittle dribbling from his rubbery lips, Krog-Kablog reached for another goat. "Oh yeah, I just remembered. My mentor, Xixos of Thropp— I wonder whatever became of him?—once told me that I should never ingest the Wine of Ygllupu. To do so would bring about the vile fulfillment of a cataclysmic prophecy. What about that?"

I nodded as I headed toward the door. "Sounds like one of those allergy thingies to me. If Grohkma brings any wine, I will dispose of it. Now don't eat too many goats—otherwise, when the sun rises, this cavern will be filled with the foul and nitrous winds that oft break from your formidable posterior. See you tomorrow. Sleep tight, and do not allow the bed-insects of V'gazzi to bite."

* * * *

Well, of course, the deity did not heed my dietary warning, and his cavern reeked in abundance, so that verily, mine eyes and those of Grohkma did water profusely when we entered that foul domain. Grohkma's leather sack of beauty treatments was filled with bottles, jars and boxes of various sizes. I asked her if she had any wine of any kind in her sack, and she assured me that she did not.

I herded the last of the goats out the door. "No more of those for you today, Oh Mighty Flatulent One."

"As you well know," Grohkma whispered in my ear, "a swamp-satyr is part-carp, part-goat, and part-human. And you are part swamp-satyr. Since your god seems to like eating goats so much, are you not afraid that someday he will eat you?"

"I have not informed him of my swamp-satyr ancestry," I whispered back. "And, his tiny eyes are not strong enough to notice my various goatlike qualities. He does have a keen sense of smell, so I splash myself with floral colognes before visiting him to cover any hint of goat that might exude from my person."

"What are you two treacherous psychopomps whispering about?" my god thundered.

"We were simply discussing the various options for making you even more alluring," I said.

"Qizami, what stinks of flowers in this cavern?" Krog-Kablog said. "It seems like every time you stop by, this places smells all sickly sweet. If I did not know better, I would swear it was you."

"Ten-thousand apologies, Oh Flabby One," I cried. "But my own humble dwelling is located in the middle of a field of odious blossoms, and I must walk through them to get to your cavern. No matter what I do, they keep on growing—horrid weeds that they are. How I hate them! I stomp on them every day. But I fear that this action only infects me with their various vile perfumes."

Krog-Kablog laughed. "No need to apologize. I cannot be mad if you're going to all that trouble to help destroy those awful, repugnant blossoms. But there must be a solution…Say, I think goat musk might help cover the whiff of those odious flowers. I do like the pleasant, appetizing smell of goats."

"An excellent suggestion," I said. "I shall buy some of that musk tomorrow. From now on, I will smell like a goat whenever I am near you." Smiling, I turned to Grohkma. "It is now time to work your magic on my god."

The silver-nailed one walked closer to the river lizard. "Where to begin…? His face does seem to have a few human qualities, which is good. Thankfully, he doesn't have any facial scales. In fact, he even has a hint of eyebrows. Are you part mammal?"

Krog-Kablog nodded. "My great-grandfather was a walrus god."

"That must be where you got the whiskers—I'd originally been thinking 'N'vakian catfish'. Like a walrus, you have large, greasy pores. Those will need to be cleaned and tightened with a strong astringent."

The river lizard bit his lower lip. "Will that hurt?"

"Not at all!" Grohkma reached into her sack and pulled out a bottle of purple fluid. "I'll just rub some of this medicinal brandy on your face and those big pores will tighten up in no time."

I watched as the silver-nailed one did her work.

"That brandy smells delicious. Let me have a taste," Krog-Kablog said.

"Certainly," Grohkma said, "I have several bottles—far more than I need." She poured half the bottle between the god's blubbery lips.

At first, the river lizard's greenish skin seemed to improve: it looked less greasy and a little more human than usual. But then it began to turn a little too blue for my liking. Then pinkish pustules began to pop up. "Say, I just had a horrible and doom-laden thought," I said. "Isn't brandy made from distilled wine…?"

Grohkma and Krog-Kablog both turned to look at me. Then they looked back at each other.

"This brandy of yours—where is it from?" the river lizard asked.

"No place special," the silver-nailed one said. "Just some little patch of Dreamland called Ygllupu. Why?"

The god responded by biting Grohkma's head off.

I was not going to wait to see if Krog-Kablog had a similar reply in store for me. I ran out of the cavern, all the way back to Phlemuria and my favorite tavern, wherein I consulted some familiar spirits.

"Alas," I said to Agzep, the bartender, after my third beverage, "while attempting to beautify Krog-Kablog, I fear that I have inadvertently released an apocalyptic nightmare of doom upon Phlemuria."

"These things happen," Agzep said with a shrug.

"If only I knew the whereabouts of Xixos of Thropp," I said. "Actually, I suppose there's a good chance he's in Thropp right now, since that's his hometown and part of his name, but there's no way for me to find out, for Thropp is many hundreds of miles from here."

"You really should try to keep up with current events," Agzep said. "Thropp was destroyed in a volcanic eruption decades ago."

"Well, I guess you have all the answers, Mister He-Who-Knoweth-Everything!" I cried. "I suppose next you'll be pulling the address of Xixos out of your malodorous bottom!"

"Actually, I will not need to dig that deep," he said with a wicked smile. "I have only to lift my hand and point a finger to the window at your left. He runs that revered establishment over there."

I turned my head, and a scream of mingled disdain, aggravation and horror winged its way from between my writhing lips.

For he was pointing toward the filthy brown temple of the insect god Blaalador.

* * * *

"Well, well, well!" hissed the giant dung beetle known as Xixos of Thropp. "Look what we have here. The High Priest of Krog-Kablog has come to ask my help. How delightfully pathetic." We were in his stench-ridden master-chamber. The building was constructed from countless tons of dried, compacted animal droppings. One might well wonder how such a temple could have attracted any worshippers at all. The answer to that puzzle can be summed up in six words: short sermons and strong ceremonial liquor.

"Do you think I like being here?" I said. "I didn't know what else to do. It's not every day that Krog-Kablog's skin turns blue with pinkish pustules!"

"Did you say blue? With pinkish pustules?" The creature's mandibles began to click frantically. "Oh, my. That isn't good. Not good at all. I hope you having been serving him the Wine of Ygllupu!"

"Actually, he had some of the *Brandy* of Ygllupu…" I whispered.

"Great knuckle-gnawing night-gaunts!" he exclaimed. "By the snake-beard of Cthulhu, that's even worse! We are surely doomed! The end of Phlemuria is nigh! And to think I own real estate around here. It's not going to be worth a slim copper prakni after this!"

"Well, what's so terrible about this brandy, anyway?" I said, shifting in my seat, which was also made from dried dung. Unfortunately, it was not *completely* dry.

"What's so terrible? Krog-Kablog is a giant river lizard, and as even the tiniest runts among Phlemuria's school-children all know, giant river lizards have very delicate livers." He shook his antennae with exasperation.

I stuck my head out of his chamber window, looking for a school child. Fortunately, a very small one was walking by at that moment. "Child," I said, "is any part of the giant river lizard especially delicate?"

"Yes, of course," the little one stated. "The liver. River lizards cannot tolerate even the tiniest drop of the Wine of Ygllupu, which twists their livers. Why, even my wee unborn sister, still damp and cozy in my mother's bulging tummy, knows well that time-honored fact. Is there anything else you would like to know? The color of the sky? The difference between 'up' and 'down'…?"

With a sigh, I threw a silver coin to the child.

I turned back to Xixos. "So tell me: what can we do to avert this ghastly and unholy doom?"

The giant beetle thought for a moment. "Well, that brandy will seep into the delicate liver of the river lizard. There it will twist the liver, creating liver-blisters. These twisted liver-blisters are the greatest danger—for if they start to quiver, all is lost!"

"I do not understand," I said. "Are we to fear the quiver of a river lizard's liver-blisters?"

Xixos nodded. "Yes indeed, for that quiver means that the liver-blisters have evolved into creatures far more vicious and deadly than the original river lizard."

"And what sort of creatures would those be?" I asked.

A chorus of screams erupted in the streets. The beetle gasped. "You will find out soon enough," he said.

Xixos led me to the temple's high tower, which wasn't really all that high, since it was just one floor up from his office. In the streets below, dozens of great glistening slabs of slime-streaked blue meat, dotted with pinkish pustules, were slithering down the streets, engulfing terrified citizens.

"But what has happened to Krog-Kablog?" I said.

"The river lizard is no more!" Xixos shrilled. "He was the first victim of his own quivering liver-blisters. They consumed him as they swarmed out of his body. And they have been eating and growing without stop since that moment. All is lost! Fear holds sway! Doom is the order of the day! Panic and mayhem shall soon ensue!"

"For an enormous dung beetle, you sure throw in the towel pretty quickly," I said. "Where's that legendary dung beetle tenacity one hears so much about?"

"Oh, are we known for being tenacious?" Xixos clicked his mandibles with interest.

"Yes, you are," I said. "Everywhere you go, people talk about the tenacity of dung beetles."

"That's right!" shouted the small school child, who was still loitering in the street below. "I hope that when I grow up, I will be as tenacious as a dung-beetle."

"Eavesdropping is impolite!" I shouted back. "Now go hide in a tree or something before one of those liver-blisters gets you." I turned my attention back to Xixos. "I would at least have expected you to call on your own god for assistance. I mean, we *are* in his temple."

"Hey, that's right!" The beetle slapped his front legs together merrily. "Quick! To the holy dung-pit of worship!"

* * * *

I knelt with Xixos in front of a great abyss, deep in the bowels of the dung temple.

"Where are all the other priests?" I said.

"Oh, they were out running some errands," he said with a shrug. "I suppose the liver-blisters got them."

"You don't sound too upset."

"Hey, I'm a dung beetle. All I really care about is dung."

I couldn't argue with that.

"Mighty Blaalador, hear my plea!" the beetle intoned. "Arise from your comfy hidey-hole of darkness! I *beseech* you. Oh, please, we really need your help. If you come to us I'll get you a whole cartload of nice, fresh dung!" Xixos turned to me. "You know, it wouldn't hurt if you gave him a little of *your* dung."

"Maybe later," I said. "For now, I'll just talk to him." I stretched out my arms in supplication. "Here's the deal, Blaalador. Phlemuria is being destroyed by a bunch of quivering, twisted liver-blisters and you're the only one who can possibly fix this situation. So get your smelly carcass up here right this minute!"

A roar of monstrous rage shook the very walls of the temple, and for a moment I thought the whole stinking structure would come crashing down on us. Then a gigantic beetle-head popped out of the abyss.

"Liver-blisters, huh?" Blaalador said in a deep, rumbling tone. "Sounds like some moron gave Krog-Kablog the Wine of Ygllupu."

"Ha! This idiot's friend gave that overgrown polliwog the *Brandy* of Ygllupu!" Xixos said.

"What a lame-brain!" the god bellowed. "Sure, I'll help. But this will be the first time I've ever left this pit, you know. I'm pretty big. In fact, I'm guessing that I'm bigger than the temple. I'll probably wreck the place just getting out."

Xixos waved a limb nonchalantly. "So what? It's just made of dung."

"Good point," Blaalador said. "The two of you had better climb onto my mandibles and hold tight, so all the dung doesn't knock you into the pit as we bust out of here. Don't worry, I won't eat you. I'm sure neither of you is as sweet as a bucket of fresh donkey droppings."

"Thanks. That really helps my self-esteem," I said, wrapping my arms around the enormous insect's left jaw.

Blaalador was right: his exit left the temple in ruins. But then, it had never been what one might call a showplace. Once we were out, we looked around to see what we were up against.

The twisted liver-blisters were everywhere, bigger and bluer than before. Even their pinkish spots were now bright magenta. Now the liver-blisters were squirting digestive juices on people, reducing them to mush in mere seconds.

"Attack them!" I cried, as Xixos and I climbed down from Blaalador's mouth.

"Attack?" the insect god laughed. "I'm a giant dung beetle. I gather dung and roll it around in a big ball. That's what I do."

"Well, then, gather up those liver-blisters in a big ball," I said, "and roll them into that pit of yours. They don't have any legs so they won't be able to climb back out."

"Oh, that's fine for you," Blaalador said, "but then where am I supposed to live? I'm not sharing my place with a bunch of liver-blisters."

"You can have Krog-Kablog's old place," I said. "The cavern in the marsh. The entrance is big enough for you, and there's loads of room inside. And goats! There are still some goats in there. Think of the dung!"

"Go for it, Blaalador!" Xixos said. "I'll stay with you and feed those goats morning, noon and night! We'll be *crawling* in fresh, nourishing goat dung!"

"It's a deal!" So saying, the insect god went to work, gathering up liver-blisters and rolling them into a ball. They squirted him with digestive juice, but the steamy fluid just rolled off of his hard shell. Unfortunately, the act of rolling that giant ball around completely destroyed what little was left of Phlemuria. Toward the end, pulsing maws, wet with froth, opened up in the meaty blister-creatures and they began to scream—they sounded much like frightened pigs and parrots. Blaalador chucked the blue and magenta meatball down into the pit and hurried off with Xixos, eager to sample all that yummy goat-dung.

Suddenly I felt a light tapping on my elbow, and I turned around. It was the little school child.

"Oh, hello," I said. "How did you escape the doom of Phlemuria?"

The boy smiled. "You told me to hide in a tree, and all the trees are outside of town. But now I can't find my dad, Agzep the bartender."

"Oh, my…" I took his hand. "The gods have sent him on an important mission, little one. One fit for a man of his great wisdom. But they've given me an important mission, too. To look after you."

* * * *

All that was several years ago. After Phlemuria was destroyed, I moved to Mu and opened a flower shop. After all that dung, I needed to surround myself with prettier odors. The boy helps out around the place. He's a good kid.

So, here I sit in my sweet-smelling shop, writing this tale upon my tail. Sha-Boom and Kyle stop by to say 'Greetings, Qizami!' every now and then, but they never buy anything. Cheapskates.

Life is pleasant. I am happy. But late at night, I sometimes remember the sounds made by that vile ball that Blaalador had rolled up. And still, the memory makes me shiver: *the bubbly, quavery squawking and squealing of the river lizard's quivering, slithering, blubbering, slobbering, insidiously twisted liver-blisters…*

THE HOPPER IN THE HAYFIELD

I. A GNAWING IN THE NIGHT

Many are the methods by which living creatures locomote over, through and under the surface of this world of ours. Some soar through the air on wings—diaphanous, membranous, befeathered or perhaps even scaled, as in the case of certain flying fish. Some swim and some simply float, allowing the currents to carry them along with the flotsam, jetsam and other forms of oceanic detritus. Some squirm and writhe, spewing primordial slime to help grease the glistening path of their progress. Some stride proudly over the land, on two, four or even more legs. Some have an odd number of legs, but that's usually just the result of some accident. Some legged creatures swing by a prehensile tail, which really isn't a limb but is in fact a handy muscular extension of the spinal column. But among those creatures that stride, one will find a small percentage that move by *hopping*—by projecting their bodies upward and forward, upward and forward, over and over and over in a pneumatic fashion, machine-like and yet suggestive in its relentlessly rhythmic ambulation. Allow me to tell you what I have observed— what I *know*—regarding such matters....

In the Spring of my twenty-seventh year, my grandfather, Winston Farthington Sorbet, passed away from a heart attack, caused by prolonged, disturbingly intimate contact with a milking machine at his dairy farm outside of the small town of Bentwhistle, Indiana. Being his only living relative, I inherited that farm. But, unlike my grandfather, I had no desire to milk, groom or engage in any other activities with bovines, so I had my solicitor arrange for the herd and milking equipment, and the tractors, wagons, and most of the excess land as well, to be sold at auction. In the end, I was left with a nice plump bank account, along with a plot of land that held a farmhouse, a barn and a bit of hayfield. I figured I would be able to live in the farmhouse and not have to draw a paycheck for at least four years—more than enough time for me to concentrate on and complete the project of my dreams. For I am a writer, and at that time, I was just starting work on said dream project: an alternate history novel that asked—and answered!—the intriguing question, "How would our world be different if Napoleon had been an elderly Asian woman?"

So finally—once all the agricultural trappings were sold off and my furnishings had been moved into the house—I was able to start my new life, out in the country. The farmhouse was a bizarre structure, with five added sections—hallways with six small rooms—built on in a slipshod, hurried fashion. They shot out from the square central house like the arms of a starfish. In many of those impromptu rooms, the only wiring was an extension cord running from some plug in the original building.

I had no idea why my grandfather had decided to add on so many rooms in such a slapdash fashion. Most of the rooms held empty wire cages, all streaked with filth, while in others I found metal vats containing stinking fluids in various shades of red, blue, purple, pink and yellow. The contents of the vats all reeked of vinegar, which must have been a chief ingredient in those problematic brews. It took me some time, but using a pump I bought at the local hardware store and several garden hoses screwed together, I was able to siphon all the colored liquids into a ditch behind the house.

I carried all the wire cages out into the barn, and just left the metal vats where they were. They were ugly and corroded, but they were also too big to remove from the rooms—in fact, it appeared that the rooms had been built around them. So I left them where they were. I was single, and wasn't planning on inviting company over, so their appearance wasn't a major concern.

At the time, I was happy to be left with the barn and small sector of hayfield, for I was at least able to brag that I was a landowner—though the land I was left with really wasn't good for much. Still, possessing any amount of land can be an uplifting notion. It pleased me to know I owned outright, and was master of, my own special albeit tiny domain.

One evening, as I was sitting on my porch, gazing at the orange and golden hues of an especially picturesque sunset, I happened to notice a sort of mild turbulence in the hayfield.

Every now and then, here and there, I would spot multiple pairs of snowy-white, fuzzy protuberances sticking up out of the hay. It soon dawned on me that my little field was populated by a large family of rabbits, happily hopping through the crisp leaves. Easter was coming up in a couple weeks, and so I called out jokingly to the long-eared interlopers, "Which one of you is the Easter Bunny?"

Imagine my surprise when suddenly, all of the ears stopped in their tracks. The rabbits ceased their hopping, as though disconcerted by my innocent statement. Then, slowly, all the ears lowered into the green growth, and I saw no more of the creatures that night.

Later, while preparing for bed, I heard a creaking and scraping in one of my grandfather's slapdash spare rooms, and so I threw on a robe and hurried through the house in the direction of the noise, to see what the matter might be.

As I opened the door of the room that contained the source of the disturbance, I heard a quick scrambling sound, like that of many little creatures rushing away. I felt a light breeze upon entering the room, and was shocked to see that a portion of a board near the base of a wall had been gnawed away, as though by many rodentlike teeth, allowing a small entrance from the outside. I then realized that one of the floorboards also had been gnawed at, though it was still in one piece. Clearly I had interrupted the vandals before they could finish their dirty work.

The gnawing had loosened the board, so I pulled up on it along one side, to ascertain what unknown treasure the night's trespassers had been trying to abscond with. The board came up with a whining creak, and there, hidden amidst mounds of sawdust and mouse droppings, I found a mildewed blue notebook. The cover had been scribbled over with a smeared but still readable title in black ink:

THE AIEE-SH'TAR EGGS OF BUG'ZHA BHUN-YEH

There was a metal vat in the middle of that room, so I pushed against it until I had moved it to the wall, covering the hole that had been gnawed there. I then carried the notebook back to my bedroom, where I opened the slender tome and gazed upon the cramped, spidery cursive—my grandfather's handwriting—therein.

II. BLOATSOME BLASPHEMIES OF THE EASTER FEASTER

I settled into bed and hugged my pillow tight as I studied that mystery-ensorcelled notebook. The text read as follows:

"I now realize why I was able to buy this place for so cheap. I was talking to some of the town elders earlier today, and they kept making the Sign of the Rabbit—index and middle fingers held aloft—as they spoke to me. And oh, the things of which they spoke!

"The age-wizened couple who sold me this place—who have since relocated to Canada—hadn't mentioned that this farm had been built on unholy ground, where once evil settlers had worshipped the great and terrible nature god Bug'zha Bhun-Yeh. Had I only known that, I might have reconsidered spending my life's savings on so accursed a chunk of rural real estate.

"Bug'zha Bhun-Yeh! I have been doing some research in the 'Rare Books' section of the Bentwhistle Town Library. Of course they had copies of the *Necronomicon* and *The Book of Eibon*—most 'Rare

Books' sections do—but I was quite shocked to see that they also owned a copy of the very rarest occult volume of all time.

"Yes, they possessed a duckskin-bound copy of *Der Kwacken-Kulten De Daf'fei-D'ukkh*—written in 1684 by that mad necromancer, alchemist and huntsman, Elmharr Fhud. Elmharr was well-versed in ancient secrets, and his mission in life had been to find and eradicate all traces of demon-adulation in his native land of Kartoonia. This was no easy task, for that small but wicked country was—and in fact, has always been, even to the present day—rife with covens, worshipping the hideous likes of Bug'zha Bhun-Yeh, Daf'fei-D'ukkh, and even that stuttering, snout-faced abomination, Por-Kyei Pe'yugg.

"No doubt the evil settlers who had worshipped dreaded Bug'zha Bhun-Yeh—on the land that is now my farm!—had come to America from Kartoonia, so that they could worship as they pleased.

"So I checked out *Der Kwacken-Kulten De Daf'fei-D'ukkh* from the library—but since it was a rare book, valued at many millions of dollars, I was only allowed to take it home for three days. But horror of horrors! I tremble still when I reflect upon what I read in those demon-plagued three days of ultimate madness!

"Many and varied were the squamous and lugubrious tidbits of elder lore I learned from that fowl-fleshed volume of unspeakableness. Now I know that the day we call Easter is in fact based on an early pagan holiday of sacrifices and ritualistic egg-dyeing known as Aiee-Sh'tar, which celebrates the foul night that Bug'zha Bhun-Yeh came to our world from his horror-hutch beyond the stars!

"In an especially hideous and rather lengthy footnote started on page 273 and continued onto pages 274 and 275, Elmharr related numerous facts regarding the appearance and origins of Bug'zha Bhun-Yeh. This fearsome and demonic presence stood over eighty feet high, and resembled the worst possible cross between a rabbit, a squid, a grasshopper and a carnivorous plant. It had a flabby body covered with fluffy white fur, with powerful, scaly legs that kicked out backward, like most hopping insects, propelling it up to a quarter-mile per leap. The body was encircled by sinuous green tentacles, that in repose, hung down from around its waist like the verdant stalks of a hula-dancer's grass skirt.

"But the head of the creature was by far its most repulsively horrific feature. It had a sleek, rabbitlike skull with moist, blinking pink eyes and a dew-flecked pink nose that twitched nervously. Beneath that nose, its ravenous, fang-lined, saliva-dripping, chomping mouth opened vertically, like the copious maw of a Venus flytrap. Atop its grotesque head reared two long, fleshy, pointed ears, forever turning from side to side, trying to catch the sound of potential prey creeping about, for the loathsome rabbit-god constantly hungered for the satisfying, tangy flavor of living flesh. The diabolical entity possessed a variety of strong mental powers, including telekinesis, as well as the unique ability to break itself down into hundreds of smaller versions of itself, to enable it to track down and devour very small creatures.

"Bug'zha Bhun-Yeh came to Earth countless aeons ago from the world we humans know as Mars. The creatures that once dwelled there used to call it W'haa-Tzupp-Dokh. The red planet is void of life now—for quite simply, Bug'zha Bhun-Yeh ate it all. And after devouring all of the red planet's inhabitants, the rabbit-eared one sealed itself into a protective capsule formed of pure psychic energy, and then used its telekinetic powers to send the projectile to our lush green globe.

"But Bug'zha Bhun-Yeh was considerably weakened by the enormous strain of propelling its own mighty bulk such a phenomenal distance. That is why it hasn't devoured all of the Earth's inhabitants—the trip to this world left it crippled, with a reduced appetite. But there may come a day when its health and all-consuming hunger will return. Woe to humanity should that day ever come!"

At that point, I stopped reading, for I was extremely tired from the evening's exertions. I tucked the notebook under my pillow and promptly fell asleep. Unfortunately, it had been a bad idea to retire after reading of such frightsome matters. Instantly I lapsed into a nightmare of mind-numbing intensity. I dreamed that I was running through a valley of maroon boulders and orange sand, kicking up clouds of bright dust as I hurried along—for I was being pursued by something monstrously huge, a behemoth that squealed with glee as it hopped after me. In that nocturnal fantasy I was a very fast creature—I appeared to have many dozens of jointed legs, like some kind of millipede—but what pursued me was even faster, for suddenly it grabbed me in a coiling green tentacle, hoisted me up and then slowly began to lower me into a multi-fanged mouth that gnashed from side to side.

The dream ended with a prolonged crackling sound, as my dream-self realized that what I was hearing was in fact the violent crushing and crunching of my own chitinous exoskeleton…

III. THE LURKERS FROM BENEATH THE BARN

In the morning, over breakfast, I read more from the blue notebook. Every now and then, I would glance out of my kitchen window and spot furry white protuberances moving up and down, out in the hayfield.

According to the notebook, my grandfather began to notice more and more fuzzy ears out in the field—the very field I'd been watching from my breakfast table. Like me, he never actually saw the rabbits. When I read the final entry in the notebook, it chilled my blood, even though

I was eating a warm, butter-laden serving of blueberry flapjacks at the time:

"Great God in Heaven! It has been months since my last entry—how I shudder as I recall, albeit dimly, the events leading up to my current crisis! For this morning, I hit my head on an open cupboard door in the kitchen, and it knocked me out of the hypnotic stupor imposed upon me by that uncouth creature.

"Would that I had never found, weeks ago, under those loose, warped floorboards in the barn, that secret entrance to the cavernous crypts under my seemingly innocent farm! Would that I had never stumbled across that unhallowed subterranean temple where the All-Hearing One, Bug'zha Bhun-Yeh, resides when it is not out prowling for small animals to devour! For I now know that the hideous creature, still weak all these aeons later from its trip to Earth, has broken itself down into smaller versions of itself to conserve energy and still allow for greater ease in hunting. In addition, I now realize that those hundreds, maybe thousands of little Bug'zha Bhun-Yeh avatars have been using their psychic powers to compel me to feed them!

"That is why, for seemingly no reason at all—as though in a trance—I have been building and maintaining so many chicken coops, adding them onto the house itself so that I could collect the eggs as soon as the chickens had exuded them! That is also why I have been coloring the eggs with the sacred dye of Aiee-Sh'tar and leaving them outside, hidden in the grass, for the small avatars of Bug'zha Bhun-Yeh to gobble down during the night! For with each egg, made sacred by that specially formulated dye, Bug'zha Bhun-Yeh grows a little stronger, until at last it will be able to merge again into one mighty creature, so that it can take over our planet and devour every living thing, just like it did on W'haa-Tzupp-Dokh!"

Then came the last paragraph in the notebook, in which the spidery handwriting grew ever more frantic and hastily scrawled:

"But no! I cannot let that happen! I am out of that hypnotic trance now, so I must kill myself so I cannot again be enslaved by Bug'zha Bhun-Yeh and forced to feed those hopping avatars more eggs! But first I will get rid of the chickens and hide this notebook—and then!—then I will kill myself! I have always had problems with my heart—perhaps I can somehow induce a fatal heart attack by experiencing an overwhelming surge of excitement. But how? How? Unless—yes, the milking machine—!"

Simultaneously repulsed and terrified, I threw the notebook away from me. The events detailed in that shocking narrative were simply too bizarre, too outlandish, too nightmarish to believe. All yet all the facts—the cages, the vats, the bunny ears, my Uncle's death by milking machine—all seemed to point to one inescapable conclusion: namely, that every word in that accursed notebook was *true*.

Clearly there was only one thing for me to do. I would have to go into the barn, search out the loose, warped floorboards and see if I could find the entrance to that secret, underground realm of terror. And if I did, I also would have to go down into those noisome subterranean depths—perhaps to fight the core swarm of those wee Bug'zha Bhun-Yeh avatars.

I finished my flapjacks, had another cup of coffee, and then rummaged around in the closet until I found a flashlight and a nice big hammer—perfect for smashing evil little bunny-heads, if necessary. I felt it would be best to act quickly—for after all, Easter, also once known as Aiee-Sh'tar, was coming up in a few weeks. No doubt Bug'zha Bhun-Yeh's powers would be at their peak on that doom-laden pagan holiday.

As I walked out of the house and down the porch steps, a flashlight in one hand and a hammer in the other, I suddenly realized that I was being watched.

The hoppers had crept out of the greenery and were standing in a line by the hayfield. Their lurid tentacles swirled about their bodies, flexing their rubbery muscles. Their fanged, vertical mouths drooled and their dewy pink noses twitched. They stared and glared with loathsome glee at me—and I suddenly found myself feeling sleepy…very sleepy indeed.…

IV. KEEPER OF THE SECRETS OF DER KWACKEN-KULTEN

Time passed in a foggy, dreamlike blur. Then one day, I stumbled over something small and furry as I was leaving the house, and I fell down the porch steps, hitting my head on a rock in the lawn.

I rose to my feet, confused. A shrill, constant cackling, as of hundreds of chickens, seemed to be coming from the house. I walked back into the building and happened to see a newspaper on the coffee table. I checked the date on the paper—it was the day before Easter.

I then walked though the various built-on wings of the house. In all of their rooms, chickens in cages were laying eggs and vats of dyes were all filled to the brim with fresh batches of their vinegary brews. It appeared that the avatars of Bug'zha Bhun-Yeh had managed to work their hypnotic spell on me, forcing me to do their bidding. How many eggs had I dyed and fed to those legions of hopping fiends, bring them ever closer to their ultimate goal of reuniting into a huge, ravenous cosmic monstrosity?

So again, I found my flashlight and hammer and marched out of the house, determined to go down into that subterranean crypt beneath the barn to do battle with the avatar-swarm that lurked below.

And again, I suddenly realized that I was being watched.

There before me, right next to the barn, stood a furry white creature, eighty feet tall and graced with a ring of tentacles around its bloated body. It gnashed its slavering vertical mouth at me and twitched its obscene pink nose. Apparently I'd prepared enough eggs during my hypnotic trance, and the avatars had all been able to combine into the mighty, insatiable beast known as Bug'zha Bhun-Yeh.

I was about to turn and run, when I remembered that hellish dream, in which I'd been a Martian creature being pursued by a tentacled horror. Running definitely wasn't the answer. No, my only answer was to think the matter through—and quickly, for the creature was examining me with delight, rubbing two of its tentacles together with ravenous anticipation.

In a fear-fraught fantasy of frenzy, I thought to myself, "What would Elmharr Fhud do?" Then it suddenly dawned on me: Elmharr had been a legendary hunter and necromancer, well-versed in the secrets of Der Kwacken-Kulten, with great and mystical powers. His spirit had desperately longed to destroy Bug'zha Bhun-Yeh. Maybe I'd be able to summon him. Besides, I didn't have much to lose by trying.

I fell to my knees and raised my arms to the heavens. "Hear me now!" I cried. "Oh Spirits of Earth and Air and Fire and Water, Demons of Time and Space, let fall the veils that separate the realities of the living and the dead! I beseech the eternal soul of Elmharr Fhud to return to Earth, so that he might help me do battle with the evil rabbit-god! Rush to my assistance, oh great hunter! The time has come at last, Elmharr Fhud, to kill Bug'zha Bhun-Yeh!"

As soon as I'd finished uttering the words, dark, heavy storm-clouds rolled across the sky. Lightning flashed and the ground trembled with sudden, violent quakes. Bug'zha Bhun-Yeh let loose with a high-pitched squeal of rage. It lashed out at me with a tentacle, but I managed to roll out of the way of the snakelike appendage.

Then a glowing, man-shaped figure of pure light appeared in the sky high above us. The spectre gracefully swooped down toward Earth, picking up speed as it descended, until soon it was plummeting with the relentless speed of a comet. I covered my eyes with my hands just before it struck Bug'zha Bhun-Yeh, fearing that there might be a blinding flash of light, perhaps in combination with some sort of explosion.

I heard a high, shrill, utterly alien voice call out, again and again— "W'haa-Tzupp-Dokh! W'haa-Tzupp-Dokh!" I now think perhaps that Bug'zha Bhun-Yeh had been trying to use his telekinesis to send Elmharr Fhud's spirit off to Mars—thankfully, without success.

I then heard a wet, heavy, resounding smack, much like the sound of a prizefighter punching the sweaty face of an older, fatter boxing opponent. That was followed a series of moist thuds, like somebody dropping countless raw hamburgers off a roof onto a sidewalk.

When I opened my eyes, I saw the luminous spirit hovering victoriously over a huge pile of dead avatars. Apparently one well-placed supernatural punch from the avenging spirit had served not only to kill the trans-planetary menace, but also to break it down into the smaller units of which it was composed. The glowing soul of Elmharr gave me a friendly wave, and then it gracefully turned and flew off, back whence it came.

I spent the rest of the day gutting the avatars, chopping them up and storing the best cuts in my grandfather's freezer. I wasn't about to allow such an ample supply of rabbit meat and calamari tentacles go to waste.

Later, I finally went down into the subterranean caverns beneath the barn. There I found a series of damp, interconnected chambers, most of which were filled with greasy rabbit droppings that had a strong fishy reek to them. I cleaned up one of the chambers, put up a few posters and turned it into my writing area. My alternate history Napoleon novel is coming along nicely.

Unfortunately, I have since discovered that eating the flesh of those horrific, though tasty, creatures can bring out some lasting physical side-effects. My body is now covered with a light coating of white fuzz…tentacles have sprouted from around my waist and my ears have lengthened to an alarming degree…I'm constantly hungry for tasty dyed eggs…and I'll tell you this: it can be rather disconcerting to find oneself chewing from left-to-right, instead of the usual up-and-down.

But at least I'm getting my exercise.

In fact, I find my daily hops through the hayfield to be rather invigorating.

TONY TAR-PIT AND MONKEY-FACE JOE BATTLE THE FLYING MUSHROOM-DEVILS: A TALE OF PREHISTORIC ARRKHUMM

"Zogga Dogga Yog-Sothoth!"

As always, Tony Tar-Pit hollered a joyful exclamation of religious fervor to his god at the end of yet another strenuous workday. Tony was a massive mountain of a man, with thick black hair and fine strong teeth—most of them were straight and white, too, not all crooked and yellow like those of his boss, Lava Larry.

Tony was head butcher at Lava Larry's Rib Cave, the most popular eatery in all of Arrkhumm. Procuring the meat was always a brutal task. First, six of Tony's fellow cavemen would use heavy vines to snare one of the free-range steggies grazing in the boulder-enclosed canyon behind the restaurant. Then Tony would pick up his favorite club, Old Boom-Ba, and crush the beast's skull with one well-placed swing.

Each steggy was so incredibly stupid, it took one a whole fifteen minutes to realize it was dead, and so the cavemen would have to keep the beast restrained so it didn't flail around too much. Excess bruising would ruin the delicious meat.

When at last the beast was done kicking and fighting, the cavemen would roll away the boulders blocking the mouth of the canyon and drag out the huge, yummy lizard corpse.

Then Tony would take off his usual tiger-skin robe and put on a work-smock made out of leathery pterodactyl wing-membrane. He would get out his big stone knife, Old Chop-Chop, and lovingly gouge, rip, slice and hack the steggy into serving-sized chunks.

As Tony sliced up the meat, he would whisper devote prayers to his god, Yog-Sothoth, He-Who-Bubbles-In-The-Night-Sky, the Great-Father-Who-Provides. He would thank Yog-Sothoth for giving the humble cavepeople such good, fat steggies and other lizards, too, for meat. Tony loved the Great-Father so much, it sometimes made him blubber like a squealing, red-faced cavebaby.

Those bloody chunks of meat were set to cook on hot rocks next to the lava-pit a few yards away from the mouth of the canyon. The enticing aroma would make Tony's mouth water until bubbly currents of drool flowed over his lower lip.

At the end of the workday in question, Tony hollered his thanks to his god, as noted, and cleaned off Old Chop-Chop with some pretty-smelling vuupuu blossoms. Lava Larry walked up to Tony and gave him a large bundle wrapped in gugg vines. The caveboss regularly rewarded his butcher with some cooked steggy steaks to take back to the Tar-Pit clan. Lava Larry always let Tony take some fine rock-fried organs with him, too, including the little steggy brains and the big steggy man-roots.

"You have killed and sliced well today," Lava Larry said with a crooked-toothed smile. "Here is good meat for you and your three mates."

Tony cocked his head to one side. "Three mates? I only have one, my wife Trixie Tar-Pit."

Lava Larry's rugged brow furrowed even more than usual. "What about Monkey-Face Joe and Yargoona? Is not Yargoona your she-wife, too, and is not Monkey-Face Joe your little man-wife? Gary Granite, who tosses the salad here at the Rib Cave, has a sweet, agile man-wife who gives him great pleasure. In today's modern caveworld, it is perfectly respectable for any hard-working man to have a man-wife just for fun, in addition to however many she-wives he might wish to fill with bouncing babies. Now tell me, why has Trixie not given you a baby yet? Are you not squirting man-root juice into her she-hole on a nightly basis?"

Tony Tar-Pit laughed. "I fill her with so much man-root juice, I am surprised it is not squirting out of her ears! When the time is right, I am sure Yog-Sothoth will grant us a fine, fat baby, full of sweet, innocent love for his cavemommy and cavedaddy. As for Monkey-Face Joe and Yargoona—they live in my cave, but do not pleasure my man-root. They are good cavepeople and I worry about them because they are so small and weak. Why, each of them is only six feet tall—not eight, like you and me. So I protect them, as Yog-Sothoth protects us all."

'But since they are in your cave," Lava Larry said, "you have the right to tell them to pleasure your man-root. Maybe they would like to do so, to show you honor."

Tony Tar-Pit laughed. "But they are so tiny, like baby pterodactyls! My man-root would surely burst them wide open, like a steggy-head I've clobbered with Old Boom-Ba. No, I do not wish to make them die screaming, impaled on the end of my massive man-root. Thank you for the meat—I will see you in the morning!"

Tony began the long walk home, swinging the meat-bundle by the end of a vine. He could see why Lava Larry might think that Monkey-Face Joe was his little man-wife. In addition to being so small, Joe also had a kind, hairless, big-eyed face and shiny golden hair. Those big eyes were blue, like those of the poo-kaka monkeys that capered in the jungle south of Arrkhumm. That resemblance was what gave Monkey-Face Joe his nickname.

Yargoona was also fairly small, though she had black hair and eyes like most of the other cavepeople, and also a nice round potbelly and a pretty scar across her forehead. Both Joe and Yargoona were gentle and fun-loving, and they enjoyed picking ticks, leeches and other funny bugs out of Tony's hair, though they didn't do a very thorough job. But, Tony did not complain, for he knew they were doing the best they could. He did have a lot of hair and quite a big body, and bug-picking can be tiring work.

Tony knew he would never need extra mates, male or female, so long as he had Trixie. She was tall, strong and boulder-breasted, and took great pride in her ability to pleasure Tony's strong, thick man-root for hours on end, coaxing his creamy juices to shoot forth again and again and yet again.

Tony thought about how happy Trixie, Joe and Yargoona would be when they saw all the delicious, bloody meat he was bringing back to the cave. The three of them also hunted during the day, but Tony was the one who always brought the most food home. Joe was very good at climbing trees, so he usually found lots of flying-lizard eggs for them to eat. Just the thought of eating some big, tasty eggs made drool start to pour forth over Tony's thick lips.

Suddenly, a lean, muscular raptor leaped out into Tony's path. It's lime-green eyes widened as it gazed at the caveman. It was only about four feet tall, but one bite from its razor-sharp fangs, as well as one swipe of its vicious talons, could easily have killed even the mightiest cave-man. It moved closer, opened its deadly mouth, jumped up—

—and gave Tony a wet, affectionate lick right across his face.

"Bloodfang!" the caveman cried. "I am happy to see you, too!" He set down the meat bundle, unwrapped some of the vines and pulled out a dripping steggy spleen. "Here is your dinner, my friend!"

Monkey-Face Joe came running down the path. "I thought I smelled steggy meat! Do not give it all to Bloodfang!"

"Have no fear," Tony said, holding out a nicely toasted lizard tes-ticle. "Here is the best piece, just for you!" He watched fondly as his cavefriend grabbed the morsel and sank his little teeth greedily into the rounded lump.

"Yargoona and I spent the whole afternoon gathering sweet, juicy farfarr berries," Joe said.

"Farfarr berries taste good in my mouth," Tony said, "but is eating plants healthy? They eat Granite Gary's tossed salads at Lava Larry's, but still, I worry about any caveman who puts too many leaves and flowers and fruits into his stomach. Like you! No wonder your belly is so flat and hard, instead of big and round and healthy like mine."

Monkey-Face Joe nodded. "Yes, I should try to eat much more meat, so I can be more like you. You are my hero, Tony Tar-Pit!" He reached toward the bundle of meat, picked out a slice of steggy liver, and took big bites out of it. "I will try to grow a big, round belly so I can be fat and healthy!"

"Since we are talking about health, I think I should point out something else. I have noticed that bottom-rocks come out of your pooper as often as once or twice a day," Tony said. "I mean, we both live in the same cave, so I notice such personal things. Letting the food come out of your pooper so often surely cannot be healthy. You are not holding in your food long enough. I only make bottom-rocks once or twice a week!"

Monkey-Face Joe looked up adoringly at his friend. "Oh, surely Yargoona and I would be lost without your grand wisdom and loving protection. Yes, I will try to hold in my bottom-rocks much longer than I do now—for many days if necessary, if that is what it takes to be as healthy and happy and bloated as you. My good cavefriend Tony Tar-Pit, I do wish I could do more to serve and honor you!"

Tony thought for a moment. "I do enjoy eating the roasted flesh of the saber-toothed star-nosed mole—a rare delicacy! I ate some several years ago, and still delight in the memory of its flavor. But I am too big to squeeze down into one of their tunnels to catch one. But you, Monkey-Face Joe, are so very small, you could go down one of their holes with ease."

Joe gasped. "Me? Go down the tunnel of a saber-toothed, star-nosed mole? That sounds very dangerous. It would be easier if I just pleasured your man-root. It is too big to fit in my small bottom, but I do have two strong hands and a mouth—"

"No need for that! Trixie keeps my man-root very happy." Tony showed his little friend Old Chop-Chop, which hung from a strap tied around his waist. "I will lend you this, and you will be safe. Old Chop-Chop is good at making animals stop moving." He patted the top of Joe's head. "Let us go meet the women and fill our bellies with steggy steaks. I do not have to work tomorrow, so in the morning, we will hunt down a saber-toothed, star-nosed mole. What great fun we will have!"

"Fun?" Joe managed a weak smile. "Oh, yes. Sure. Fun. Much fun…"

A short while later, at the cave, Trixie and Yargoona were pleased to see their menfolk, and doubly pleased to see so much steggy meat.

Tony Tar-Pit announced to the women that Joe would be hunting down a saber-toothed, star-nosed mole in the morning.

"My big strong husband-man!" Yargoona cried. "How happy I am that you will be dealing death to a blood-thirsty creature tomorrow! The picture in my head of you, wrestling and stabbing a savage beast, makes the happy cavelady-parts between my legs tingle! I hope your man-root will be able to handle all the pleasure I will bring to it tonight!"

Joe patted the hand of his scarred, potbellied wife. "That would indeed please me, but remember, I must get much sleep tonight before the big hunt. Much, much sleep."

Later that night, after hours of lovemaking, Tony Tar-Pit and Trixie cuddled on their mattress of animal skins stitched together with monkey guts and stuffed with dried steggy dung.

"Tony, I am worried," Trixie said. "Monkey-Face Joe is so small and pitiful and weak. Are you not afraid that the saber-toothed, star-nosed mole will rip out his heart and stomach and liver and kidneys and other soft inside parts?"

"He will be fine! He will have Old Chop-Chop with him!" Tony exclaimed.

His gigantic wife shook her head. "Joe can barely lift Old Chop-Chop," she said. She thought for a moment. "Tie together many gugg vines and then wrap one around Joe before he goes down into the tunnel. That way, if he screams for help because a mole is chewing on his leg or arm, you can pull him out by the rope, and maybe it will pull out the mole, too, so you can club it to death. Just be careful you do not club our little cavefriend Joe to death as well."

"My wife," Tony Tar-Pit said, "you are so smart in the head, if you ever die, I will eat your head so I can then be smart."

"Your words of passion make my blood boil like lava," Trixie purred.

* * * *

In the morning, Tony Tar-Pit and Monkey-Face Joe found a mole-tunnel in the hills behind their cave. Tony followed Trixie's suggestion and tied together many strong lengths of gugg vine. Then he wrapped one end around Joe's waist, tied it in place, and handed him Old Chop-Chop.

"Now crawl down into the deadly darkness," Tony said, "and if you hear something snarling with rage directly in front of you, stab it to death. Will you remember to do that?"

Joe nodded. "I think so." With a heavy sigh, he crawled down into the tunnel.

Tony watched as yards of gugg vine snaked down into the earth, pulled by his little cavefriend. He listened carefully. No screaming yet. So far, so good.

Overhead, a flying lizard squawked, and he looked up at the winged creature and all the pretty, fluffy clouds. Truly the Great-Father, Yog-Sothoth, was a fine and generous provider. Soon his friend Joe would emerge from the ground, coated with blood, dragging the mangled corpse of a flesh-eating burrower. Yes, life was good.

"Old Chop-Chop is too heavy," Joe shouted from underground. "I am very tired. Can I come out now?"

"Have you spilled the blood of a wild beast yet?" Tony shouted back.

"Nooooo..."

"Then stay in there."

A black-winged butterfliosaurus floated through the air, bellowing delicately. Tony lashed out with Old Boom-Ba and crushed it. He had no way of knowing, but the after-effects of that action would eventually lead to the sinking of a heavily populated island called Atlantis.

"What a boring day," Tony said. He sat down on a rock. "Nothing is screaming or rampaging."

A little orange beetle crawled onto Tony's big toe. It was pretty, so the caveman didn't hurt it. Eventually it crawled off and slaughtered a tiny ant. This simple act led, many thousands of years later, to the birth of a funny little man named Adolf Hitler and a mighty conflict known as World War II.

"Tony? Are you still out there?" Joe cried.

"Yes! Did you kill the star-nosed, saber-toothed mole yet?"

"No, but I just found something soft and really dead-smelling, and it has a funny-shaped nose and big teeth. I think something else killed the mole before I had a chance."

"What a pity!" Tony cried. "Well, grab it and I'll pull you and the dead mole out. Maybe it is not too rotten to eat. Trixie and Yargoona can make pretty necklaces out of the teeth!" He began to pull at the gugg vines. "What a heavy load!" he shouted. "That must be a huge mole!"

"Blecchh!" Joe shougged, which is a combination of shouting and gagging. "This long-dead thing smells like rotten fish mixed with the goo that squirts out of a cavebaby's pooper! I want to let go of it—it can't be good to eat!"

"I will be the judge of that!" Tony Tar-Pit roared. "Besides, there are still those teeth for pretty necklaces! Yargoona will look so sexy with rows and rows of sharp mole-teeth draped under her sweet, scarred face! I bet just thinking of such a vision makes your man-root hard with lust! Does it, my friend?"

"Ummm…Sure, Tony. Oh, I am almost out of the hole—I can see daylight! Hurry, pull faster, I need to get away from this stinking corpse!"

Tony Tar-Pit spotted the welcome glimmer of his friend's blond hair at the mouth of the tunnel. He grabbed the smaller man by the shoulders and dragged him up to his feet. Tony then reached into the tunnel and hauled out the dead carcass. Yes, this dead saber-toothed, star-nosed mole was indeed extremely rotten, and covered with maggots and worms and other squiggly things.

"Say, what is this?" The potbellied caveman pointed to a strange creature hanging onto the mole's hips. It appeared to be a cross between a large insect and a mushroom, a little bigger than Tony's head, shimmering with all the colors of the rainbow. It had a round, puffy body and ten spindly legs, all stuck deep into the mole's flesh. Three wet, bulbous bug-eyes stared up at Tony, and a long, unfurled proboscis waggled at him.

"What an ugly little monster!" Joe said. "It looks like some kind of evil mushroom! If I am going to kill anything today, let me kill that thing with Old Chop-Chop!"

Suddenly the extended proboscis unfurled a bit more and licked at Tony's face. "Oh no, do not kill it!" he said. "It likes me! It is licking my face, just like my dear pet, Bloodfang." He pulled the insect off the dead mole, and it responded by crawling up his arm and curling up, purring, in his hairy armpit. "Look how friendly it is! Be nice to the poor, lonely mushroom-devil!"

Tony grabbed Old Chop-Chop from Joe and used it to cut off the mole's rotten, toothy noggin. "There, now our women can have pretty necklaces. Carry the head—I want to cuddle my new pet!" He fished the creature out of his armpit and rocked it in his arms like a cavebaby.

"You are going to keep that thing?" Joe said. "In the cave?"

"I have to," Tony said. "It is so small and helpless—just like you! I think I will call it…Monkey-Face Joe Number Two! But no, that's too long a name. I will call it Buggoth, since it is a bug and, like you and I, a child of Yog-Sothoth."

When the cavemen arrived at home, Tony and Joe told their wives of their morning adventure. The cavewomen were divided in their opinions of Buggoth.

"I do not like this new pet of yours, Tony," Trixie said. "It will probably grow big and try to suck out our blood or eat us! Surely you have brought death into our happy cave."

Yargoona thought otherwise. "I hope it does grow big. Very big! If we raise it with kindness and love, it will protect us from even the fiercest of meat-eating lizards, like the chomposaurus or the savage mutilatosaurus."

Buggoth must have somehow understood the meaning of Yargoona's words, because at that moment, the creature leaped out of Tony's arms and onto the scarred cavewoman's bosom, where he began licking her neck with gentle affection.

"See, Trixie?" Tony said. "Buggoth responds to love with sweet kisses! What a good monster!"

"Perhaps you are right," his wife said. "Very well, the mushroom-devil can stay—if Bloodfang does not object!"

The pet raptor, who had been napping in a far corner of the cave, awoke upon hearing his name. He trotted up to Yargoona and Buggoth and sniffed at the fungoid insect.

Buggoth let loose with a giddy squeal and jumped down onto Blood-fang's back. The two hideous creatures began to wrestle playfully, just like happy cavebrats.

"Zogga Dogga Yog-Sothoth!" Tony Tar-Pit exclaimed. "They love each other! Maybe someday when they are both full-grown, they will mate and create some kind of funny lizard-mushroom-bug! I would like to see such a thing!"

"Tony!" cried a low voice from outside the cave. "Can I come in, or are you rutting with that beautiful cavewife of yours? I can come back later!"

"Lava Larry?" Tony shouted. "Is that you? Come in, we are not rutting right now. Though if we were, you could certainly watch! Joe and Yargoona watch all the time!"

Tony's hugely fat boss shambled amiably into the cave. "I was just passing by and I thought I'd say 'Hello!' to my favorite worker. Hello to you, Tony, and to Trixie, too, and Monkey-Face Joe and Yargoona and Bloodfang and—" He stopped and stared at Buggoth. "By the dripping beard of the sea-devil Cthulhu, why do you have one of *those* in your cave? Are you insane with crazy madness?"

Tony cocked his head to one side. "Is something wrong with my new pet, Buggoth? Do you know what he is? I do not, but I am very fond of him!"

Lava Larry's squinty, piggish eyes grew wide with fear. "That, my friend, is one of the deadly star-crabs! They are evil, undying creatures that came from a strange place up in the sky, way past the moon! Many of them live in the mountains a few miles from here. Others live in damp underground caves. Have you not heard of the evil star-crabs?"

"Of course I have!" Tony said. "My cavemother Gungoona used to scare me when I was a little cavebrat with strange tales of their wicked ways. But she never said what they looked like, so I did not know

Buggoth was one of them. I thought he was some kind of walking mushroom. Though he does look a lot like a crab, now that you mention it."

"A star-crab? In our cave?" Trixie shook her head. "I see I was right the first time. That little devil will surely kill us all."

Buggoth stopped playing with Bloodfang and moved toward Tony. With a soft, sad little cry, he jumped up into the caveman's arms. The creature stared, whimpering, up into his master's eyes.

"Look what you have done, Lava Larry!" Tony said. "You have made my little friend sad! I do not care if he is a star-crab or not. It is clear he loves being with cavepeople! Maybe the other star-crabs were mean to him. Maybe they hit him or made fun of him because he was small and friendly and good!"

Monkey-Face Joe burst into tears. "The poor little mushroom-devil! Tony is right! Listen to Buggoth's pitiful moans! He knows he is being judged, and it is making him feel bad inside—because he wants to stay with us!"

"Yes, his tiny crab-heart is filled with kindness!" Yargoona said.

Buggoth turned his malformed head to stare at Trixie. A wistful sob wheezed forth from his proboscis.

The cavewoman sighed heavily. "Very well. The star-crab can stay."

Lava Larry nodded. "Yes, I now see that this young star-crab is not an evil killer lusting for human flesh. Surely he is the strangest—and also the sweetest—of all the children of Yog-Sothoth." He flashed a crooked-toothed smile. "Let me hold the precious little abomination."

Tony handed the creature to his boss. Buggoth instantly began to pick ticks out of the flabby caveman's stinking chest-hair, gobbling them down his long, curling mouth-organ with relish.

"Oh, see how useful he is!" the bloated caveman observed. "I have been meaning to pluck out those ticks for weeks!" He looked down at Buggoth's back. "Oh, look at this!" He tapped on two odd growths spouting from the creature's shoulders.

"Hmmm, those funny little fins look like they might grow into wings someday," Tony said. He glanced over at Bloodfang and smiled, again hoping that his pets might rut and create strange offspring someday. A *flying* lizard-mushroom-bug! Zogga Dogga Yog-Sothoth!

* * * *

Weeks passed, and Buggoth proved to be the most helpful pet in all of Arrkhumm. He excelled at sucking ticks, leeches, lice and other assorted vermin out of the various nooks, crannies, wrinkles, creases and folds of Tony and all his friends. At first, many were hesitant at the thought of allowing a voracious star-crab to touch their flesh, but once

Buggoth did his work, those he treated always agreed that he performed his task with agreeably gentle thoroughness.

Trixie and Yargoona used the teeth of the saber-toothed, star-nosed mole to make two lovely necklaces: Trixie's was made from the teeth of the top jaw, and Yargoona's came from the bottom jaw.

"With those classy mole-tooth necklaces, you two are the sexiest caveladies in all of Arrkhumm," Tony said one morning while they were eating their breakfast pterodactyl eggs.

"Oh, husband," Trixie said, blushing. "Your tender words make creamy juices trickle down my heavy thighs from my eager she-hole."

"I am curious about one thing," Yargoona said. "You told us the saber-toothed, star-nosed mole was dead when Joe found it. How did the beast die?"

"Hmmmm..." Tony Tar-Pit thought for a moment. "I do not know, really. I recall that Buggoth was clinging to its corpse like an adorable baby possumosaurus."

"I wonder why?" The scarred cavewoman gazed at Buggoth, who was squatted on the floor nearby, sucking out an egg's raw goo through a hole in its shell. "He would not have been cuddling with a dead thing for warmth."

"Do you think Buggoth killed the mole?" Monkey-Face Joe said. "He is much smaller than a mole. He does not have sharp teeth or claws. I do not see how he could have done it."

"Maybe Buggoth has a secret deadly talent!" Tony cried.

"A secret deadly talent?" Trixie echoed in disbelief.

"A secret deadly talent!" Yargoona repeated with wonder.

"A secret deadly talent..." Joe whispered fearfully.

"Ruff ruff-ruff ruff-ruff ruff-ruff!" Bloodfang barked. He hated to be left out of anything.

* * * *

That night, Tony Tar-Pit pleasured Trixie three times with his massive man-root. He began to pleasure her a fourth time, but stopped in mid-stroke.

"What is wrong, husband?" Trixie said. "Do you no longer find me desirable?"

"Be silent!" he hissed. "Listen! What is that noise?"

Trixie and Tony listened, as did Monkey-Face Joe and Yargoona, who had been watching the frenzied coupling from their bed in the shadows.

Outside of the cave, a loud, curiously rapid flapping of wings sounded. "What a strange noise!" Trixie whispered.

In his little sleep-nest of pelts and dried grass, Buggoth whimpered. Tony slipped out of bed and crept toward the mouth of the cave.

"Be careful, brave friend!" Joe cautioned, covering his head with a fur blanket. "Let us know what you see!"

Tony left the cave and peered up into the sky. Overhead, a strange creature was fluttering about thirty feet above the ground. It looked like Buggoth except it was much bigger—almost eight feet across—and sported crooked, batlike wings that beat the air with incredible speed.

Its long proboscis was completely unfurled. The creature whipped its mouth-organ in wide semi-circles, tasting the air.

"Whoop!" the creature whooped. "Whoop-whoop-whoop!"

Having whooped, it soared off into the night sky.

Tony hurried back into the cave, where he scooped up Buggoth into his arms. The frightened little star-crab was shivering with fear.

"My poor baby!" Tony cried. "You must have heard the evil whoop of that which lurked outside. One of your cruel kin has found our home, sniffing you down like a relentless bloodhoundosaurus. But do not fear, I shall protect you if it returns!"

"*If?* I am *sure* it will be back," Trixie said. "It will no doubt bring others, too. We cannot stay here. But where can we go?"

"We shall hide out at Lava Larry's!" Tony said. He looked down at his shivering pet. "We must take Buggoth, too—but since they can sniff him out, we must do something to cover his scent." He thought for a moment. "Is anything in this cave smelly enough to cover his natural scent—which is actually rather pleasing, like that of a vuupuu blossom?"

"I know!" Monkey-Face Joe said. "Yargoona's woman-hole has a very ripe, fishlike odor. Surely you have noticed it."

"Yes!" Trixie interjected. "How it makes me jealous! My she-hole only smells like a single, tiny, insignificant sardinosaurus. Hers boasts the powerful reek of three-dozen man-eating bronto-clams."

"That is true!" Fred handed his pet to Joe. "Here, my friend. Rub our gentle pet Buggoth against your beautiful wife's fuming love-pit. Rub like you've never rubbed before!"

Yargoona laid back on her bed, pulled up her fur nightgown and spread her legs, revealing a loose-lipped opening that distinctly resembled the glistening maw of a ravenous flytraposaurus.

First Monkey-Face Joe rubbed Buggoth's back against Yargoona's steaming passion-patch. The mushroom-devil began to purr in the most curious fashion. Then Joe flipped the creature over to do the front—

Instantly, a strange, fleshy flap in Buggoth's lower abdomen opened up and out surged a massive cylinder of spongy yet rigid tissue—easily four times the length of the creature—that plunged with lusty accuracy right into the depths of Yargoona's she-hole.

"Zogga Dogga Yog-Sothoth!" Tony bellowed.

"You can say that again!" Yargoona moaned, bucking her thick hips against the invading phallus.

Buggoth shook free of Monkey-Face Joe's grip and began to ravish Yargoona with the gusto of seven rampaging sexosauruses in heat.

"That must be what killed the saber-toothed, star-nosed mole!" Tony said. "I bet Buggoth skewered it with his mighty crab-pizzle. No mere animal could withstand a pounding from such a monstrously meaty man-root."

"It is fortunate," Trixie said, "that Yargoona has a she-cave as spaciously deep as the night sky itself!"

"Joe," Tony said, approaching his diminutive friend, "are you not concerned that Buggoth is mating with your cavewoman?"

"Better him than me…" Joe muttered.

Buggoth uttered a shrill whoop of delight—and with that, his rigid power-pillar instantly went limp and shriveled back into the creature's abdomen. The fleshy flap pulled shut behind it.

"We are wasting time!" Tony said, snatching up the satiated mushroom-devil. "I think Buggoth is stinked-up enough to avoid detection. Let us leave immediately!"

The four cavefriends threw on extra furs and hurried out of the cave, with Bloodfang scampering close behind. They rushed through the night, straight to Lava Larry's Rib Cave. Up among the clouds, huge dark shapes fluttered and whooped.

The eatery was actually composed of several interconnected caves, and Tony marched up to the entrance that led to the sleeping quarters of his boss. "Lava Larry! Wake up, my good, protecting caveboss!" he shouted. "We need your help!"

The obese caveman shambled sleepily out of his bed-cave. "Hello, Tony, Trixie, Joe, Yargoona—Bloodfang and Buggoth, too! Is something wrong? Having a problem with cavebats? Roachosauruses?"

"Worse! Much worse!" Tony moaned. "Buggoth's evil relatives are coming to get him! Please hide us!"

"I knew this day would arrive," Lava Larry said. "The star-crabs are too evil to let one of their own try to live a life of gentle happiness. It is up to us to do what needs to be done." The entrance to his bed-cave was halfway up the side of a large hill, and Larry craned his neck upward to view the top, which was covered with tall, vine-draped trees. "You know, the lava-pits of my restaurant are on the other side of this hill…"

Tony clutched his insect pal to his chest as he gasped, "Are you saying we must burn Buggoth to death to escape the wrath of the evil star-crabs? Never!"

"Ummm, no, Tony," Lava Larry said. "Follow me up to those trees. I have a plan that might save us all—including our dear friend, Buggoth. But hurry! Hurry! We do not have a cavesecond to lose!"

* * * *

On top of the hill, Lava Larry shared his plan, and Tony Tar-Pit and his cavefamily followed the obese caveman's detailed directions.

"Keep weaving those vines! Please hurry!" Lava Larry said to Trixie and Yargoona. He turned to Tony and Monkey-Face Joe, who were constructing a curious figure out of branches, large leaves, vines, rocks, and some of their furs. "Put longer arms on that thing! It has to look just like a caveman. And stuff the belly with more rocks—it is way too skinny! Put in as many rocks as you can!"

Up in the sky, a mad flurry of wings rattled and buzzed through the air, growing louder and louder still.

Tony and Joe pushed the figure to the edge of a cliff just above one of the lava-pits. There they tied a stout vine around its rock-stuffed waist. Then the two friends backed off into the shadows beneath nearby trees.

Four enormous star-crabs hovered down out of the night, approaching the figure on the cliff. One of them wrapped its spiny legs around the shape's head and shoulders, and the others drew closer so they could all help the attack by sinking their sharp limbs into the figure's bulging stomach and rear.

"*Now!*" Lava Larry cried. With that signal, the four cavemates all rushed out of the shadows and threw nets of strong vines over the flying mushroom-devils. The ends of some of the vines were tied to heavy rocks, and Tony and Joe threw those rocks over the edge of the cliff.

The four monstrosities fought to free themselves from the trap, but their crooked wings were hopelessly tangled in the weighted vines. They slowly began to drop down, down, down toward the bubbling lava pit below.

The cavefriends rushed to the edge of the cliff to observe the anticipated demise of their enemies. Suddenly, one of the flying creatures began to break free, and it tore at the vines with its pointed feet.

"Noooooooo!" Monkey-Face Joe cried. "Evil mushroom-devils! You must die no matter what!"

So saying, the brave little caveman threw himself over the cliff and landed on top of the huge star-crabs. The added weight caused the tangled mass to descend faster, and just as it hit the molten rock—

—Joe jumped off the monsters and over the rim of the lava-pit.

The squirming space-demons instantly sank to a fiery, bubbling death.

"Zogga Dogga Yog-Sothoth!" Tony crowed. "Monkey-Face Joe is a hero!"

The sun was just beginning to rise, so Lava Larry and Tony Tar-Pit cooked up some steggy steaks for a hearty victory breakfast. Buggoth and Bloodfang frolicked without a care as the cavefriends gnawed on the delicious dinosaur meat.

Little did they all know....

Nine months later, Yargoona—impregnated by Buggoth's alien seed—would give birth to the world's first ghoul.

A ghoul is not really an undead creature, as many historians and students of the supernatural have supposed. It is actually a human/ alien-demon hybrid, which can be summoned through full-moon rituals involving bloody sacrifices. Yargoona's baby grew up to be especially hideous, with a hairy muzzle of a face, thick black hair, vicious talons, gnashing fangs, a massive phallus that hung down to his knobby knees, and two insatiable lusts: warm flesh and hot blood...

But hey, boys will be boys.

DER FLEISCHBRUNNEN

Der Fleischbrunnen was based within a warehouse with boarded windows. There were no signs on the building, which was—and still is, in fact—just one of many dozens of warehouses in the industrial sector of a filthy, boring city. This city is located on an island, and very few people there speak English—or German, for that matter. You would never be able to find the building, based on those few vague facts.

But then, you would have no reason to seek it out. It is empty now.

My grandmother on my mother's side grew up in a poor family from a small fishing village in Crete, which is not the island in question. She had been a very beautiful woman in her prime, and had married well. Several times, in fact—always to very wealthy men. I'd been her favorite grandchild. I used to call her Jia-Jia, and when I was little, I was surprised when I learned that Jia-Jia was Greek for 'grandmother' and not her actual name. I knew all the adults called her Ellie, but I thought that was something adults called old women. Ellie was, in fact, short for Elena.

When she died last year, she left me fifty-seven million dollars and several companies in different countries. I have plenty of business experience—I worked for decades in the soft-drink industry, in marketing—so I felt confident in my ability to continue her legacy.

One of my grandmother's businesses was in that filthy, boring city I'd mentioned. A month after my grandmother died, I called Mr. Pileggi, the man who was running that business.

I had a nice talk with him on the phone—he had a little trouble speaking English, but we were able to understand each other. He seemed very helpful. He made arrangements for me to be flown to the island, so he could give me a tour of the business. He even made plans for a car to pick me up after I got off the plane. It would be early evening, so the driver would take me directly to the restaurant where I would be having dinner with Mr. Pileggi. I was only going to be staying two days, so I wouldn't be bothering with any luggage—only a carry-on bag.

The day came for my trip. The flight went as scheduled. I arrived on the island, got off the plane and found the car. The driver, a dark-haired man with a huge smile, opened the back door of the maroon Buick for me and I got in. After he took his seat behind the wheel, he turned around and said, "Where to, my friend?"

This caught me a little off-guard. "Oh. The restaurant. I'm having dinner with Mr. Pileggi. Nick Pileggi."

The driver raised his eyebrows. "What restaurant? We have many here."

"I can't remember the name," I said. "But I do recall it wasn't in English…I asked Nick what it meant, and he said, 'The Hungry Bear.' No wait—'The Fat Bear.' Does that help?"

The driver shook his head.

I tried to remember more of my conversation with Pileggi. "We talked about the name for about five minutes—but it's just not coming to mind. Maybe it was French…or German…?"

"We have no French restaurants," the man said. "So maybe German."

"Now let me think…What would be German for 'The Fat Bear'…?" My command of the German language was virtually non-existent, but I gave it my best shot. "How about—'Der Fattenbearen'? No, that's not right. 'Der Flabbenbruin'? No. I think 'fleisch' means fat or meat…How about 'Der Fleischbrunnen'?"

Later, after the adventure was over, I found out that I'd had both the language and the type of animal wrong. And 'bear' was something different in German anyway. But evidently that wild guess had hit upon something, because the driver's eyes shot wide open and he said, "You are having dinner at Der Fleischbrunnen?"

"There is such a place?" I said, amazed by my luck. "Well then, yes, I guess that's where I'm having dinner. It's a restaurant, right?"

The young man stared at me. "I've never been inside. Maybe they serve food. I don't know. I thought it was a club. A private club. Members only. Mr. Pileggi is a member there?"

"I guess so! So let's getting going. To Der Fleischbrunnen!" I was getting a little impatient, because it was a couple hours after my usual dinner time and I was getting hungry. But at least I was well-rested, since I had fallen asleep on the plane.

The driver gave me a worried look, but then we started off down the road. On the way, he said, "My best friend's sister, she once went to Der Fleischbrunnen. She never told us what happened there, but later that year, she had a baby and it was born dead."

"I'm sorry to hear that," I said.

"The baby was all wrong. It was too small and bony, and its eyes were…funny."

"That's very sad, but you can't blame a restaurant or a club for something like that. And she only went there once, right?"

"Once was enough," he said.

I was surprised when he turned down a road that was lined with huge, unlit buildings. Eventually he parked in front of that unmarked warehouse with boarded windows. "This is it," he said. "You get out here. I don't like looking at it. It makes me remember that thing. That devil-baby."

"But this isn't a restaurant!" I said. "There aren't any lights or cars or customers or—or anything!"

"Just get out!" the driver said. He turned around—his eyes were streaming tears. "Get out right here! I'm going home now! Get out, Mr. Fancy Big-Shot!"

What could I do? The man was extremely upset. I figured I'd be better off taking my chances on the street, even though it was getting dark. I'd done some reading on the island before my trip, and it had a very low crime rate. The lights of the city were less than a half-hour walk away, so I really wasn't in any danger.

So I got out.

The man screamed "To Hell with you!" as he drove off.

I had a few protein bars in my carry-on bag, so I fished one out and ate it as I thought about what to do next. It was a warm night and nobody else was around, as far as I could see.

I decided to check out the warehouse. Der Fleischbrunnen. Why? Just for the heck of it, really. Plus, I was curious. Seeing the place evidently had brought back some unpleasant memories for the driver. Why would a club have anything to do with a deformed baby? Had the place ever really *been* a club? After all, it was just another warehouse among many others. It looked like it had been deserted for decades.

Bag in hand, I walked up to the door and jiggled the knob. It was locked, but a woman's voice on the other side said, "Yes?"

I was completely startled, since I'd figured the place was abandoned. "I'm looking for a restaurant called Der Fleischbrunnen," I said.

The woman laughed. "*Restaurant?* What makes you think we're a restaurant?"

"Well, is this Der Fleischbrunnen?" I asked. "Is Nick Pileggi in there? Can I come in?"

"Yes, this is Der Fleischbrunnen, and no, we don't have a Nick Pileggi in here." A bolt clacked and the door swung open. Inside the entryway stood a thin, elderly woman with an angular, incredibly wrinkled face. A few wispy tufts of white hair stuck out from under her lime-green turban. She held an odd little lantern that appeared to be made mostly of yellow glass, with a stone base and handle. There were no lights behind her in the building. "We're not a restaurant, mister. Do you still want to come in?"

"I'm supposed to be meeting with Nick Pileggi," I said. "But I don't know the address. I have his home phone number, though he's probably already at the restaurant. Wherever that is."

The old woman smiled at me. "Poor man. You are far from home, yes? And lost! Ridiculously lost! You have no idea where you are! We don't have a phone here, but there's plenty to eat. Let me find something for you. Then we'll decide how to get you to this Pileggi fellow."

She took my hand and led me into the building. We headed down a hallway lined with large paintings—some were so huge they stretched from ceiling to floor. I couldn't make out too many details by the light of the old woman's strange lantern, but basically, they all seemed to depict elderly people with their hands raised in the air. After we'd gone about ten feet, she let go of my hand.

I pointed my forefinger like a mock gun—thumb raised, trigger-style—at one of the paintings. "Stick 'em up!" I said in a Bugs-Bunny-like gangster voice.

The old woman stopped. "Stick what up?"

"All these people have their hands raised, like somebody's pointing a gun at them." I pointed my finger like a gun again. "When criminals rob somebody, they say, 'Stick 'em up!' and the victims put their hands in the air. Well, they do in American movies, anyway."

The old woman laughed. "Oh, I never go to see movies. I don't watch television, either. Isn't that terrible? I feel I am missing so much!"

I shrugged. "You're probably better off. At least you're living your life, instead of just watching other people you don't even know. Most of them are just made-up characters anyway. Except for the ones on the news. But why don't you watch TV or movies? Is it against your religion or something?"

The old woman continued to walk, and gestured for me to follow. "A man who also lives here, he went to a movie, a few years ago. Something about the light made his eyes bleed. The same thing happened to a woman who lives here when she tried to watch a television. The light—there is something about the way it flickers, so fast, so strong. It is not good for us."

"So you live here with some other folks?" She didn't answer my question, so I went back to the original topic. "Well, movies and TV don't flicker for me. You and your friends must have really sensitive eyes. Is that why you're using that lantern?"

"Yes, exactly right." The woman led me into a large, dim kitchen, lit by a few yellow candles set in wine bottles. The place was a complete mess, with filthy pots and plates scattered on the table and across the counters. "Forgive the way our kitchen looks." The old woman wheezed out an exasperated sigh. "The others here, they leave it all for me to clean up. And I'm the one with sore hands! Every year they get worse. I wish you were a doctor. Then you could give me some pills for my poor, aching hands." She turned to look at me. "Maybe you *are* a doctor…?"

"Sorry." I watched as she opened a breadbox and took out, not bread, but a large leather pouch. She opened it and pulled out a long, lumpy chunk of what looked like beef jerky.

"Here," she said. "Dried lamb. Very delicious."

I took the shriveled mass of meat from her. She pulled out one for herself and began to gnaw on it. I smelled the meat—very spicy, lots of garlic and maybe oregano. I chewed on it a little—it was really very good. Pretty soon I'd eaten my share, so she gave me another chunk to chew on.

"So what's your name?" I asked.

"Oh, you must forgive me! I should have introduced myself when we first met. My name is Maria."

I suddenly realized that the old woman had a bit of an accent—an accent so familiar I'd taken it for granted. "Hey," I said, "you're Greek, aren't you? I'm half-Greek. My mother's side of the family."

The old woman stared into my eyes. "And what is the name of your mother's family?"

I told her.

The old woman nodded. "I see. And your grandmother. Was her name Elena?"

This time, it was my turn to nod.

"Of course!" Maria grabbed another stick of lamb jerky and began to gnaw with great excitement. "By any chance did you come to this island to claim a family business?"

"Yes…" I said, suddenly unsure of how much I should reveal about myself. It was unnerving, watching her tear into that meat with such happy fervor. I guess she still had all her own teeth.

"Of course, of course," she gushed, mostly to me but I think to herself, too. "This Pileggi you mentioned, he must be the fat man who comes by during the day! We've never known his name. He doesn't stay to talk to us. The pig, he's not nice like you! Maybe you should fire him and be the one who works with us!" She suddenly threw back her head and laughed, once, twice. "You don't know, do you? You own this place! You own Der Fleischbrunnen! So how did you get here, anyway? And why did you think it was a restaurant?"

I told her about my conversation with the driver, and when I was finished, she laughed again.

"That is good, good!" she crowed. Then she looked me in the eye. "I shall tell you this. In all the universe, there is no such thing as a coincidence. No such thing as an accident. You think you came here by mistake, but all is happening as it was meant, by powers beyond our control. Events are like the teeth on the gears of a clock—they fit together and move each other along, and when all is done...Then, my friend, we shall both know the time."

She bit off and chewed some more dried lamb, swallowed, and then continued with her ravings. At least, they seemed like ravings at the time. "Oh, I can tell we are going to get along! Yes, we're all going to be good friends! That fat man, he treats us like animals—your grandmother, a very dear woman, she simply had no idea. She stopped visiting us after the fat man began managing the place for her, so we were never able to tell her! Now come with me, come, come, come! It is time for you to see what you have inherited! It is yours, all yours! Der Fleischbrunnen!"

She grabbed her lantern and ran past me, out of the kitchen, whirling around every few steps to gesture for me to follow, follow. She was a very nimble old lady—I'm surprised she didn't fall and break a hip.

"So what's a Fleischbrunnen, anyway?" I shouted to her as I ran. "I guess it's not a fat bear—"

"No, no, no!" she cried. "It is German for 'meat fountain'! Hitler named it that when he visited the island, so many years ago. Such an odd man—and such greasy hair. The smell of that grease filled whatever room he was in. It smelled like bacon mixed with lilacs. Sickening!" She stopped right in front of an enormous wooden door. It was open about six inches, though I couldn't see in from where I was standing.

"Hitler used to come here? World War II Hitler?" I said. "I own a business that used to have Adolf Hitler for a customer? Lady, that is just too weird for words!"

"Oh, really, my dear friend, my good sir? You think that is weird?" She licked her lips. "Then tell me what you think—of this!" So saying, she pushed the door wide open. She really was terribly strong for her size and age.

There it was, right before my eyes, in the middle of a huge chamber lit by yellow candles in lanterns. It was surrounded by dozens of extremely old men and women. Some were slowly dancing with their hands in the air. Others were carrying wooden buckets, and large wooden spoons, too.

But what was *it*, you ask?

It looked like a five-foot high volcano of pink flesh, spouting up from out of a wide broken area in the floor. A thick, bluish slime rolled slowly down from the mouth of the hideous thing. Some of the elderly workers collected the ooze with their spoons and plopped it into their buckets. All of them kept whispering the same long phrase or sentence over and over. I couldn't make out everything they said, but a foreign word which sounded vaguely African—'gah-tam-bah'—was repeated often.

I walked through the door, right up to the horrible little hill. As I reached out, about to touch it, Maria hurried up to me and grabbed my hand.

"No metal," she said. "*Never* metal." She pulled a ring off my finger and put it in the breast pocket of my jacket.

I touched the side of the mound. It vibrated slightly, and pulsed, too. It was rubbery and very warm, almost feverish. A glob of the blue slime trickled down the meaty hill and wet my index finger.

I raised the finger to my nose for a sniff. It smelled like a mixture of sweat and rice pudding with cinnamon.

"Do not taste it!" Maria whispered. "It is highly addictive."

I had no intention of tasting it, though I did appreciate the warning. I wiped my finger on my pants.

One of the old women carried a full wooden bucket out of the chamber through a side door. A few seconds later she returned without the bucket, with another woman by her side. They talked for a moment, and then they began the whispering chant. They raised their arms and began to circle Der Fleischbrunnen—the meat fountain.

I pointed toward the side door. "Where does that go?"

Maria took a newly filled bucket from one of the women and walked toward the door. "Come with me," she said. "You deserve to see it all. The miracle belongs to you!"

This new room was a candle-lit laboratory. Maria walked to the center of the lab and dumped the contents of the bucket into one of three stainless steel vats, all heated by gas jets.

"You're putting that juice in metal containers," I said. "So how come you had to take my ring off?"

"The 'juice', as you call it, is the Milk of Time," Maria said. "It can be stored in any type of container. But the source of the Milk cannot be allowed to come in contact with metal. Do you like our laboratory? We are very scientific, yes?"

On tables and counters, the blue fluid was being tested and processed by about a dozen workers in white smocks. "They all work in shifts," Maria said. "Production never stops. There is a great demand for our product. That is why it is so expensive. Only the very rich can afford to use it on a regular basis. And they do. Even though long-term use has its side effects, like sensitivity to most forms of light. And of course, the extreme dependency. The addicts eventually come here to work in their old age—they give the fat man all their money and in return, they get to live here and have the Milk for free."

"But—what does the stuff actually do to people?" I said, watching one of the workers pour the goop into a test tube.

"This marvelous compound," Maria said, "makes a person feel like God. Your grandmother never let a drop touch her lips. Me? That's another story. The scientific principle is a bit too complex to explain quickly, but basically, it interacts with the body's hormones, male and female. That is why only the very old are allowed to work with it. Their hormones have dried up, so they won't be compelled to swill it down like hogs all day long. They only need a little every day—enough to keep them alive."

I thought about this for a moment. "So it's some kind of aphrodisiac?"

Maria shrugged. "Perhaps. If you think that God is sex personified. I don't know. I am far too old to remember how it felt. That is another side effect. It makes a person live a very long time. Even after the wonderful feelings go away." She sighed sadly. "We have a very nice room for visitors. You can stay there tonight. The fat man will be here in the morning. You can fire him then."

"There's a lot I still don't understand," I said as we walked through the lab and into another passageway, Maria leading the way with her lantern. "Maybe I'll fire the fat man—Nick—eventually, but I don't think I should do it tomorrow. I need to talk to him about some things. Like how this stuff gets sold, who buys it. Maybe I don't want people to have it any more. Hell, maybe I should shut this whole place down."

"Elena talked that way sometimes," Maria said, "back when she used to visit us. I would say to her, 'Ellie! The Milk of Time is the only thing keeping your poor old Jia-Jia alive! Do you want to see me die?'" The old woman wagged a finger at me. "Now I ask you the same question. Do you want me to die? Your own flesh and blood—your Jia-Jia's Jia-Jia! Is that what you want?"

"I wouldn't wish death on anyone," I said, wondering if she could possibly be who she said she was. My grandmother's grandmother! I tried to figure out her age in my head. All her talk of death suddenly made me remember the driver's story about the dead baby. "Did a young girl once visit here and…?" I wasn't sure how to continue. Finally I just said, "Her baby was stillborn."

Maria waved a hand slowly, dismissively. "A stupid whore. The fat man arranged for her to entertain a business associate here. A very handsome man. That crazy whore, she got drunk and didn't even do her job. Instead she somehow managed to wander into the forbidden areas of the building. Then she passed out and some of the old fellows who help gather the Milk of Time had their way with her." She barked out a dry laugh. "Not all of us are completely dead below our belts! Men with seed so very old…older than you or anyone else from the outside might guess…what sort of awful baby would that make? You cannot make fresh bread from moldy flour! Better off that it died, I think. Ah, here is your room for the night. A very nice room."

The nice room Maria mentioned was in fact a spacious, well-furnished suite, with redwood furniture draped with quaint old doilies. Thankfully, it had modern lighting fixtures, along with a refrigerator, television, and a bar. So the building did indeed have an electrical connection. Maria didn't enter the room. I asked if she wanted to come in, but she just shook her head and hurried away, down the long hall. Maybe all those modern conveniences scared her. But I did notice one thing, just before she turned and rushed off. She took just a moment to stare—with an odd look of what might have been fear, worry or curiosity—at a beige door in a corner of the suite.

In a cabinet at the bar, I found bottles of vodka, whiskey, gin—and a half-dozen old bottles of ouzo. I recalled that my grandmother used to enjoy the occasional nip of the stuff. It's not the sort of drink one can chug down. It's too strong, thick and licorice-sweet. Perhaps Mr. Pileggi enjoyed it, too. There was tonic in the refrigerator, so I made a gin and tonic. I looked around for a phone, but apparently Maria hadn't been lying when she'd said there wasn't one. I suppose that had something to do with their need for secrecy. Even then, Der Fleischbrunnen wasn't such a secret—the driver had known its location and a little more, too, though most of his facts were wrong.

As I finished my drink, I looked over some of the books on a shelf by the television. I was amused to see a book with the title, *Put A Little Greece In Your Cooking!* There were many other dusty old cookbooks there—those must have been my Jia-Jia's. I then saw that all the cookbooks had the same name on the spine. My grandmother had written them. She'd always had some difficulty writing in English, so she must have had the help of a ghost-writer who knew both Greek and English.

One book on the shelf had the intriguing title, *The Seven Blasphemies of Ghattambah.* I recognized part of the title as the word I'd heard the old people whispering as they gathered the Milk of Time. It was a very large book, bound in leather that had thick, bristly black hair sprouting from it in spots. Utterly disgusting. The title had been burned—or rather, branded—onto the spine and front cover. Certainly a unique printing process. I wondered what kind of animal the leather had come from, and decided it must have been a pig.

I opened the book. Each page was divided into quadrants, each in a different language: English, Greek, German and another I didn't recognize. Also, in the middle of each page was an illustration. These depicted a variety of nauseating subjects: mostly bizarre sexual practices and cut-off or cut-up body parts. I stared at one picture for about three minutes—basically because I couldn't decide what the thing in the picture was supposed to be. It had a puffy, tubular body with a multitude of pincer-legs, like a caterpillar. It also had long, heavily veined spiral wings. I had no idea how any creature could fly with wings like that. The head of the thing didn't have a brainpan—it was just a huge, gaping mouth filled with sharp, crooked teeth. The thick lips were dotted with small, black eyes.

At the base of the wings was a large, knobby hump. Perhaps that was the location of the brain, if indeed the thing had a brain of any size. A cluster of extremely long tendrils grew out of the top of the hump.

The caption informed me that this creature was Ghattambah.

I wanted to read the book, but decided I could do that later. In fact, I would take it with me when I left. I put it back on the shelf and decided to try opening that beige door. I wasn't surprised to find that it was locked. I thought for a moment. If the key was in the room, where might it be hidden…?

I reached up and checked the top of the door-frame. Nothing.

One by one, I opened the books and shook them, hoping a key would fall out. But it wasn't hidden among their pages.

Then I thought about all those ouzo bottles. I went back to the cabinet and examined them. Sure enough, a rusty old key was taped to the side of an ouzo bottle at the back of the cabinet. A fine hiding place, since ouzo is not for all tastes, and there were five other bottles of the stuff in front of it.

I unlocked the door—and found myself staring down a crude tunnel supported by wooden beams, with thick planks for walls, ceiling and floor. On a small shelf on the tunnel wall I found a box of wooden matches and a glass and stone lantern with a yellow candle inside.

I lit the candle and walked down the tunnel. I simply had to. I'd already seen so many bizarre sights in that building, and the fact that Maria had cast such a strange look at the door made me intensely curious.

As I walked down the tunnel, a thought entered my mind. I knew the soft-drink industry pretty well. A drink that contained the Milk of Time could easily enslave the world. After all, millions of people were already addicted to caffeinated beverages. The addiction of that Milk would just further strengthen the enslavement. But did I want to enslave, therefore rule, the world? Of course not. I was already filthy rich. Why would I want the extra responsibility? I wasn't about to let greed evolve into destructive stupidity.

The tunnel took a turn and sloped gently downward. As I followed the way, I began to hear noises: movement, voices, and incessant dripping. Suddenly the tunnel opened up into a huge cave.

And I was not alone.

I put down my lantern at the mouth of the tunnel, since there was already light in the cave. Dozens of lanterns were set in niches cut into the rock of the cave walls. Several of the old workers were dancing and whisper-chanting, while others collected the Milk of Time from the cave floor with wooden spoons. They ignored me as they went about their duties. The Milk itself was dripping down—

—down from an enormous cocoon, which was lashed to the roof of the cave by hundreds of thick ropes of silk. The cocoon was about the size of two bulldozers parked end to end. The surface of the huge pod was rough and filthy, with several oozing holes along the sides.

I thought about how far I had walked, and the direction the path had taken...The cave was directly under the huge room which housed that fleshy volcano. That meant that the volcano was growing out of the top of cocoon, extending through a hole between the cave and that warehouse room. The cocoon seemed to be constantly oozing fluid—plenty for the workers to collect. As one of the dancing workers moved past me, she whispered, "Ghattambah."

I noticed a structure along a wall of the cave near the cocoon. Steps built onto wooden scaffolding led up to a platform at a level less than five feet away from the pod.

As I watched, an old man with a long wooden pole, sharpened at one end, walked up to the platform and began to prod at the cocoon, ripping a couple more holes into it. These began to ooze the Milk of Time almost immediately.

Milk? A quaint euphemism for blood, or ichor, or whatever that vile slime was.

I decided to get a closer look.

I walked up the wooden steps to the platform. I passed the old man on the way and he simply gave me a small nod.

I stood high above the cave floor, watching the cocoon. The liquid oozed from the holes with a slow, gently pulsing regularity. I was in awe of this creature. What sort of being could constantly lose vital fluids without dying? It couldn't be a creature from Earth. I was eager to read that hide-bound book—hopefully it would shed some light on this nightmare scenario.

At this point, I did something utterly senseless. And I did it without thinking.

I thought about the name Hitler had given the place—Der Fleischbrunnen. Maria had mentioned it meant 'meat fountain.' Everyone knows it's good luck to toss a coin into a fountain. So I absent-mindedly dug a penny out of my pocket and flicked it toward the cocoon—and it landed right in one of the gaping, oozing holes.

Only then did I remember what Maria had said.

No metal. Never metal.

It was a stupid thing to do, but I guess I was meant to do it. Maria had said there was no such thing as an accident.

The cocoon began to rock back and forth, faster and faster. I hurried down the wooden steps. Writhing tendrils began to tear through the holes in the horrible bundle. A deafening, high-pitched shriek of rage echoed off the stone walls. I ran back to the mouth of the tunnel—and just in time. The agitated cocoon tore free of its moorings and fell with a sickening thud to the floor of the cave. There the casing tore open and a huge, slick, squealing thing scrambled out. It looked like a twisted, sickly version of the creature in the book's drawing. The ravenous mouth-head whipped around, looking for prey, and fastened upon the nearest worker. That insane turbine of a mouth shredded the old man to red ribbons and sucked him down in a matter of seconds.

With this nourishment, the body of Ghattambah began to plump up. The creature ate another of the workers, then another and yet another. The strange curving wings of the creature spread majestically. I wanted to run, but I found myself transfixed by the sight of such ravenous carnage. Soon the head whipped in my direction. I regained my senses, grabbed my lantern from where I'd set it earlier, and ran back through the tunnel. Fortunately, I couldn't hear anything following me. The lantern slipped out of my hand and broke about halfway back to the room. I actually yelped when its feeble yellow light went out. I ran with one hand tapping the wall beside me, so I would be able to find the turn along the way.

Once I was back in the room, I grabbed *The Seven Blasphemies of Ghattambah* and popped it into my bag. Then I hurried out of the room, through the labyrinth of the building's halls, in a direction that I hoped would return me to the main entrance. The halls were dark, so again I had to run with one hand madly tapping the wall to my side. I could hear plenty of running and screaming, though I couldn't tell what direction any of it was coming from. Soon the floor began to shake, and the squealing of the monster pealed through the building. The creature was trying to break out of its confinement—probably through the hole in the roof of the cave. As I ran through the halls, I kept thinking to myself, *That thing is mine! Mine! And now my own property is going to kill me!*

I turned a corner and suddenly I saw Maria, holding a lantern.

"What is happening?" she said. "I was sleeping and—"

"We've got to get out of here!" I said. "The door! Where's the door?"

She took my hand. "There is another way out that is close," she said. "Follow me." She led me down a nearby hallway. "Is there a fire? Is the fountain safe?"

"The fountain has dried up," I said. "It's over. All over."

"What? That cannot be!" she cried. "I will die. I need the Milk of Time to survive!"

"There must be some stored somewhere," I said.

"Of course," she said. "Hundreds of gallons. But the customers—"

"To Hell with the customers," I said. "It's mine, remember? Get me out of here and you and the other workers can have the rest. Every drop."

"Ah! I *knew* you were a good man." She flashed a huge grin at me. She still had a stringy piece of lamb stuck between her front teeth. "Just around this next corner. An emergency exit."

Maria did indeed get me out of the building, but she did not accompany me any further. She simply slipped into one of the other warehouses. As I ran from the building, I heard a crash of timber and turned just in time to see an enormous, shrieking shape soar up out of the ruined roof.

In flight, Ghattambah looked like a nightmarish four-way cross between a moray eel, a caterpillar, a bat and an eggbeater gone berserk. Green static danced upon its impossible spiral wings. Suddenly there was a flash of dark-green light and the creature disappeared.

I eventually did meet—and fire—Mr. Pileggi. I moved Maria to a nice little house in the United States, and she now has all the Milk of Time she could ever need. I also made similar arrangements for the rest of the workers who had tended to Der Fleischbrunnen. That's the nice thing about having loads of money. It makes taking care of problems that much easier.

I also hired some folks from the island to fix the damage to the warehouse. It's a big, sturdy building. As I said before, it's empty now. And in the future, it's only going to be used for storage.

As for that abhorrent hide-bound book—I have read it from cover to cover. I now know all the mysteries of Ghattambah the Undying, whose soul dwells beyond time.

The creature's cult has existed on this world for thousands of years. Some of the pharaohs of ancient Egypt used to make sacrifices to Ghattambah. The island's great cave had been a center of worship for centuries. Somehow the cult had evolved into a business, which had eventually found its way into my grandmother's possession.

Having read the book, I now know how to bring the creature back to this world—as a rampaging winged god, as an enormous larva inside a cocoon, even as a black, octagonal egg. But I have no wish to summon the thing.

And yet I cannot bring myself to destroy the book. I know I should. It contains secrets of incredible power. I hope there will never come a day when I'll want or need that sort of power.

Still, who knows what the future will bring?

That book is filthy. Wicked. Dangerous.

Yet it feels so comforting to own it.

ABOUT THE AUTHOR

Mark McLaughlin's fiction, nonfiction, and poetry have appeared in almost one-thousand magazines, newspapers, websites, and anthologies, including *Living Dead 2, Black Gate, Galaxy, Fangoria, Writer's Digest, Cemetery Dance, Midnight Premiere, Dark Arts,* and two volumes each of *The Best of the Rest, The Best of HorrorFind,* and *The Year's Best Horror Stories* (DAW Books).

Collections of McLaughlin's fiction include *Beach Blanket Zombie, Motivational Shrieker, Slime after Slime,* and *Pickman's Motel* from Delirium Books; *At the Foothills of Frenzy* (with coauthors Shane Ryan Staley and Brian Knight) from Solitude Publications; and *Raising Demons for Fun and Profit* from Sam's Dot Publishing.

An expert on B-movies, McLaughlin writes two columns on the topic. HorrorGarage.com features his online column, *Four-Letter Word Beginning with 'F'* (the word in question is Fear). Also, GravesideTales.com features his horror-movie history column, *Time Machine of Terror!*

McLaughlin is the coauthor, with Rain Graves and David Niall Wilson, of *The Gossamer Eye,* which won the 2002 Bram Stoker Award for Superior Achievement in Poetry.

With regular collaborator Michael McCarty, he has written *Monster Behind The Wheel* (hardcover from Corrosion Press, ebook edition from Medallion Press); *Partners In Slime* (Damnation Books); *All Things Dark & Hideous* (Rainfall Books, England); *Professor LaGungo's Delirious Download of Digital Deviltry & Doom* (Darkside Digital); and *Professor LaGungo's Classroom of Horrors* (Bucket o' Guts Press).

He is also a successful marketing and public relations executive who regularly writes articles for business journals, newspapers, trade publications and websites.

To find out more about his work, visit:

www.Facebook.com/MarkMcLaughlinMedia

and his blog:

www.BMovieMonster.com.